D0878372

THE
GOLD HUNTER

THE GOLDFINDER SERIES, BOOK ONE

PHILIP ATLAS CLAUSEN

BALBOA.
PRESS
A DIVISION OF HAY HOUSE

Balboa Press books may be ordered through booksellers or by contacting:

Balboa Press
A Division of Hay House
1663 Liberty Drive
Bloomington, IN 47403
www.balboapress.com
1 (877) 407-4847

Because of the dynamic nature of the Internet, any web addresses or
links contained in this book may have changed since publication and
may no longer be valid. The views expressed in this work are solely those
of the author and do not necessarily reflect the views of the publisher,
and the publisher hereby disclaims any responsibility for them.

The author of this book does not dispense medical advice or prescribe the use
of any technique as a form of treatment for physical, emotional, or medical
problems without the advice of a physician, either directly or indirectly. The
intent of the author is only to offer information of a general nature to help
you in your quest for emotional and spiritual well-being. In the event you use
any of the information in this book for yourself, which is your constitutional
right, the author and the publisher assume no responsibility for your actions.

Any people depicted in stock imagery provided by Thinkstock are models,
and such images are being used for illustrative purposes only.
Certain stock imagery © Thinkstock.

Print information available on the last page.

ISBN: 978-1-5043-7158-2 (sc)
ISBN: 978-1-5043-7160-5 (hc)
ISBN: 978-1-5043-7159-9 (e)

Library of Congress Control Number: 2016920911

Balboa Press rev. date: 01/18/2017

CONTENTS

ACKNOWLEDGEMENT

The complete story, of which you hold the first volume, is called *The Goldfinder*, and it took thirty-years for the story to reveal itself to me. I thank my sons Pete, Jeff and Troy for spending at least a part of their childhood listening to me clack away in the basement, lost in a different world, a different time. I'm sure they wonder about me. I thank my wife Sally for endless patience and electronic magic—uploading and downloading—a totally unfathomable magic to me, as is she. I thank Balboa Press for doing a great job of design as always.

PRELUDE

John Valory had no interest rushing into the Gold Rush. California was a long walk away, a mule killer, and a man killer. He worked at Cates Saw Mill in Harrisburg, Pennsylvania, a dollar a day and glad to get it ripping pine logs into planks, and he became a drinking man. But a letter arrived, February of 1851, a letter so tattered and worn it looked as if it had fallen from the moon: *John, You want timber mountain and saw mill so come and get it. Dain King of Gold Nation Mining Company buys every stick of lumber you make.* Sketchy directions followed having to do with bearing northwest from Pyramid Lake out of Nevada Territory and then into California through Beckwourth Pass, and thereupon to North Fork of the Feather River. *Keep asking for Colonel King. He is well known in these parts.* Handwriting simple and clear, but the signature smeared from a stray drop of rain as to be unreadable. Maybe M, maybe K.

Maybe every drunk is but a man with a broken dream—and one dream away from sober. Here was a last chance. John quit whiskey and bought a good used Studebaker covered wagon for fifty dollars and three mules for seventy-five dollars. His wife Magya was easy because he told her they would go to San Francisco where she could restart her opera career. The little girl Annabel was persuaded by the promise of a pony for riding in the hills. Petr needed no promises. Petr Valory was sixteen and sure a shovelful of California dirt would produce enough gold for all dreams to come true. Mostly good dreams, but a few scary dreams he couldn't talk about.

September 1851 the Valorys made it to the eastern slopes of the Sierra Nevada and found a foot of fresh snow, and more on the way. A gold hunter named Big Jack helped them build a cabin. In the spring John began cutting trees for Colonel King and his lumber business took off. The letter had been true enough. But after John realized who "Dain King" was, he wasn't happy. Then Petr found his goldmine and all hopes of happiness died in the strangling hands of greed.

"The lightning bolt is buried in these mountains. If you find it you gonna buy a castle? Get a dozen wives like a Mormon? Maybe you buy the moon?" He meant gold—the lightning bolt was Papa's word for gold. Papa didn't believe in gold, he believed in trees. Trees were his gold.

John Valory stood atop a Ponderosa pine log two feet in diameter. King of trees compared to the mere princely pines back east. He was pulling hard on the upstroke of ten feet of ripsaw steel until his muscles bulged, and then coasting while his son pulled the sharp blade back down. The log lay horizontally split over a pit. Down in the hole his son was pulling hard on the down stroke, covered in golden sawdust, imagining the dust as showers of precious gold, the blood of kings and pharaohs. The son of John Valory had dreamed the great valleys of gold. He had dreamed gold all the way from Harrisburg, Pennsylvania to California. He imagined what his father had not imagined. He had a secret he didn't tell anyone.

He believed he would find a treasure-lode in these mountains.

Today he would find gold. *Today* he would become the hunter not of deer or birds, but of precious metal. *Today* the dream would come true. He would find his treasure right after they finished eating cake.

Today, June 12, 1852, was his birthday, the magic of seventeen. Petr John Valory (his Russian mother skipped the second 'e' in Petr to save ink) would get a few simple presents on this beautiful bright blue California Sunday. Then he would go gold hunting. What his father didn't imagine was that he didn't want to get presents, he wanted to give them.

Rumors of California gold ran wild. An ordinary man could make a fortune in a day. Rivers of solid gold lay hidden in mountain valleys and could be found and harvested with a pickaxe and a shovel. Indians could be relied on to trade frying pan sized chunks of gold for a pretty scarf or a few dozen beads. These stories were for fools, he knew that. But a young man like himself could find a reasonable amount of gold in California, enough for his dream of *giving*.

He stopped sawing. He answered his father, "I'd build Mama a white house with blue shutters and I'd buy her a piano. I'd buy Annabel a good horse so she can ride around and stop pestering me."

John stopped. "Yea?—and nothing for me?"

"After I build you a water-powered saw mill," he looked at the tired face of the old Dane for a moment. "After that I bring a steam engine from San Francisco. Then you can pull levers and mind gauges all day while steam makes piles of lumber."

John Valory laughed a good hearty laugh. "How soon can you find this goldmine?"

Papa had quit drinking on the way west, but he was worn thin from cutting boards for other men, for pennies. The old man wanted a lumber mill. Was that asking too much? California was for starting over. He knew it could happen. Petr Valory would make it happen.

In the valley north was a mining camp called Gold Nation where a big man named Dain King was hauling buckets of gold out of the river. Buying every stick of lumber the Valory men could whip from the pit. Getting gold and was hungry for more. Building a long wooden trough called a flume to carry the river out of its bed so men could harvest its golden bottom. Dain King was dreaming big. Petr had seen him from a distance, a great bull of a man, a bronze dome of a head.

Papa kept Petr away from him. Papa wouldn't let Petr go near him; he didn't explain why. People had soft spots in their head that weren't rational. Petr had his own soft spots. His dream of finding gold was a big one. But he had a bigger soft spot in his head. He had fainting spells when he was a kid that sent him into a dream world. Strange dreams that were more like memories than dreams.

He dreamed he had lived long ago in a far lost land of sands and pyramids and pharaohs. He was a flying prince—he could become an invisible falcon soaring across great yellow deserts finding big veins of gold beneath the sand. He was called *The Gold Falcon*.

He had learned to keep that to himself because it was best not to talk about soft spots. The doctor called his fainting spells seizures, but he called them 'jim-jams': the picture in his head flipped and sent him into one of his strange dreams. He was simply gone for a while. Being 'away' was more interesting than real life. In Egypt his name was Mahrire. And a pharaoh named Horemheb always sent him on a mission to find gold; and Mahrire fell in love with a beautiful dream girl named Mirael. It was better than life. He couldn't talk about it.

Papa jabbed him with the long-saw. "Where's your lucky creek?"

"Past the far end of the Valoryvale, past Big Jack's cabin, past that ridge beyond his lake—to the west—I have a good feeling about that far west valley. I dreamed about it."

Every gold hunter had a feeling about a far west valley. Men searched for it. Papa knew about the lost valley with its lake of gold. Everybody knew the story. He said it was a big lie.

Late in 1849 a man named Tom Stoddard found a lake filled with gold but Indians chased him away. (But what would Indians really care about gold?) Spring of 1850, five hundred men went with Stoddard and couldn't find the lake again. Dain King was one of the 'Gold Lake men'. Was Gold Lake still out there in some hidden valley?

Half a dozen small lakes lay hidden in that high west valley. Was one of them Gold Lake? He reckoned he would find it—if it was out there.

Papa laughed. "You find it this afternoon, and we don't have to do this anymore."

There was a piercing steam whistle scream, "Eeee-eee! Yoo-hoo!" His eight-year-old sister, Annabel Rochele: the little Fifty-pounder, little Rocky, little Puzzle-puss, little Bee-bee, little Monkey-bump, dashing up to the pit.

"Come home now. It's lunchtime now—then it's you-know-what time!"

The sun rode high noon. After his birthday party, he knew she would follow him into the high valley. What to do with a lovesick puppy? That's why he had to find some gold today (a reasonable amount like a hat-full). Then get Annabel a good horse; then a nice house for Mama; then a saw mill for Papa. Then things would work out.

Father-son-daughter, walked hand in hand, three hundred yards back to the Valory log cabin. What happened late that afternoon in the high west valley changed things forever.

Gold Lake was a dream that turned into a nightmare.

2

Those who came later were always surprised by the small size of the pioneer cabin. Men with gold fever didn't spend much time building shelter, especially when most likely they would be moving on in a few days or weeks, wherever the next rumor of gold called them.

The Valorys hadn't come for gold. John was a timber man. As for his cabin, the Valory cabin was bigger than most: 20 x 20 feet square with a loft for the children, Petr and Annabel, and a good fireplace with a stone chimney (not stick and mud) up the backside of the cabin—by Sierra standards, a palace.

The woman was Magya Pavlovich Valory, who had never been less happy in her life. Her life had been reduced to living in a wooden hut in a vile wilderness in the middle of nowhere. How had she ended up here? By age fifteen she had been a rising star in St. Petersburg, Russia. She could sing like an angel but was not an angel. John Valory, who was a handsome American sailor, who said he was the captain of a ship, had swept her off her feet—but in reality was a ship's carpenter. True love propelled them to America to the dreary humdrum Harrisburg where the dashing husband slowly became the town drunk. Next the dreamer promised the glory of San Francisco. They would go west! She could rekindle her singing career!

Instead John Valory had marooned them in a pine forest on slanted waves of stone in a land of dirty men. Her voice remained musical, how she didn't know. Whether she complained or said the plainest things, "Please pass potatoes and gravy to sister, please you"—it became a song.

They finished four big wedges of white cake, then came birthday presents. Annabel gave Petr a foot-long pinecone she had painted red. Saying, "This is for my favorite brother."

John excused himself. "I am right back." He went to his toolshed.

Magya took something from her apron, small and bright. A beautiful watch, enamel on gold, too beautiful for a man, its fancy blue case with a circular painting of a man and woman harvesting wheat— she looking away, him leaning forward. What a precious keepsake Annabel should have. Magya pressed it almost violently into Petr's hand.

He opened the case. The pointing hands were gold with sunbursts on the ends, pointing at 12:30.

She said musically, "Now you know when to come home to mama." Beneath her music a sharp bright anger like the edge of a knife.

Petr pocketed the watch. She hugged him squashing her big bosom into him, whispering, "Don't ever forget I was your mama."

Annabel screamed, "It's mine! How can you give it to him?"

Petr tried giving Annabel a brotherly hug, but she shrank away hissing at him. She made a funny, whiny voice, "We'll see about this, buster."

She scrambled up the ladder, quick as a monkey, into the loft— where it grew very quiet.

John returned with a small, efficient-looking rifle, holding it out like a magic wand. Its revolving cylinder was engraved with a hunting scene of men shooting buffalo. Curiously it had "U.S." stamped on its stock. Where did Papa get such an amazing thing in the wilderness?

"A repeater shoots six times. You gonna be king of the mountain: shoot bear and deer." He handed it over to Petr. Petr took it, admired it, set it down, and hugged Papa.

John warned him: "Top all the cylinders with grease—always!—or bullets go off at once." He pushed Petr roughly away. "Go now. Be a man now. Bring home some meat."

Petr said, "Guess I'll get a bear or a deer or a big chunk of gold."

John laughed. "Your birthday—you get what you wish."

Magya didn't smile. In Harrisburg she was slightly plump and beautiful. The journey west had ruined her. She was gaunt-looking and her once proud skin had yellowed from the miserable death march across the Nevada desert. Now her musical voice was sad.

"You come home by four o'clock, okay. You have the watch, okay?" She looked pained.

He told her he would be home by four o'clock—but he wouldn't, and he wouldn't be okay.

FALCON INTERLUDE

High on the gray cliff above the Feather River, a browngold falcon sat beside a silvergray falconess warming her eggs. Looking down, he saw three ducks skimming the river and he instantly leaped, flicking his curved wings, diving upon the blueflashed ducks. They heard hissing speed and immediately leaped across emerald water, splashing up silver footprints, honking frantically, their incurved faces hard with anger. Quickly they slid beneath a harbor of low silver rocks ledged over the water. The browngold falcon veered away at the last whisper of a wingbeat and headed downriver to find food for his mate.

On the cliff, the female arose fluffing her silver feathers, repositioning herself upon two pale eggs, as she watched her heartshaped mate disappear far down the river canyon.

Now the rising sun warmed her niche in the high cliff, and the breath of morning wind fluffed the delicate feathers on her creamy speckled breast. Later she would fly down and cool herself in the stone pool by her emerald river and preen her wing feathers drawn one silver plume at a time through her sharply hooked beak.

Hunting seldom took very long, so she began looking downriver for her browngold mate.

Beyond the hushing white rapids, beyond where green river curved silently into silver mountains, she watched and waited. And she grew hungry.

A moment later she felt a strange booming up the river an instant before it struck her. "Choof! choof!" Like a huge snake stomped on hard, expelling its pellet. The shock penetrated her delicate feathers sending a cold thrill up her back. The sound held the force of thunder, but there were no black-bottomed clouds, no yellow talons of light. Here was bright clear morning pleasant with warmth after long white silence of winter. Here was the *Eyah,* the green brown earth bird now warming herself below the long yellow feathers of skyfather, *Yahee.* But she had heard the false thunder before, and she feared it.

She swiveled her head back and forth scanning river and sky for her quick flying mate. Nothing. She tilted her head all around listening for her mate, but heard no familiar skirling cry. Her only terror was that one day she might watch those browngold wings disappear on the wind and never see them again. And for some reason she knew that the day of terror had come.

Below her the scratchy-voiced birds swooped and pecked at shiny insects making their clicking noises. Her hunger grew and where was her mate? Again she looked downriver and did not see him. She rose from her eggs letting the beaming sun warm them. Now she must eat. Now the river was awakening with noisy hungers: darting flights of starlings; looping, stalling flights of sparrows—all too stringy to interest her. Watching them swoop and peck made hunger's sharp gravel tumble in her stomach.

Suddenly a pigeon flashed below her.

She flamed into air without thinking, following its zigzagging flight.

The fast flyer did not escape her, as she quickly closed and at the last instant lowered her talon, striking the pigeon in the back. Her clenched golden feet held the limp prize as she flew swiftly to her nest. She landed feeling slightly confused after her mindless rush. With her beak, she plucked mouthfuls of white feathers, and when she saw blood—she ate.

Again she gazed downriver, now a sparkling curve glazed by sunshine flowing into the mountains. Her eyes were light drinking wells of blueblack, circled by gold rings, facing forward, bigger than man-eyes. Focused as one—they magnified things—one of her secrets other creatures did not know.

Scanning the first rapids below, she saw blue dragonflies hovering above the water. The sun grew higher and brighter, and still she did not see her mate returning. Cliffs warmed under the yellow morning sun; geysers of wind wafted upward from the flowing band of light, the river below. She sensed the first hot day of spring rising, a gift to her wings.

She gazed upon her eggs. She turned them making her love-sound, "Chee-yup."

She faced the rising sun, tipped forward her broad head, and then dove from her cliff, as sparrows and starlings screeched and scattered out of sight.

Invisible flames of wind pushed her kite-body into the sky, rising swiftly, letting wind do all the work, windlift so hot and powerful her wings felt twice their normal size, as if inflated with air exhaled from the motherbreaths of the many-feathered earth below. Geysers for wind-sensing wings, she danced on hot risers, following an easing path into the sky, her heartshape dancing upward in powerful hops.

Up–pause. Up, up–pause– Up, up. Until many hops later, aloft on blue silent heaven, aloft where even the wind made no sound because there was nothing for it to sigh upon—she bobbed buoyant as a cork atop an out-of-breath windgusher. Feeling its warmbreaths fall away into the cool dregs of sky, she tipped her wings so she could spiral atop the expended wind, slowly widening her flight into descending circles. She saw how unusually high she was, because—

The river below was a silver line, smaller than she had ever seen it.

Far away east, she saw a band of redmen toiling on the ground, towing a string of horses. They were coming slowly toward her river. It was unusual to see them coming from the east, and bringing horses, but it did not frighten her. Redmen came and went over the land disturbing nothing. More often she saw a new kind of two-legged being, men with white hairy faces, men who disturbed everything. Worse, they carried thundersticks that blasted creatures from earth and sky. Mostly the red and whitemen hunted each other, and not falcons. But she had been alive seven seasons and the whitemen were coming with each sunrise as steadily as streams of ants.

The pigeonblood tasted good on her beak and now the hot-flying strength poured into her. This was the way all things, to pour into one another. One day her own strength might be consumed into that of the silent nightkiller, the owl. Then the big-head-on-two-legs might one day be consumed by howldogs. Nothing lived forever. She had seen death many times with her blueblack eyes. Yet every new day warm life floated down from blue sky into the great green domes of earth.

The falcon circled the twin panoramas of blue silent sky father above, and the great green mother below. And again she watched the toiling redmen.

They moved closer towards her bend in the river but that did not disturb her. They never harmed her nest, and when her mate returned all would be well. She relaxed on the highwind feeling its exultation. Never was there any need to fly this high merely in search of food. This knowing of the blue dome—from where *Yahee* threw down the first bird and all other dreams into the green world where they became real—this was the *thrill* lower creatures would never know. This was another of her secrets: the joy on the wind.

Looking up, nothing but the sun flew above her.

The windsinger shrilled her air-splitting shriek: "Keiiieeey-eeeeeeerk!"

Creatures on the ground froze because her voice flew everywhere at once. When nothing happened—they relaxed again. And the gray falconess gazed down upon her world again.

The redmen were approaching from sun's nest, the far mountains of the dry brown land. Now they crossed the long fingers of hills and valleys that led to her valley. Why did they come? Why did they pull a long string of horses?

She looked where the sun falls at day's end into pinefeathered mountains reaching all the way to the ocean. Now she knew her mate was gone too long. It was time to search for his body.

She sailed high over the river where emerald pines leaned across silver banks giving the water its rich color. When she wished it, her magnificent eyes magnified everything to double their size.

Gray rabbits scurried and posed; a few timid deer drank deep, looked up, water dripping from black muzzles; a grizzly bear flattened on a gray slab lay sunning himself, bouncing with hiccups, looking at shadows in the water, dreaming. Perhaps they all once knew, perhaps they had forgotten. Perhaps they had lost their flying in the great becoming and unbecoming of all the animals. All at once the animals left the river in silence—and they were hurrying.

She ignored them. She studied every cliff for a shadow of the familiar browngold shape.

Again she heard the "Choof! Choof!" but this time much closer than before. Seconds later the force of the shockwaves slapped her wings sending needles into her stomach, spreading into her wings, and she grew weak. Instinct drove her into a mindless attack dive.

Now! Scatter all enemies with flaming flight!

Bluejays shrieked, squirrels warbled, deer scurried, bears waddled—all hurrying away. She could see everything—everything except her browngold mate—and now she saw feathers floating down the river.

Sometimes the river carried feathers.

Hawk, owl, pigeon, jay; geese, duck, eagle, swallow. Never falcon. Any of these she could knock from the sky when the sun was high at her back and they never saw her coming from the wild eye of the sun. None matched her matchless wings. None reached her blinding speed of invisibility. Swooping across the river, she saw it floating on the water below, and now the weakness that had poisoned her stomach and wings entered her womb.

Browngold feathers floated down the river—so that life was ended.

Instinct told her to fly to the cliffs. But when she saw them coming from the mountain, the tree smashers, the hairyfaces riding horses and carrying thundersticks in their arms, coming towards her cliffs and coming towards her eggs—hot rage filled her. She flew up and then tipped her body downward. She attacked.

She screamed from the sky, "Screeee-iirk!"

A man raised his stick and she saw and heard—*flash-cloud-choof!* A spray of hornets streaked past her and she knew instantly what had happened to her mate and why he would never return again.

She veered wildly west beating fast towards the green mountains deeps as if death now pursued her darkly as a flying shadow. The joy on the wind was over.

CHAPTER ONE

THE GOLD HUNTER

1

She watched him from the loft window. Scurrying up the natural stone staircase that led to the waterfall, then he crossed the timber lot. She knew where he was heading: Big Jack's cabin on the big lake, and then the Sierra ridge—-the Great Beyond. Petr announced the time when he left with his new watch: one o'clock. She would wait until two. She'd planned this day very carefully.

Annabel Rochele was only eight years old but she knew two things were wrong with her family. First, Papa had promised Mama San Francisco—but instead they had settled on the eastern side of the Sierra Crest because Papa loved trees more than he loved Mama. She had been humming and singing her beautiful voice all of the way to California in anticipation of San Francisco—Magya Pavlovich Valory, the Russian woman—now trapped in a stone valley they called the Valoryvale. That was part of the second wrong, her own wrong.

Annabel Rochele Valory was trapped in stone. After making big sacrifices; giving up friends in Harrisburg, making new friends on the wagon train, and losing them four months later—her only amusement now was following Petr around.

Today was *his* birthday and more crimes were being committed by both Mama and Papa. Mama gave Petr the gold and blue enamel pocket watch that should have been hers. Papa gave Petr a new rifle that he would like even less than the watch. She knew Petr hated guns. Mama and Papa got stupider every year. But it didn't matter anymore. She was getting out. She had an escape plan.

If Petr found gold so would she. He talked about it in his sleep.

They slept only two feet apart on straw sacks so she knew today began his hunt for Gold Lake. And Annabel Rochele Valory would be right there when he found it.

At one o'clock (according to his new watch) he left with his big stupid, happy-dog grin on his face. At two o'clock (by her calculations) she was supposed to be brooming her room.

Wrongo. At two o'clock she would sneak out the window and jump off the roof and say goodbye to childhood.

2

His time had come, he even had a gold watch to prove it: he was running free in the Sierra high country where he would find gold. The long way west broke many men, and families died, but that was over. Now was time for the Sierra dream, the most beautiful mountains on earth. From a distance they looked like silver shields shining in the sun, beneath which lay a paradise of gleaming granite dripping with gold in secret places. But where were such places? Today he would find out. He had to find out. Because Mama and Annabel were suffering, he had to find out.

He ran up the steep valley of the Valoryvale that led to the Sierra Crest. He was young, tall and fit, and today what he really wanted for his birthday was not a pretty watch or rifle. What he wanted was a gloryhole full of gold.

Rifle shots snapped in the distance off the north ridge beyond which lay the big mining operation of Dain King on the north fork of the Feather River, about three miles away in the next valley. It was being called Gold Nation, where they were building a flume—a hundred yards of wooden trough that would carry the river of the North Branch out of its channel so King and his men could rob its river bed of gold like robbing a bank. But to finish the flume, King needed Valory lumber.

John and Petr Valory were his cutters, small players in the drama that couldn't be done without them: They were supplying all of the wood for King's flume; the big man needed the little man; and for some reason Papa didn't like the big man.

Petr had seen King up in his wooden tower, a big brute of a man, gazing down on his kingdom, this wild rich stretch of river, soon tamed by his rising flume. Some said he was a handsome devil. Some said he was wanted by the Army. One thing was certain: After they unloaded their wagonload of yellow planks beside the flume, John quickly hustled Petr away as if they were in a death camp loaded with cholera. Petr remembered now where he had seen the fancy rifle before.

It was a Colt revolver-rifle, and all of Dain King's men had them.

Petr started running up the valley to the crest. There was more than one mystery to solve in these beautiful mountains—and Mama expected him home in three hours.

Petr ran into forest so thick it blocked out the sun. This was Papa's gold—big Ponderosa pines—easy to find but hard work turning it into lumber. Gold finding would be much easier.

Gunshots rattled over the ridge. Not a battle. It was Sunday afternoon hunting out on the river. Nothing to worry about. Certainly not Indians. The Maidus carried bows and spears. They might steal a rope or an axe with the innocence of a child. But they were fierce as grizzly bears if interfered with or provoked. And they weren't the greatest danger in the Sierras.

The greatest danger was finding gold.

Papa warned him. If you find gold you better keep your rifle handy. Gold drew men like iron to a magnet. But the Valoryvale claim was a rolling wonderland of Ponderosa and Jeffrey pine that made fine yellow boards smelling sweet as powdered sugar. The other wealth of their tree kingdom was a mountain stream flashing through the Valoryvale like liquid crystal. It splashed into the Feather River a few miles below, but it contained no gold. He had looked. So no one would ever bother the Valoryvale. But he would be wrong about that.

John and Petr harvested straight yellow timber growing from the forest like beams of light encased in brown husks. Magya claimed the Valorys were so poor they couldn't afford ink for the second "e" in Petr's name. So naturally he wanted to find gold so his family would never feel poor again. The desire pursued him sharp as a gnawing hunger.

I will find the great gold of Earth and I will be rich and happy.

He knelt beside the crystal stream made delicious from melted snow. He drank. When he glanced up, a gray squirrel and a bluejay were watching him suspiciously. He whispered to them, "Where do I find gold? I have to find it. Papa won't last another year if I don't find gold. He needs a saw mill with a waterwheel, maybe even steam-powered, so he doesn't work himself to death. Mama needs a proper house with painted shutters so she doesn't go crazy. Maybe I'll take her to San Francisco so she can have her dream too. Annabel needs...."

Thinking of Annabel made him smile. That girl needed many things. A horse might keep her happy, might stop her following him around like a puppy. Hopefully she wasn't following him right now.

"Annabel needs a pretty horse, please."

He laughed and began running again, long smooth strides across the forest floor.

When he emerged from the thick forest marking the upper end of the Valoryvale, he knew he was in Gold Country: Bright sun was a blazing copper pitcher pouring heat from the sky; the Sierra Crest a rising kingdom of gray towers; black flies buzzing around his head aroused by the heat told of early spring. He cupped his hands beneath a miniature waterfall and again drank icy swallows of water until his throat ached. He was *alive!*

Might find Indians, or lost cities, or fire-belching caves! What secrets lay hidden in these mountains? Why couldn't he hunt gold six days a week and cut lumber just for one, like Big Jack or Dain King?

He heard a faint, skirling cry, high on the wind: "Keee-iiirrrk!" Looking up, he saw a good omen: scimitar-shaped wings carving circles on the sky. It was a falcon.

He believed it was the same one he and Annabel had taken food scraps to down by the river. He waved at it, yelling: "I *will* find that gold lake and I *will* be free as you, high flyer."

With the rifle sights he scanned the high cliffs of the Crest. No need to go there. Gold wouldn't be there. He didn't know much about "goldfinding" but he had heard gold was the heaviest substance on earth. Gold would run downhill. It would be in valleys or rivers or at the bottom of lakes—somehow. The biggest chunks would be in a high river or lake.

He scanned the rifle south.

There lay the big blue lake called "Loch Loong" by its solitary dweller, Big Jack—Jack Gorgius Frazier. He had helped them build their cabin last fall. The Scotsman had found no gold. No need to go there. But Petr would share the gold lake with Jack when he found it.

He scanned the rifle north.

There rose a sharp ridge that, once crossing it, led down into the North Fork of the Feather River; the wild rich mining camp called Gold Nation where they took a wagonload of lumber each week and then Papa always hustled him away as if the place was full of disease.

Why?

The watch made a pretty, singsonging: *ching-ching!* It was two o'clock.

Mama's gift was awareness of time. Why? Why was there always secret unhappiness under everything she did?

Papa's gift-rifle was getting heavy. Papa had warned him. Top those cylinders off with grease or they will all blow off at once and remove your face. Papa had properly loaded it. It was ready to fire, a powerful tool that could shoot six times. That meaning was clear. *Petr, you're a man now.* But he never wanted to kill anything. The rifle was useless to him as a stick of lead.

He ran fifty paces, walked fifty paces, hopped over countless rivulets of spring runoff. Not far away was a small paradise of blue lakes held in rocky bowls made like giant cups. Big Jack had told him all about it. Three years ago Tom Stoddard had found a lake somewhere. It was filled with gold—so they said. But five hundred determined men failed to find it.

Petr vowed: "I *will* find it." Another thought hit him: Dain King was one of those determined men, you can bet on it. That's why he explored the Feather River. That's how he found gold on the North Fork; what he was now calling The Gold Nation. It all made sense.

The rifle was unbearable. Sweat dripped down his face. Getting hot. Getting thirsty. It was the first hot day of spring. He was running on naked stone up a lower crest that led to the Sierra Crest. A hidden gold lake might lie somewhere in the bowl between the two crests. He would bet five dollars on it, if he had five dollars.

It was a steep climb up the mountainside. When he heard the falcon again he looked up.

He couldn't find it, but high on top of the rising cliff was a deer, a big one.

The biggest buck he had ever seen posed silently a hundred yards away on a sharp gray ledge. It was white. Pale as cream and smooth and its antlers spread like tan flames. What would Papa say if he brought home a white deer? Petr aimed the rifle and the deer disappeared like a puff of smoke. He set the rifle aside, scanning the trees, and moments later the buck reappeared atop a dry waterfall above a small circle of boulders. It made a high whistling laugh. Petr shouted back at it.

"I won't hurt you. You're beautiful. You're magic—a white deer— you're a manitoo."

Jack had told him all about it. Jack knew all about such things. The manitoo was a forest creature that lent you wisdom; it could help you prosper. Jack had seen this white buck and said it would be bad luck to shoot it. It was a good birthday gift. Now it was watching Petr Valory.

It doesn't like the rifle. Okay. Be rid of it then.

He ran downslope until he found the biggest cedar tree he had ever seen in his life.

Massive survivor of centuries, it was tent-like, with branches that covered the ground. He crawled inside. It was cool and dry and fragrant. He set the rifle against the trunk. There. Good. Crawl outside again. He made a stone pyramid to mark the tree. Come back later.

He didn't know he wouldn't see that rifle again for twelve years.

He searched upslope but the white deer was gone. Probably wasn't a manitoo anyway. Still, you didn't see a magnum buck like that every day. Just a good luck sign that today was a lucky day: Head for that dry waterfall. See what you see.

He scrambled up until he was atop the smaller crest with its big view. Little Rocky would never make it up here. No worries about that. Again he would be wrong.

To the south lay the big blue expanse of Long Lake. Jack's cabin looked like a toy house on a peninsula of pines jutting into the lake. To the north lay a gray valley holding two blue-jewel lakes, primitive and wild. A strong sugary wind breezed up from the valley, a sweet pine wind. It was beautiful. Go there—to the valley of lakes. He checked his watch: 2:15.

Plenty of time before sundown. That was another miscalculation.

There it was again. The manitoo deer stood beside the first small lake, lapping up water. It raised its wide antlers and gazed at him as if to say: Well, are you coming? Then it trotted away westward.

Petr ran down the crest leaping manzanita brambles that crashed beneath him like mattresses made of twigs. He fell laughing a dozen times and couldn't stop running and falling. When he reached the bottom he fell like a blown horse. Thank god he was rid of the heavy rifle.

While he caught his breath, he studied the lower lake with its smaller twin. No glimmer of gold, just big bowls of cold water. No gold here. How on earth did anyone ever find gold?

The big deer whistled and ran into a high valley. There it vanished. He's leading me on, isn't he? No, that's a silly idea.

He glanced along the shore. Between the twin lakes lay a grove of pinenut trees, all cut down and rotting. Who had done such a crime? He walked slowly into a graveyard of stumps. He remembered the delicious taste of the pinenuts. They were so hungry at the end of their journey last fall. Jack had shown them how to knock down pinecones from the tree using a long stick. They had been grateful for the nuts. The Indians needed pinenuts to survive. Who did this? He ran again. A dark thought hit him: *Evil is hidden beneath beauty.* That couldn't be true. Where did such an awful idea come from?

He stumbled onto a rock slab pitted with bowl-shaped holes. Indian work—a big grinding floor. Here's where they ground nuts into flour. He ran his hands along the smooth hollows and felt a strange thrill. How long did it take people to make such holes, centuries? The holes wavered like a mirage on a desert, a warning he might be having a *jimjam* fit. That meant jerking on the ground and twitching, while the picture inside his head flipped and flipped and flipped. No, not today! Not this gold hunting day!

But it didn't happen. He hadn't had a fit all the way west. His vision steadied.

A few yards off he saw ruins of an Indian village burnt to the ground, a dozen smudges like dead bonfires in a semi-circle. These had been huts the Indians called *canee,* now fading in the earth. But who had torched them, the Indians? Dain King? He suddenly felt cold even though it was a hot day.

He sat among the ruins for a long minute, feeling bad, feeling sad.

Something happened here. Indians were murdered here. Or simply moved away? This was a mystery within an hour of the Valoryvale. Thank God Annabel wasn't here to see it.

His wrong guesses were piling up.

The white buck made its high keening cry again. Standing on a small peak at the end of a high valley, it looked back at him and then suddenly jumped down, and disappeared.

Was there a hidden canyon at the end of the valley?

The watch chimed: *Ching! ching! ching!* He glanced at the sun. Three o'clock already. Circling the high silver canyon was the falcon making its sky skirling cry-song. "Keee-iiirrrk!"

The falcon and white deer—foolish to believe they were calling him or that they were manitoos—but they *seemed* to be. He felt a terrible urge to follow them. Time was speeding up.

Find out what happened here later. Find that deer. Find the Gold Lake. Hurry up.

The manitoo is guiding you.

3

She was punished for not doing her Sunday Bible reading. It was a crime against Magya Pavlovich Valory. Mama ordered Annabel into the loft to sweep her room. She went up. It was according to plan. Annabel had plotted it out. She looked down at them both.

Magya reading the big family Bible; John making one of his little bottle boats. Annabel smiled. Make the broom whisper. She took up her broom and held the rough straw in her lap—and lashed a flat piece of slate (there was a crumbling wall of it by the waterfall) onto the straw. She hung the broom from a rafter—and pushed it.

Hush back and forth, hush, hush. It would last maybe a minute. They would forget about her. *Did we used to have a little girl?* Who cared about Annabel?

Climb out the back window. Petr had an hour head start but so what? He said where he was going in his sleep. He was heading for the high valley. He called her "Rocky" in his sleep. Today we show what little 'Rocky' can do.

She returned to her doll. She said, "That's who I am now. Never mind the ground eight feet down. It cannot hurt a boy. Now I am Rocky, the boy."

Blue skies blazed high above; pine scent filled the air with the sweet smell of freedom—

She edged down the roof. She jumped. She hit the ground.

Good God! Her feet stung like nails were driven in with hammers. But nothing worse. And she could still move. She startled away like a deer.

She ran uphill to the Valory waterfall where there was a clearing. She looked up the valley and couldn't see Petr but he was easy to follow. He was about two miles away. She could tell. The falcon was circling a hundred feet over him like a kite on a string.

Their falcon, the one they had been trying to tame by putting sugared meat atop a dead tree. She was sure of it. She caught her breath and started laughing. My wandering brother.

Hunting for gold! She was only eight but already knew something important. "Men seek gold and women seek love!"

The falcon circled near the Crest and was no longer moving away. What did that mean? *The falcon loves Petr and follows him as Annabel loves and follows him?* (Yes?)

Afterwards she would have a long time to ponder over that.

4

Petr got closer to where the white buck had disappeared. It had disappeared down *into* something. He marked the spot mentally because if it was a canyon it was hidden from below. After five minutes of steep climbing he found the entrance. Well, well, well.

A crevice choked with brambles, cut and carefully placed—dried and withered and pale as if they had been placed long ago—to hide a hiding place. But why hide a canyon? What lay beyond the narrow gap? This must be something special. He went down on hands and knees.

After a few feet of scratchy crawling he exited a bramble tunnel and was inside a narrow canyon of silver-colored granite; Indians had hidden it, and used it—but for what?

What would Indians hide from the rest of the world? What did Indians really care about?

The canyon was V-shaped, remote, and forbidding. For the first time that afternoon he thought: Maybe I'm not home for supper.

He had a sudden, unexpected memory, a nightmare he'd had since he was ten, when he began thinking of girls differently from boys. It returned powerfully as he walked slowly up the strange narrow ramp of the little canyon. In the dream he saw a beautiful girl with a face much like his own, a sun-ripened beauty. She was living sunshine. He was strolling arm-in-arm with this perfectly matched to him female, perfectly happy. Then as in the way of dreams, he lost her. Searching everywhere, he seemed to have missed her only by minutes wherever he went. And yet—in his dream—he never saw her again. He could picture her, almost feel her, but he had lost her forever, leaving a terrible loneliness inside him as if his soul was dying.

Now that aching loneliness was hitting him hard.

He sat on a rock and covered his eyes. A breeze wafted faint odor as if someone had struck a match. Sulfur? His next thought was a double lightning flash.

Don't go any farther. But it's the gold lake!

He scanned the loose gravel for what had to be there: Silver-dollar-sized-deer-tracks. But there were no tracks. The path was smooth. No one here for a very long time, not even animals.

He swallowed hard and walked deeper into the canyon, now steeply uphill. An icy chill shivered up his back. He saw something up ahead, man-made, Indian-made.

A hundred yards more was a level clearing where white and black stones lay in circles. Seven stone circles where seven chiefs had been buried. Why would he know that? The hair on his arms stood up. He realized something and it was loud and clear.

The California Mountains were enchanted, the sunshine, the fresh air, famous for healing sick people. But this place—whatever that energy was—was jacked up way too high. Petr felt his neck hair *bristling*. He was terribly thirsty. The first big fear temblor hit him hard in the gut—blossoming out his first irrational thought:

Whitemen don't belong here—and don't get out alive.

He tried to laugh but his throat was so dry it felt cracked, he choked. He put a pebble under his tongue, an old trick he had learned in the Nevada desert when they had no water all day every day.

Go on. You know *he* wants you to go on. You mean (he wanted to laugh but couldn't)—

The deer? And where was the deer, anyway? This was a box canyon for sure: no way out. The buck was in here. It had to be. He was going to get a good long look at that big white buck.

He walked for five minutes until he saw the ending backwall, a steep red cliff. For some reason it was *shimmering* like a gold lake. What Tom Stoddard found and couldn't find again? Another blast of fear hit him in the gut. He stopped.

If there was a lake—where was its outfall stream running down from it? All lakes had them. Where was it? He scanned a gully for a seasonal stream and there wasn't one. Maybe there was no gold lake either. His skin went cold as if from winter wind, but there was no wind. Just beyond the chieftain graveyard was something that made him freeze.

It was so stunning he swallowed his pebble. Upthrust from the canyon floor was a quartz tongue, pure, thick, white, unbelievable.

It was streaked with gold veins.

He coughed up the pebble. His knees crumpled, he gasped, "Holy mother of Jesus!"

He crawled until he gripped the cool slipperiness of the *thing*, pulled on it but it didn't budge. It was rooted in the earth. He began patting it reverently whispering.

"Mama, Papa, Annabel, look what I found."

The gold-streaked tusk proved no gold hunter had been here before—except maybe Tom Stoddard. Who claimed he'd left this place...*this very place*...in a hail of arrows!

"Must see...must see if it's all true," he whispered. He had to go on, had to see the lake.

The burnt match smell very strong now, tainted by something worse, skunk-worse, something rotten and dead. Was the lake lined with dead bodies?

You came to find the legendary Gold Lake, didn't you? Go on now. Find it.

His legs shook. He was entering a cloud of rotten stench. He moved forward covering his nose, trying not to gag.

Another hundred yards he heard the steady hiss of a waterfall. Maybe there was a lake or at least a plungepool. Even small waterfalls produced prodigious amounts of water. Why was there no stream running down the narrow valley? The mystery urged him onward and suddenly he was running scared with a big yellow gob of fear in his stomach.

He found himself crouching awkwardly forward, expecting a whizz-thump of an arrow in his chest. His shoulders ached. His eyes popped so wide he couldn't blink. Nearing the end wall at last he would see the big white buck close up and it would be worth the trip. There couldn't be any gold here. (*Could there?*) On the other hand California *was* the Promised Land.

This *was* an unexplored canyon. (*Wasn't it?*)

At the back of the canyon fell silver threads of showering water, a small waterfall. He forced himself forward feeling the stinging arrow that would end his life. But water promised a lake and he had to see it *now*.

Then he saw it.

Round as a red moon, it was small, its backwall curved like a piece of broken cup. The water was blood red, nothing growing within twenty yards of the red pool, its perimeter arid and stinking of gas, the starkness relieved only by the hissing jet of water. Was *this* Gold Lake? A bubble rose to the surface and that awful smell again. The smell made him think of giving birth to eggs or *something bad* and he didn't know what or why he thought that way. It was a creepy place. Something could jump out of the lake at any second. His hair stood up and his skin crawled and his vision wavered towards a jimjam fit. A chill ran up his back and his arms goose-pimpled.

Please don't let me pass out right now.

The jimjam didn't happen. No shimmering halos of purple light; no mental holiday into the ancient past. But it was close. His vision wavering, he gripped his head willing himself not to have a fit. He looked around.

Where was the big deer? No way out, the white deer had to be in this canyon. But it wasn't and that wasn't possible. He whispered, "Got to be...so strange...not to be."

The deer wasn't here. Somehow—the deer was somewhere else.

The head of the canyon formed a tall red crown fifty feet above the lake. He scanned the rim but didn't see the white deer. *(Deer or manitoo?)* He studied the lake.

At the edge there was a finger *pointing* at the water, a shiny black finger, and when he walked over to it, he saw it was a primitive, beautiful stone knife made by the redmen.

Go on, pick it up. You know you want it.

He picked it up. He flashed the knife in the air feeling a strange savage power in his blood. He dashed around the lake swinging the knife, yelling, "Bad old Indian, you gonna mess with me now?"

Then the bad old Indian appeared out of nowhere.

5

The bird circling high overhead marked his location so exactly she was able to avoid the steep climb and instead took a gently rising valley to the north, a quicker path to her goal. Her brother was north of Big Jack's Cabin almost two miles and just below the Crest. It was probably an hour worth of running but she was good for it.

Her white dress had shredded into pitiful rags in the manzanita mazes but she didn't care at all. She wasn't a boy—that would take time. But she was getting dirty. Boy was she ever. She was a brown rag of a girl! That was a start. A boy was dirty and tough. Things might hurt but a boy didn't care.

One hour later she reached a granite bowl with twin lakes. The bird was circling the far end of a high valley so she headed there. A minute later she was within a grove of dead trees and found a flat slab of stone pocked with holes like a meteorite. Beyond this lay a dozen scorched spots, all spooky and sad, making her sense something terrible had happened here. At the far end of the valley was a dark slit in the Crest that might be a box canyon, or it might be nothing.

The bird was circling above it. He had to be there. She sprinted for it.

Getting dirty, getting tough, not caring. On my way to being a boy.

Getting to the box canyon was a serious five minute climb. Without the bird marking it she would never have found it. The small entrance to the canyon was covered with tangled shrubs that had been pulled aside so there was a small gap in the tangle. If the shrubs were fresh she wouldn't have noticed it. But the shrubs were brown and dried out. Maybe whoever maintained this entrance was dead.

Either a bear or Petr had gone into whatever it was—a gully or a canyon. She was pretty sure it was Petr, and that she was getting close. She felt like making a good old steamboat joy whistle scream but decided to wait. Wait until you see him.

She low-crawled through the ragged hole and was inside in seconds.

The canyon was narrow, a jaw that made her feel like she was being swallowed up. She tried to escape the feeling by running, but it didn't help. A few minutes later were circles of black rocks and white rocks like a small graveyard. Beyond this was a tusk of white quartz, like a crude pulpit sparkling with gold. None of this interested her. What she wanted was to sneak up on Petr and scream, *Ha, ha! Thought I couldn't find you?*

A minute later there was a lake that smelled like rotten eggs and dead frogs.

You didn't go in there, did you? Then, Don't get all little girl scairdy-cat now. The place was revoltingly creepy. Red water stinking with frogs? *Definitely.* Definitely entering boyhood.

Her entire being quickened with an electric thrill when she heard a faint welcoming: *ching, ching, ching, ching!* The watch—it meant he was here! She ran up to the lake.

Worse than creepy. Beside the dead pool sat a neat pile of clothes— and the realization of what that meant sent a chill up her spine.

There his faded red shirt. Boots with the tops flopped over. The watch nestled in the shirt like a jewel. Spectacles neatly placed. Why brother, why—have you gone swimming?

Kneeling at this soft altar she handled the watch fondly, kissing The Lovers painted on its case. *The watch should have been mine.* Directly overhead the falcon cried, "Keee-iiirrrk!"

She looked. High on a ledge of rock, high above the water, there he was.

Annabel gasped, but barely a whisper came out. "Peh...."

He stood painted on the sky. Shirtless, stripped to his blue pantaloons. Why? What for? A cannonball-sized rock hoisted overhead—he looked oddly *old.* Eyes clenched, mouth gaping like he was getting ready to do something crazy.

Annabel shrieked long and hard, not the happy steamboat whistle, but the scream-train bound for Hell. "Eeeeeeiiiiiiiiii!" And it didn't do any good. Petr jumped.

Tipping into a dive, down he went. Down, down, down, then a stone-first smash into the lake that made it splash and boil. Annabel waited open-mouthed.

Red rings formed silent farewells and Petr did not come up.

6

The big man gutted, then salted the bird and when he was done tied it to his saddle horn. It was a smallish bird, a golden brown falcon. He'd missed the larger female but it wasn't his fault or the rifle's, one of the six-shot repeaters he had stolen from the government. That bird had flown like winged hell. Earlier in the day he was disappointed by the rifle's killing power when he shot a grizzly and it grunted and ran away. That would be one dangerous bear the next time it encountered a man.

Munson rode in looking very used-up. King asked, "Pah Utes coming?"

"Big bend of the river right where you want em, waiting like corn-fed ducks."

"And horses?"

"There's six Injuns bringing thirty horses, nice big ones."

King grunted with satisfaction. "All right then. We hit them at dawn. Get the men down."

Did the Indians really think they'd get rifles for horses? Sometimes life was too easy.

7

When Petr saw the Indian he froze. The knife in his hand felt foolish. The Indian held his bow fully drawn with an arrow ready to strike—a small black point gleaming in the sun. And his eyes glittering obsidian points somehow too bright—like he was half man, half lightning.

He barked, "Heya-hey!"

Petr jerked as if his body was operated by strings the Indian pulled. He felt his scalp rise. He was seeing a force of nature. This wasn't just an Indian.

This was the supreme Warrior Being, King of the Indians, like a bear or a mountain lion formed into a man. He was magnificent, broad-shouldered, in bleached white buckskins.

Then he relaxed the bowstring. He pointed the arrow at a narrow cliff. "You go up there, you see?" He gestured to a ledge of rock at least 25-feet above the small lake.

His voice was deep, "You jump—you swim down—I tell you where. You strip—shirt and shoes."

Petr nodded. Put the knife down. No question of not obeying. He was pretty sure disobeying meant death. He piled his shirt, boots, glasses—and the pretty watch.

The Warrior said, "You come up too soon, I put arrow in you." He gestured for Petr to go up. His voice commanded, "Swim to mouth inside mountain, and go down fast as you can!"

Petr hurried to the back of the lake where he could climb. At the base of the cliff, on a broad slab of gray rock, were Indian drawings blazed as if made by flaming fingers. Had he intruded on an Indian sacred place?

Wiggling pairs of snake lines; circle within circles and W's like birds. Most stunning of all was a big white deer with big antlers and a bird tangled in the horns—or flying from it.

It was the great deer he had followed—the great manitoo—now falcon, now deer, now Indian? He brushed his fingers over it and felt a rising reverence.

It *is* their sacred place and the warrior is going to kill me.

He moved beyond mere thinking. His brain was no longer telling him what to do. He felt brilliant clarity and daring that bordered on insanity. He could do anything. *Anything.* The Indian was somehow feeding him energy, sending him courage.

The Great Warrior watched him closely, nodding encouragement, but not smiling. Petr knew what this was. It was a test of manhood. Indians were big on bravery and manhood and showing it.

Petr climbed smoothly up the granite face. He felt as if he had been scaling cliffs all of his life. It took only a minute to reach the high ledge above the calm water.

This altered its appearance. Seen from the ground the lake was a red-rimmed eye, a dead eye. Seen from here it was an icy blue eye, a turquoise mirror. His burst of fearlessness suddenly evaporated. *You jump? You swim down?* He couldn't do it.

The Indian was poised like a statue, watching him, waiting.

Petr called down, "What do I do now?" his voice quavery and weak.

The strong voice replied: "You gonna find out pretty soon. You jump. You swim into that hole. You gonna see. You find place you can breathe again. You believe me or you gonna die. Now get a big rock."

The voice was so deep and powerful Petr found that he wanted to obey. He found a smooth cannonball-sized rock. He looked down. The lake now seemed the size of a small blue bucket. He leaned over the ledge and felt his stomach shrink. His vision made pinwheels of purple fire, the beginnings of a jimjam fit. He closed his eyes tight. His voice sounded childish.

"Why are you doing this to me?"

The Warrior laughed. He said, "Indian boys jump from here, long ago. They become real men—real Indians—or they die. You gonna find out right now."

Petr opened his eyes. The lake seemed a mile down. "I'm afraid...I can't."

The Warrior's voice was deep as forest wind: "All boys afraid. Now you be a man. Now you gonna see. You do what I say, you live. You don't do it, I kill you."

Petr grimaced. He was seventeen today. Not a boy. Not a good day to die. I refuse to die.

The Warrior nodded as if to say, *now,* but he looked sorrowful, his lips didn't move but—and this had to be some new version of the jimjam fit—Petr heard him anyway only now it was inside his head, and even louder than before. The Indian said: *I watched from this place for a long time—I wait for you—Now hear me. I am with you when you hear me. I am in your heart when you need me. Go now and find me in your heart.*

Petr didn't understand what this meant, only that this was it. This was *manitoo.*

The words gave him strength. He took a step backward and hoisted the stone over his head. Either you're a man or you're not. If you're not, you die. Simple as that.

For one brilliant moment he considered the possibility that he had gone completely mad. Sorrow filled him to a degree he had never experienced before. He wanted to bawl like a baby. Other thoughts entered that were stronger and braver than his usual white man's store of knowledge: *It is The Luminah...I will be with you...You will know what to do...You will not be afraid...not ever again...I am with you...Tell no one!*

Then his own thoughts returned: Do it quick now. Or he'll kill you.

Must jump into Gold Lake suddenly because it is so shockingly cold. No other way to go in—deep. He lunged for the edge, but stopped again.

Need lots of air. The Indian said he would swim into the mountain, into a hole. He would find a place where he could breathe. It sounded impossible but he had to try.

He filled his lungs until they felt like hard balloons of air. Then he exhaled and inhaled again. Holding the stone high overhead he leaned out and felt the heavy rock pulling him forward, felt waves of fear. The forest voice whispered again:

Go deep into the lake...It is The Luminah...I will be with you...You will know what to do. You will not be afraid again...ever...I am with you...Tell no one!

The forest voice pulled him forward.

Now! He swung the stone high and leaped into the air and tipped into a dive.

Plunging full of hope, flying, falling, strange words trailing after him like streamers of smoke: *You will find yourself in The Luminah.*

The last instant he prayed: Let me be born alive!

When he hit the water he heard a little girl scream like steam whistle.

8

John climbed up to the loft, looked over the rail, and laughed. Then he came back down. Magya watched him nervously. What was so funny? He hadn't talked to Annabel, only laughed.

He went to his shed for ten minutes. When he came back inside he was stinking of whiskey and grinning like a fool. The demon was back! Where did he get whiskey? From that evil mining camp?

She yelled, "Get away from me, you filthy swine!" But it did no good this time.

Twenty years before he was drunk with the smooth lines from Shakespeare. That's how he charmed her. After they married he lost Shakespeare and took whiskey every night. But for seven months—the journey west—he had been sober. Now the dirty beast returned.

He tossed his round glasses aside and plunged at her. "Now you— be my wife again!"

She cried out, "Help me, Annabel!" She jumped onto the ladder and climbed as fast as she could, but John was right behind her. Laughing, gripping her legs as she screamed tumbling into the loft. John followed and she backed away quickly. She grabbed the broom but it wouldn't come loose. He brushed it aside, laughing. The rooster! No more of that. Not ever. Rather die.

She said, "Stay back, you dirty beast."

He peeled his filthy gloves revealing the horrid nubs of his fingers. "My hen, she's all alone now." He was chortling, giddy, all roostered-up.

She held her bosom in her hands but her hands were too small to cover them. She tried reasoning. "Remember, I raise him like my own boy—and you said you'd leave me be." Her voice trembling, "You need dirty thing you go to King's tavern and buy you an Island girl." Shocked that she'd said that to him, then she screamed, "Leave me be!"

He grinned, lunging at her.

"No! Keep back!" Must not let this happen. Not another baby! Their first two were born dead. Then giving birth to Annabel had nearly killed her. When he began kneading her like dough, she gasped.

He laughed again, "Oh, that pretty song, too." He tore at her buttons. There were fifty white buttons down the front of her black Sunday dress.

She slapped him so hard it sounded like a rifle shot, but he didn't stop. Finish him off, say anything. "Annabel and I leave—"

John pulled with all his strength and buttons flew like shining stars.

9

Red rings lapped the shore, one by one disappearing.

Annabel sat repeating over and over, mentally, Please come up, please come up, please. She looked at the beautiful watch: Four oh-two. Take a deep breath. Count slowly. She began their hold-the-breath game. Annabel always fizzled out after sixty seconds. Amazingly, Petr could hold for nearly three minutes. He claimed his secret was to think of a faraway story.

Go away mentally. Take a little trip. Forget about breathing.

She exploded after thirty-two seconds.

Okay, too excited. Don't count, don't think of minutes.

She stared at the pool, whispering: "Come up, oh please come up."

The water was a blank red mirror. Nothing appeared. No dripping brother saying, Rocky, I really fooled you this time! Any real boy would try the game again. Hold your breath!

She sucked in a big lungful of air. This time she tried remembering a story Big Jack told when building their cabin last fall: Don't ya go dandling off into the woods now, little darling. Ya hear them whispers in the stream? Them's voices of lost children! She laughed but Jack continued sternly. Water kelpie's got em. He's the prettiest pony ya iver seen. But onc't ya hop on, ya niver get off. Yoor stuck like glue. Takes away many a fair lass and laddy ivery year, sad but true. He nearly got me onc't when I was just a yoong soncie. *Beware of the Water Pony.*

She laughed, her breath exploded—and the red mirror held nothing at all.

How long has he been under? The watch read four oh-four. Petr underwater four minutes? *Impossible.* Maybe the water kelpie got him too. Maybe he was playing a game just to scare her. But that was no good. *He doesn't know you're here.* She stared at the red pool.

"Okay, you won the game, Petr. Now please come up, please, please."

Still there was nothing and Petr wasn't coming *up*, and then Annabel must—

She touched the water. It felt like cold teeth biting her hand!

You cannot go down into that faceless mirror of death. It's suicide. It's—

Go down brave boy! And find what? His bloated body stuck beneath slimy rocks? Not Petr anymore but a terrible clay cocoon?

She dried her fingers on her dress. She put the gold watch in her pocket—where it belonged. She picked up his shirt. She pressed it hard into her face and it smelled good: salty, tangy, sweaty leather aroma of Petr. She pulled on his floppy boots. They came up over her knees. They comforted her. Wearily, she lay down using the shirt for a pillow but she began shaking, trying to hold back tears. Not a very boy-like thing, was crying. Just keep your eyes on that lake!

Exhaustion rolled over her. She was worn out. All that uphill climbing and downhill running and hopping streams, had done her in. Go to sleep now. Get some rest.

No, I won't sleep! Maybe close my peepers a quick minute. I'll be right here when he—

She barely whispered: "When he comes up... please... come... up."

She couldn't help it. She fell deeply asleep dreaming a long dream that began with children laughing, crying, playing. She knew all about them: the lost children who thought they knew better than big folks, thought they could wander off alone in the mountains. She knew because Big Jack had told her. But why did they sound so happy? They would never be seen again because the Water Pony took them away. Jack warned her about the Water Pony. It took children and drowned them.

The day was getting worse because now she saw it. The Water Pony galloped around the lake. Now it stood before her. It was beautiful.

Shimmering blue, with a coal black mane, its tail brushed the ground. What fancy blue eyes and bright teeth you have! Annabel spoke clearly: I need to go down right now to find Petr. Can you help? That's why you're here, to help me—aren't you? Water Pony nodded three times. Down there, is he? Water Pony stomped the ground. I'm only dreaming so why not go?

Annabel grabbed its long black mane and climbed onto its round solid back. They slid into the water, not cold at all, it was dreamy cozy warm. But what Jack said was true. She was glued to Water Pony's back. She could not get off.

It took her down to a gloomy, honeycombed bottom, thirty feet below.

They entered an underwater cave sloping *upwards* like a teapot spout. Since it was only a dream she could breathe underwater. The pony trotted up the watery tube and after what seemed like ten minutes they entered a cave chamber holding a dark pool nearly identical to the one outside the mountain only this one was deep inside the mountain, its shore fine black sand.

Around the lake were caves like small dark eyes. Above each cave was the drawing of an animal. Bear. Deer. Wolf. Turtle. Twelve caves with twelve different animals.

Next she noticed a small stream that exited the back of the lake and disappeared down yet another tunnel. That tunnel was flickering with gold light. And carved above its entrance was a blazing gold falcon. The Water Pony didn't hesitate. It went down the falcon tunnel.

Downhill for five minutes into pulsing yellow light, the channel ended abruptly at the lip of a waterfall. Here the Water Pony stopped. Its job was done.

Annabel saw a great, huge crater littered with gold. At the crater center a pool bubbled with liquid gold. That was impossible—just dream-stuff—but then she saw him.

Petr! There he is!

Halfway down the crater, holding something tightly against his chest, a shinybright moon, a little round moon. But why is he crying? Then she knew.

He's trying to come home to Annabel but it's too hard because of the terrible weight of the moon! He turns and waves goodbye to her.

But it can't be Petr. His eyes are glowing like disks of gold.

10

Someone— some*thing*—was dripping over her.

Cold fingers brush her shoulder. Gently as a feather. Gently as he—

She twitched, couldn't help it, but kept her eyes closed as a husky voice breathed on her.

"Why...child...why...An-uh-bell?"

That wasn't—couldn't be Petr. That was a wicked creature's voice trying to remember a forgotten tongue. Forget that wonderful stupid fairytale Water Pony dream. Petr is dead. Cold logic told you that. He is underwater dead. Five minutes underwater, maybe more. You don't walk away from that. So who was this cold drippy thing hulking over her, some creepy Indian?

Annabel made razorblade eyes and saw wet blue pantaloons and legs long enough to be Petr's strong legs. And strong arms, a carved face, dark amber eyes and hair the color of whiskey in sunlight, as Papa liked to say. But that skin was lobster red. Petr got sunburned underwater? His face was wrong, too. It had meteor streaks like something exploded in his face.

The Thing said, "Why did you...follow me...Annabel?" She winced as it stroked her hair, brushing it from her face just as Petr would have done. Thankfully, Big Jack had told her all about such vile creatures. This was something called a *haunt,* a walking dead thing.

She scuttled back, kicking off the boots and bringing up her fists.

"Keep away from me, you creepy haunt." Tears burned down her cheeks, and couldn't be helped. "You're not Petr. I had a brother once, but I don't anymore. He drowned in yonder lake."

The Thing seemed calm and patient, just as Petr would have been.

Smiling tiredly, sitting on a rock, it pulled on the boots, then the red shirt. It didn't put on the spectacles which was the tip-off. Petr always wore his specks everywhere he went. The haunt's amber eyes blazed unnaturally bright and lively. Feverbright. Now it searched the shoreline and found a black knife she hadn't noticed before. He stuck it in its belt. But then he kept searching for something else.

"Annabel—the watch, did you take it? Tell me...what time is it?"

Annabel backed away and clamped her breast pocket. "You can't have it. It's all I have left. It was his—now it's mine—till the day I die." Wishing she hadn't added that last part.

The Thing smiled slyly. "Just tell me the time. We won't mention

24

this to Papa or Mama—about the watch, or the lake." Smiling sadly, he said, "All right, little monkey-bump?"

Without agreeing to anything, Annabel read the time: "Five thirty-six."

That jolted him, head snapping back, he swallowed hard, "God, an hour—under there."

There was something beside him she had been too terrified to notice before, something so amazing it couldn't be real; something impossible from the dream, shiny and wet.

A gold moon the size of a pie. Real solid gold.

Her eyes widened and her mouth fell. "You...found...Gold Lake?"

He nodded wearily. "That's part of our deal. You keep the watch. You keep your lip buttoned about all of this." He waved his hand around. "Agreed?"

Annabel nodded. She wanted to agree. She asked suddenly, "I gotta know: How could you stay underwater an hour? How did you do that?"

He shook his head. "There's a cave that goes under, a long ways under. There's lots of gold. For some reason I can't remember what happened. It's blanked out—actually—*blazed* out. It's called The Luminah. Don't ask me what that means. I can't remember. Don't tell anyone."

She was thinking: Looks like Petr, sounds like Petr, acts like Petr—but what about the glasses? "Don' cha want your specks?" she asked innocently.

He picked them from the sand, blew on them, and pocketed them. "I don't seem to...to need them anymore. Pretty funny, huh?"

Yeah, that was real funny, a great answer. Proof Number One. She sought more of the same damaging proof. "Where ja get the funny old knife? It looks like black glass."

He sat like Papa after a long hard day. "It's none of your beeswax business, little Bee-bee. You already know way too much." He rubbed his arms as if he were real flesh and blood.

She thought: That's right, I do know too much—as much as you—if you really were Petr. The haunt didn't look like a creature from Jack's tales, just a tired, wet man. Could it be Petr?

She reviewed her strange dream. Water Pony took her into a hole in a lake, a cave into the mountain. Was it a real place? The real Petr... could he have...just possibly-maybe might have...if it were real...swum into? Could he have breathed—inside what he called The Luminah? Could he....

Keeping low, she approached him as if he was a hot furnace, slowly, carefully—while he was absorbed in tying his boots. Would a haunt even know how to tie laces? She stared into his big whiskey eyes. He had a new sparkle in his right eye. She inched closer. He stared without needing to blink. There was a sparkling speck and it was a real humdinger.

A tiny gold star. Right there in his right eye. Wow.

This was new. The old Petr Valory had no such speck. Not to mention it. Not on your life. It might set him off. But she grew crazy bold. She touched his cheek. He was on fire! Did dead men have hot skin? She withdrew quickly.

She said in a small wary voice, "Why's there no second 'e' in your first name? Why's it spelt funny?"

He tied his boots. "Because Mama said it would save ten dollars worth of ink, over my lifetime, not having to write another 'e'. It's her idea of economy."

And that was true. But there was a bigger, more important burning question in the world. She blurted, "Who's your favorite sister? What's your nicked-name for her?"

He laughed, turning to her tenderly, "Oh Annabel. Oh Little Fifty-pounder. Our Little Puzzle-puss. We have dozens of names for you." He tousled her hair—and she let him.

"But you're my little Rocky. You're my *favorite* sis. The one I love the best."

Annabel threw her arms around his neck, gasping, "Oh! Petr, I thought you was dead! Oh Petr, oh God, oh Petr! I thought...I thought...." Tears spilled down her face.

Petr swung her around in a circle until her feet flew outward, until she giggled.

She said, "Oh, is it really you?"

"Rocky, don't you worry. I'm more alive than you'll ever guess. And don't ever doubt I love you the best." She clung to him looking up at him. He shook his head. "You're due a good spoon-beating from Mama for ruining your dress, but first things first."

He glanced left and right. "Let's get down this mountain before grizzly's suppertime."

Petr turned modestly away tucking the gold moon under his shirt, halfway down into his pants, cinching his belt. He grimaced and smiled. "Finding gold is hard, painful work. But the Valorys are rich now. You'll wear a silk dress and be riding a fine big horse very soon."

He hoisted Annabel onto his shoulders. "Okay, whirly-girl: You keep the pocket watch and we keep our big secret. Now let's get home."

The watch *chinged* six o'clock in Annabel's pocket. She said, "I found a good path from home. Can we take it? I'm a good pathfinder."

Petr laughed. "You are—unfortunately. Point the way, Rocky Pathfinder."

She gripped his ears and prodded him with her toes for speed. "Giddy-up, horsy!" Then he carried her down the mountain towards the Valoryvale.

But their day was not done yet.

11

Halfway home Annabel fully recovered, trotting behind him like a talking puppy. The sun-painted mountains grew cherry red. His vision was now razor sharp, all colors dark and rich, all pines emerald spears, all mountains hammered walls of molten iron.

"God in heaven," he spoke warily. "My eyes are light-drinking wells."

He was a wildcat roaring with energy. The world sparkled in kaleidoscopic rainbows of green, yellow and red, the sky a rich vault of cobalt blue. Never had he felt such *vitality*.

Yet he felt anxious, as if too late for something. He slowed to let Annabel catch up. She was breathing hard.

"What did you say? Ain't you gonna tell me what happened down there?"

Petr shrugged. "It was like a dream. I only remember snatches."

"Tell me snatches then."

"I dove underwater and found a tunnel. I swam until I reached a chamber filled with stale air. It was filled with gold light coming from *below*. That didn't seem possible. So I went down another tunnel for a look. I found a room full of bright light. It was hot. That's all I remember. That's probably where I found the gold moon. But I don't remember. I passed out for a while. I dreamed I was in a land of pyramids and pharaohs and I was looking for gold."

She said, "Was there a beautiful girl?"

He didn't answer. That was enough for now. They could hear the whispery welcome of Valoryvale waterfall that fell twenty feet to the valley floor. Just one more steep rise and—

Then he heard something very bad.

"Wuh-wuh-wuh," like a big dog.

He knew what it was. A rolling mound of flesh was heading towards them and he reached back and gripped Annabel's head. "Stay put like a rock."

She crouched behind him. She looked more like a noodle than a rock. Jack had been right to scare them with stories. Kids alone in the woods without a weapon had no—

He remembered the Indian knife and pulled it out.

The grizzly sniffed the air, gazing at them. His head was big as a bushel-basket, his body a dark sack of hunger. When it reared up Annabel screamed. Six feet of raging appetite stood on its hind legs. A greasy patch of blood smeared one shoulder—a wounded grizzly—very bad news. He remembered the gunshots earlier today. The bear made a low rumbling grumble.

Then it charged.

Petr screamed: "AWAY! AWAY from my sister!" Amazing thunder in his voice, the warrior screaming in his head: *Attack!*

Suddenly he ran at the bear, the knife cocked at his hip, ready to strike, ready to meet the bear, and the bear kept coming. A little girl-scream sounded a thousand miles away. And then the bear filled his eyes.

It halted abruptly—and swung a hooked paw. Petr ducked and amber eyes blazed hatred at him. It bellowed and Petr smelled rotten fruit and death. Its gaping blue yap filled with yellow teeth. Petr struck the knife into the huge mouth.

With all his might he drove into the slimy hole, down the slimy throat, plunging until his arm was engulfed in a meat grinder. The bear gagged humid breaths and vomited purple geysers spraying Petr's shoulder and neck. He was clamped up to his shoulder in an iron jaw. Below his embedded fist a powerful savage heart pounded like a buried drum—

Chooomba-chooomba-chooomba!

Nothing existed in the world but him and the heart of the bear.

The bear toppled sideways and Petr felt his shoulder pop. The grizz made a curious whining cry, turning its mouth gingerly aside. Its legs coiled like springs and Petr knew his stomach was about to be churned out like spaghetti from a bowl.

Thick claws raked him but clicked against metal as something round pounded his gut. And for some reason he knew what to do next. He forced the knife into a grisly circling stroke. Hot greasy fluids boiled over his hand and the big beating heart popped like a balloon. The grizzly stiffened. Blood poured from its mouth.

From somewhere a keening wail had been going on forever. "Eeeeeeeiiiiiiiii!" A little girl pulling on him, screaming and kicking and beating.

Blood rivered over him in big red gushes—but the girl was there to help free him. She didn't stop screaming as she pulled his arm from the gushing throat and his arm floated out like a newborn baby. Red teeth-marks sliced from his bicep to his wrist.

He did not want to believe that arm was part of him—or his hand—a dead-looking blob that no longer held a knife. Well, it was a good place to leave the knife. He crawled away.

Collapsing on his back, wiping sticky goo from his face, he was coated in purple puke. No girl should see such a sight. Poor Annabel, where was she? Was she all right?

He didn't have strength to stand so he twisted around. Annabel was standing over the dead bear with her fists clenched and her voice even higher than usual.

"Bad old bear! Why did you do that? Bad old bear!"

He gasped, "Annabel...it's...not much...farther. Get help... get Papa."

She crouched beside him, hands on knees, staring at him, her dress a bloody rag; her voice awestruck. "That was *amazing*. Where did you learn that—that was real Injun fighting. You jumped, you swung, you rolled, you—"

"Rocky! Get Papa and don't tell Mama."

She nodded and ran away. She was a girl, but she was reliable.

He had one last thought: That was one hell of a birthday.

Then everything went black.

CHAPTER TWO

KILLINGS

1

Two miles below the Valoryvale twelve men were bedded down on a ridge above the Feather River and they were supposed to doze right off and get up at 5 A.M. and kill Indians.

Curl Watney tipped his flask taking a fiery nip of whiskey and King would have shot him if he saw that. No drinking before a fight, he insisted.

Watney wished to hell he was back in Iowa. Wished he was hitching the team to a plow, getting fields ready for corn. Instead he was on a rocky ridge overlooking a river, waiting to kill, all for a sack of gold. King promised a thousand dollars for a year's work.

God damn the gold. Get it. Get back to your wife.

He hadn't signed up for killing—just tending mules and helping build the big flume; nothing about killing Indians for their horses. There was a lot he wouldn't be able to tell Martha.

2

Sabbah slept dreaming he was awake and seeing everything from a cloud. The thin-lipped moon kissed the crest of the big silver mountain beyond their camp. Not a puff of wind disturbed this peaceful night. The stars made tiny countless campfires overhead. The small band of Indians slept in Long Green Valley beneath the mountains by the whispering river, six Pah Utes lying in a circle of grass, his cousins, and his son. Thirty ponies stood a short distance off, their legs hobbled with rawhide, unaware they were being watched. Together they had

31

traveled over the big desert to the big cold river at the base of the silver mountains. The People journeyed here each summer to hunt deer. Sabbah was dreaming of the good hunt that brought them here and the fat deer they would bring home to wives waiting by the pale blue lake three long days away in the east. And he was dreaming of rifles that shout six times. The white man said he would trade thirty horses for thirty rifles.

Something inhaled sharply and his dream spirit quickened. That part of him knew—

Something is watching you! Awaken, don't move! Let the illusion of sleep continue.

⚜

Above the river the falcon slept on her eggs until a stone rattled down the cliff sounding just like a snake. Small pebbles hit her chest startling her into a short, wobbly flight and what she saw next was worse than an invasion of snakes.

The horse gods were riding along the high rim of the canyon, making a shower of stones.

When she returned her eggs were smashed. She circled the nest screaming wildly. She clenched cold gravel in her talons and let it go. She could not bring her eggs back to life. Now she would never show the young flyers the joy on the wind.

She jumped skyward and when she did she remembered her lost mate. Her sickness returned as if the smashed eggs were inside her stomach.

⚜

The sound did not repeat itself and Sabbah relaxed, stretching lazily, inhaling the good strong smell of his elkskin robe, heavy with dew, warm and good like a woman's scent. He smiled. Dawn would bring a new day to show his son *Nojomud* the joys of the hunt. The boy was a small version of his father, homely, dark-skinned as smoke. The whites called Sabbah—Smoke Sam, because he was dusky, bowlegged, thin-chested and dog-faced. Sabbah works harder to run, to hunt, to get a wife! Ten years ago Sabbah found a Mahdoo woman who married him, and gave him a son. Nojomud was different only in one way: he was always smiling. Father and son were unlike their athletic kinsmen, the Numah, who the whites called Paiutes.

Today Sabbah would show his son that he could do something big: bring the power of rifles to their tribe. Coming down the long valley his little band had seen two new cabins full of whitemen. Those bad people chopped down trees like crazy beavers. You could not share the hunting ground with them. They needed to be rubbed out. Where was the man Munson who promised guns? No matter. This bend in the river before the high cliff was the meeting place. Sabbah would trade with the white savages and when the time was right—use the rifles on them.

He remembered seeing the owl-faces the first time. Nine summers ago when Chief Truckee was still alive—

The owl-faces came staggering across the dust, men half-dead from ignorance of how to live in the desert. The People fed them and guided them West through the mountains. When the owl-faces left with round bellies they thanked the People—and gave nothing in return. Sabbah remembered what he said at that time: So this is our pale brother we waited so long to see!

Next came the gold-crazy dogs—men who were digging up the mountains for their yellow god-in-the-ground. More came every day now, beggars who traveled in rolling huts bumping along with their empty-faced women inside. Ugly beings! Pouring into the Silver Mountains like streams of hungry ants. His wife's people, the Mahdoos, would be stuck with these thankless creatures. Sabbah knew what to do. Get guns. Kill the invaders. That was why he was here.

He heard the snuffling sound again. He sat up slowly as moonrise.

Ten paces away stood the biggest buck deer he had ever seen. Stone still. Beautiful white face with tree-like antlers; powerful body rising like mist from the dark grass. Black eyes staring at him.

Sabbah thought, Stay my friend, sah, sah, sah. I will do a beautiful thing for you. My heart is true, and I will hurt you only a little.

From the elkskin he drew his bow and quiver. My friend, better you to come with us—enter our bellies, become one of the People—than wander off in the mountains where you will be killed by wolves, eaten by skunks, and become one of them. I will make you Numah!

He pictured a beautiful robe for Nojomud, moccasins for his little feet, sinews becoming strings for a fine bow, antler tools to chip arrow points. He pushed the strung end of the bow into the ground just below his crotch, and pulled the other end slowly into himself compressing his arm. The greasewood eased towards him and he slipped the string onto its notched end. Good and tight, the wildcat's gut making the singing voice of my bow.

From the soft wildcat quiver he drew a single rosewood shaft. Careful not to touch the point, he gripped the feathered end and drew the silent bow into a smile. He whispered, "Hear me now: You will be Numah, you will be strong, you will not be sorry."

Wing-like ears rotated towards him. The buck snorted and bolted away.

Gone like smoke in a breeze! Sabbah sat blinking. Nojomud lay sound asleep. He reached over and combed the boy's hair, his black forelocks rough as a pony's tail. The boy turned but did not awaken. Sabbah would have much time later to think about this last touch.

He ran to the horses calling to the spotted one that made Sabbah more than a man. "Talldog, hssst." It came instantly and he released its hobbles and instantly they followed the clicking music of the running deer.

Long moments they chased following the deer down the Long Green Valley through mist and wet grass but could not close ground. The scent and clicking grew fainter.

No choice but to follow: God has taken the shape of a white buck deer!

Then show the sleepyheads in camp the biggest deer they'd ever seen. Nojomud would whoop, seeing the war bonnet of antlers, and of course, gazing at his father with pride. The picture was spoiled by an unsettling thought: Sabbah has only one arrow! His quiver of arrows lay inside his elk robe, now over a mile away.

Talldog was a good horse. They caught an occasional glimpse of a ghost flickering through the mist. It was dangerous to run at night:

Talldog might step into a hole; spirit creatures roamed. Yet darkness couldn't last because already the great light of Apu had begun its first kindling and would soon flame the horizon.

Hunting time is dream time. He could not tell how long he followed the deer. He guessed if he yelled aloud, no one in the camp would hear him, guessing he was three times beyond his yelling voice being heard. A bad thought came: My big friend you are leading me astray. But then he saw it again.

Exploding from the grass it splashed into the river, crossed, and disappeared again.

Sabbah forgot to breathe. What was that thing? God come to life on the ground? Where was it?

Moments later it re-erupted on the opposite bank and shook itself off. Above the buck, tall dark cliffs rose to the dusky sky where stars twinkled and faded.

Sabbah hobbled Talldog, whispering, "There may yet be work for you." He stalked towards the river but before he reached the edge of the water he saw movement along the cliff. Did it fly up there?

The white buck looked as if it was standing on the sky. Lifting its head, its pink tongue flickered like flame, as if to say, Now you see why I am so big?

Sabbah would never forget this moment. The deer climbing so fast as if lifted by wings, fading stars behind him, how could Sabbah know this was the last sweet moment of his life?

He called softly: "My friend, you are too beautiful to kill. Perhaps the Good Spirit wishes for you another son." He smiled, wondering if he too might someday have another son.

Then he heard the sound that ended all good dreams forever.

3

There was a second attack of noisy stones. The falcon flew wildly up, her heart beating faster than her wings. Quicker than thought she sailed across the flat green valley, seeing—

The horse gods were on the move again! Coming down the cliff, down the river. She could see where they were heading. Closing in on a circle of redmen sleeping in the grass, they dismounted, they crossed the river. At the edge of the camp they leaned on rocks and pointed their long sticks.

Fire tongues stabbed at the sleeping men. Horses bucked and cried but hobbles and ropes kept them from running away. Raucous explosions slapped the air and she veered away with flame-stabbed eyes, slowly fading. When she could see again—

Red men lay like broken eggs thrown to the ground. And killers crept up like spiders, closer and closer.

4

While rifles boomed Curl Watney snuck off into the grass and threw-up. The sickly sweet smell of blood had gotten to him. Now the sun was rising. If some righteous soul saw this evil murder work, what then? Men weren't supposed to slaughter peaceful Indians. This was America and here in California there was an agreement that guilty whites and guilty Indians would be treated equally to a trial. And there was a regiment at Honey Lake to back it up. He didn't want to die.

Better get back so the men won't know you're gone.

Watney burst in among them yelling, "Hurry it up, boys!" Raising his pistol he dashed to the side of the camp where the men were finishing the work. He held the pistol against the head of a small Indian, maybe just to pretend he was—

"My God," he cried, "This one's only a boy!"

The big man Dain King grabbed the gun away, his hands and face splattered red. Placing the barrel onto the forehead of the wounded child, he fired.

"That's how it's done!" King yelled. "You wanna get paid? Or go back to Iowa and sit on corn?" Curl trembled. He saw the hole in the boy's head.

King turned away in disgust. "Ah, go back to your corn."

A narrow-eyed, efficient looking man prodded a heap of leather beside the dead boy. He spoke softly, "Empty bedroll. Looks like one of them got away. That's bad luck."

King kicked the bedroll into the air, he was furious. "Let'm crawl back to his squaws. Tell'm this is a bad place to come. Let's git. Gather the horses, now!"

Some of the men would claim later they saw something hurled from the sky and then a sharp sound like ripping cloth, a small gray blur that made a peculiar popping sound. Then a man screamed.

"Jeez, I'm hit!" Curl Watney twisted sideways holding his head. "I'm hit...I'm scalped."

It was a comical sight but nobody laughed. Watne was on his knees holding his head and his hat was rising into the air, circling upward. He looked around, bleating, "Ga-a-wd help me."

The narrow-eyed efficient man called Tiger, pointed skyward where the hat continued to rise in tight circles. He jeered, "Looks like an Indian scalping-bird got you."

A bucktooth, mule-faced man aimed at the circling hat. King snatched the rifle away from Deef Petty, the worst shot in the bunch. The rifle looked like a toy in King's hands. The hat flew higher and higher, an impossible target, but King braced and fired.

The bird shuddered and plunged out of sight. King thrust the rifle back at Petty.

"Killed it. Think you could 'a done that, Deef?"

Deef Petty looked at the rifle, then at the big man. "You shot the bird! I'm gonna have this yeer' rifle bronzed. See if I don't!" He kissed the cylinders knowing he would do no such thing. The rifle held six shots same as a pistol. With this repeater he could fire fast as snapping your fingers. He'd never seen anything like it. Where King got such rifles he didn't know, and it was best not to ask. Immediately he began refilling the holes with black power, ratcheting the lever that rammed half-inch balls of lead into the cylinder. Before he could finish he heard the scream.

Tiger said calmly, "Watney's gone crazy."

He was running in long grass, rowing his arms wildly in a green ocean, a silhouette swimming for the dawn. Deef swore, "Damn, he's running back to Ioway."

King grabbed the rifle again and took long careful aim. The first two cylinders clicked empty. "Goddamn you, Deef!" The running man staggered and fell, and got up again. He ran and they heard him bawling like a baby. The third cylinder was full. *Bam!*

Curl Watney slapped forward into the grass.

King stared at his eleven remaining men. "Anybody else wanna run back to Ioway?"

Nobody said anything. King looked at them. "All right, now you got a taste of it." His face hardened into a grim mask. "Our sacred duty is to wipe these *skraelings* from the face of the earth." He used that strange word like a blasphemy. Gazing into the sky he was talking to himself. "They murdered my men...the last true men of earth." Then he returned to them with his anger. "Next time won't be so easy, now git. He-yah! Take their horses to the hideout. Make a corral. Come back to New Viksburg in a week saying you caught them in the hills." He sounded drunk, only he wasn't.

He took something from his saddlebag, something they didn't want to see or know anything about: a foreign-looking axe, curved and with a short handle. He pulled out something else nearly as bad, a T-shaped branding iron. It was a good time to leave. The men drifted away.

"Go back," he said. "I'll settle up with these Injuns."

The men drove the captured horses across the river. They didn't look back.

King made a hot campfire and waited for the iron to turn red as he slicked a sharpening stone across his axe, repeating, "Bad time has come for you, *skraelings*."

5

The shots were random, but each time Sabbah flinched as if he was struck in the face. Oh my heart, do not run ahead of me. Do not see bad things. Spirit visions belonged to *poohagum*, Sun Eagle, and his strange daughter, Minoah. But he couldn't help it. He was seeing bodies twisting on the ground and red spirits flying to the sky. He cried out: "Oh my heart, lie down, lay still—oh my son."

He counted twenty gunshots and knew something terrible was happening. White coyotes did terrible things. Where the Mahdoos lived these tricksters made rivers run into wooden houses in the air to get the sun metal hidden in the water. He hated the whites with all his heart. They were hurting the beautiful Mother.

He had a horrifying vision: His horses were all gone; his family dead on the ground.

It was as if his chest was struck by a rock. Oh my heart, oh my son.

The red ball of sun balanced on the horizon and he knew he had been gone far too long. Sunshine meant new life, but not today—"Oh my son is lying on the ground!"

He neared their campsite.

He entered a thick sweet smell like vomited berries which made Talldog skitter sideways. Sabbah jumped down and fell into the matted grass. There were bodies all around. His cousins twisted and sprawled, blood leaking from many holes and their eyes staring and empty of life.

Then he saw Nojomud with his eyes still closed, he had never wakened.

Sabbah screamed long and high like a wounded animal.

He wrapped his son into himself, the arms and legs dangled limply. He had never cried in his life and didn't cry now. Moaning, "Oh, no—my son."

Still holding the little boy, blood running down his chest, he visited each body. Now he saw the white coyotes had been very busy. All bows and arrows were gone. All of the bodies were full of wounds: a hole in the back of each head. And what was worse—

Each forehead was charred with a black T. Branded.

Why? What did this mean? And there was something worse.

All thumbs were gone—collected—chopped off.

Sabbah, kill yourself, you cannot endure this. He sat rocking his son and moaning. Finally tears streamed down his face.

Stop looking at The People gone from the Land, never to return, cannot be replaced!

But he could not stop. They looked like leaking, broken pots.

Pain had cut deep lines in their faces; the white coyotes had disfigured them. Sabbah shook his fists in the air. I cannot make life run back into them, cannot repair broken pots. Cannot make People live again. Cannot make day run back, or make dreambuck not happen, running away from death like a coward. Good Spirit, what did you save me for?

He clenched his jaw so hard a big tooth cracked.

His tears stopped. After a while he knew what to do. He laid Nojomud gently down. Then, one at a time, he went to each corpse. He dipped his finger into each head hole.

He streaked blood from the bridge of his nose over his eyebrows like a wing, one streak for each man until red bloody wings formed above his eyes. Then he returned to Nojomud.

He dabbed his son's blood, painting an X over his heart. He could do this because now he was dead, because the river from his heart to his head was dry forever. He was a ghost.

Blood cried out from the ground: *Sabbah, kill them! Kill the killers!*

But he answered wisely: Not yet. The coyotes would only complete their killing work. Sabbah will destroy them *tonight.*

Bury your People; protect them from animals. This was the good voice of the hunter. It said something else: *Hold them with your eyes. So long as Sabbah walks, they also walk!*

He responded with deep conviction, "I will do more!"

He held his boy and waited for the last tears. Then he was ready for the next terrible thing. The man who had never been big or strong or fast as the others pulled the stone knife from his belt. He hardened his mind.

No longer human, you will now make yourself a spirit being.

He touched his chest with the blade welling blood as if a mouth had opened. Then he cut an X over his heart. He gazed at the bloody X on his heart.

He gasped, "Nojomud!" inhaling sharply as the pain spirit entered him.

He gazed at the sun and pointed the knife at his eye. Then he cut along the lines of his dried tears. Sabbah gasped, "My People!" He felt the bloody lines on his forehead and then he cut the first wing angling toward his scalp. He gasped, "Hazzabuk!" Then cut the other side, crying out, "Sah wah neebo!" Now there was a bloody wing on his forehead. He cut twice more across his face. "Mog wah nah!" Another gasp, "Daw zaw mah!" His face burned as blood ran into his eyes. When he closed them he could not stop seeing his People.

When the bleeding finally stopped the sun was nearly overhead.

He buried the bodies and covered the mounds with smooth stones from the river. When he finished, the sun was high over the silver mountains, yet he fell asleep as if it was midnight.

Much later when he awakened, he was curled around the short mound that was his son. When he got up to leave his eyes would not open. Sabbah has died, he thought, the Good Spirit has pitied me.

But flies were buzzing around his head, biting him, stinging him. He was still alive. He heard his own strange voice rasp: "Open the grave of your eyes, Sabbah!"

But they were stuck shut. He had to pry them open.

Now there were five fresh grave mounds. He sighed; he had no desire to breathe again. He saw something sticking up in the middle of the camp where Nojomud had made a small fire last night. It was a black metal shape that he recognized. It was sticking up like a warning.

It was the branding iron that had been used to disfigure the People.

He pulled it from the ashes. It was a drooping T with a hole drilled in the back, and a green stick jammed into the hole. He tore out the stick. He said, "I will do more."

He tied the thing around his neck using a piece of rawhide, then held his hands skyward. He uttered a powerful oath: "Good Spirit gave men stomachs so they could feel hunger. Now I am full of hunger stronger than food. I am hungry to kill!"

The sun fell into the silver mountains. He was done here. He leaped onto his horse. He galloped around the graves, circling them five times, yelling his war eagle cry. "Kiii-yiii-yeee!" He completed his powerful oath.

"There will be five deaths—and one child."

Screaming, he rode towards the silver mountains where the white coyotes dwelled, where Sabbah would not sleep until he had killed five times—and killed one child.

6

A hundred miles away an old chief sat before his canee warming himself in the morning sun reflected from the big blue desert lake of his People. His vision had made his thoughts sweet.

Every shadow deepens mysteries of God's Spirit. From harvest moon to hunger moon, all things are good. Grass grows, ponies fatten, pinecones fall—all returning to earth. The way of spirit is the way of Pah Utes. Take nothing not made from the Land—such as repeating rifles. Sometimes young men did foolish things.

He had watched them ride off with a string of horses. That was ten days ago.

Dotso cried for little Nojomud to stay. The wives of four warriors cried their goodbyes. War chief Numaga watched with expressionless eyes as usual. Everyone knew it was dangerous to trust whitemen. It was never good to leave the Pananadu, their lake, the big desert heart, the life-giver, the source of strength. Certainly you did not leave it for rifles. In the spring the People netted ducks and cut fresh cattail shoots. In the summer they caught giant trout and harvested rice. In the fall they gathered pinenuts, made the big rabbit drives, and made big piles of dry wood and food. In winter they made tools, wove baskets, and told old stories of when the lake was much bigger and magical creatures lived in the water.

Sun Eagle was thinking of all these things because he had seen his ending dream. This summer he would die. Just now a shadow passed over his shoulder and he looked up.

His daughter, tall and beautiful as her mother had been, now nineteen, too skinny, too opinionated to be a good wife, yet she had received many offers. "Please wake up, father."

"My daughter wakes me from my dreams. Why? Did she marry someone while I sleep?" He remembered Lanno and Caddo riding their ponies sitting backwards. Once they had walked on their hands past the canee, calmly turning their heads to say good morning. This made him laugh. But she ignored all offers because she would be a healer like her father—*poohagum*—not wife to any ordinary man. Some were flower girls, some were rock girls.

Minoah handed him a bowl of warm pinenut mush.

"Why didn't you stop them? Rifles will only make them proud and foolish."

Sun Eagle ate slowly. "I see the men returning to Stone Mother with weary legs and empty arms. Desert wind blows itself out in three days."

He would not tell her how worried he was about Sabbah's little tribe so he changed the subject. "I dreamed a hunting bird was wounded in the air, and then was found by a young man painted red and white. The bird was dying and the young man was wounded in the heart. He inhaled the bird into his nostrils and when he breathed out again, he was healed. He was some new kind of man. He came to us in a boat. But he is a rare one. He can fly."

Minoah laughed. "Such a man I would consider."

Sun Eagle did not mention the other dream about a metal bee hitting him in the head.

She returned to her subject. "You did not say enough."

He smiled. How strong-willed she was, like her mother, but hard as manzanita, too. She was four years old when her mother died, a snakebite while gathering pinenut cones, and he could not save Lickee. Maybe if he had, Minoah would be softer—a flower girl. Heya-hey, welcome everything—every loss has its secret food. He waved his hands like graceful wings.

"I have said enough. Sabbah and his followers will return in two more days with their tails dragging, or I will look for them myself."

The days came and went and Sabbah's tribe did not return.

7

Everything felt like a dream except for the smell of whiskey and sweat. His father had carried him down the mountain in his arms—and a little girl held his hand. The trio stumbled in twilight of a half-familiar landscape heavy blue with night. The girl whispered: Don't worry. I'll hide the moon down in the ravine. He was starting to remember things. Had he fought a grizzly with a knife? Had he been killed?

Papa brought him inside the cabin and laid him on the table and Mama saw his bloody, puke-covered body and went crazy. She shoved John violently out of the way.

"What have you done? He goes out good boy and comes back drunk! Like father, like son! His real father—the damned halfbreed!"

Petr was having trouble seeing, everything blurry. But Papa sounded happy, his voice rich and rolling: "Better than reading the old books, huh?" Then he turned to interrogate Annabel about when and where and how. Annabel made short tough replies: Sundown above the waterfall; killed a bear with a knife. Papa brimming with pride: "Kills big grizz with a knife, huh? I go get the axe."

None of it made any sense.

Petr slept for a while and when John returned he burst into the cabin holding two hairy forepaws, shaking them so they clicked together like rattles.

"Long as a man's fingers," he cried. "Look at em!"

Magya pushed him away, "Get those devil things out of this house!"

John laughed. "He's man now; he's bull of the woods now."

Petr closed his eyes and passed out.

8

He was a falcon flying over the big green meadow where dead Indians lay on the ground. Just a dream, the bodies turned into grave mounds. His wings stopped working, and he fell from the air. "Help...me...."

Annabel squeezed his good hand, waking him up. He was safe in the loft, with Annabel crouched beside him as if she had been watching him all night. She asked, "You under the lake again?" She looked worried. He shook his head at her. He looked around.

Early morning, dark blue, dead quiet, and he was filled with immense pain. His parts felt all crooked like a twisted rag. He said "No, it was nothing."

Truth was, it was an awful dream: Flying and falling and dead bodies on the ground. He shook his head again. He gripped her small strong hands.

"Tell me sister, where did you hide the-you-know-what."

She told him. The ravine. Same as in his dream. So how much was real?

"Stay," he said. "Don't move."

Then he went out the window. Then he went down the ravine.

When he returned five minutes later the house was still dead quiet but it was daybreak. Papa lay sprawled in the kitchen, smelling like whiskey. Where did he get it? Gold Nation. Dain King. Magya had withdrawn behind purple bedroom curtains.

Petr returned to the loft where Annabel waited breathlessly.

"Lemme see it again." He held it out, the gold disk. Annabel gasped. "Oh God *amazing!*"

Petr tucked it under his pillow. Annabel excited was not a good thing. She collected jars of small pine cones and pine needles and flowers that smelled like sugar. She had created a wall of blue jars on her side of the room. These things kept her busy, kept her calm. Would she settle for such trifling tame stuff after this? He knew what she was going to say next, and she did.

"Can we go back to the lake and get me a little moon? I'm a real good swimmer."

He pinched her cheeks. "Too cold, too deep, too dangerous, little puzzle-puss." Adding, "I barely made it myself. I won't *ever* go back." To cheer her up he said, "After I'm done working tonight we'll visit the falcon. And I'll show you where a mommy and baby deer live."

She was good at pouting. She sighed. "Okay. But I still want to know what happened. Nobody holds their breath for an hour." He tousled her hair and said he'd try to remember.

But truth was, he *couldn't* remember.

9

There was no time for pain or sickness—or adventure. There was work to do.

Petr's arm had to heal while he was working in the saw-pit. Papa wanted to know about the bear. Petr said it happened so fast it was a blur. But that wasn't really true. Death was in slow-motion.

John grinned. "Old grizz, he was already bled out from a gunshot when you stuck him." He laughed. "But don't tell that part when you're telling it."

Petr remember the gush of blueberries and blood. No, not quite bled out.

They quit at three in the afternoon in a good mood. After carrying the last plank from the pit, John took Petr's hand and rubbed it gently across the wood. "She's smooth one way, rough the other." He winked. "Know what board I mean? Don't run against her grain, okay?"

Magya made supper of rabbit stew, barely warmed up. Papa elbowed Petr, whispering, "Cross-grain." Then he announced grandly, "I take that bear to town and sell it, okay?" Petr nodded, he didn't want to see it again. John nodded back. "I take a load of planks along. You get rested up, okay?" Petr left the table and Magya muttered something.

Sounded like, "Yeah, we just go." She retreated to the bedroom and pulled the purple curtain. John rubbed his palms crossways, smiled and winked at Petr, and left for Gold Nation. He looked too happy for simply delivering lumber.

Petr whispered to Annabel, "Let's go feed the falcon." He shredded a small piece of rabbit meat and Annabel sprinkled it with a pinch of sugar.

They walked briskly to the Feather River taking twenty minutes. They came to the falcon feeder pole, a pine tree struck by lightning, leaving an eight-foot high stump, and he was relieved to see his dream wasn't true. There were no dead Indians. He boosted Annabel onto his shoulders gripping her skinny legs to brace her. She glanced left, then right.

"Petr?" Her voice worried. "The rabbit meat from yesterday, it's still here."

He said, "Maybe she wasn't hungry. Brush it away, leave the fresh." Last night in his flying dream he saw dead Indians. And then he fell from the sky. He said, "Stay here and watch for the falcon while I go check on something."

He set her down and right on cue she said, "Can I come with you?"

"Not this time, this could be bad...really bad. I gotta find something out." He hugged her, and for all the trouble she caused, he couldn't believe how skinny and small she was. She'd never bloom roundly into a woman like Magya. When he turned to go, Annabel's voice became teasing.

"Know how I tracked you yesterday? The falcon circled above you."

Petr yelled over his shoulder, "Everybody likes you for bringing food, even animals. I like you for frosting my cake yesterday."

"I'm glad you *like* me—I *like* you."

"Well, if you really *like* me, stay here. I won't be gone long."

Annabel blurted, "If you ever...*disappear*—I'd just die! That's what I found out yesterday. When you were under the lake, I was *dying*."

Petr stopped. He returned to her because yesterday *was* pretty bad. He knelt before her trembling little stick girl body. "If I ever lost you, Rocky, I'd die too. Okay? Now stay put. I'll be back in five minutes at most."

She hugged him tightly. "Say you won't ever leave me—*ever*? Okay?"

He hugged her back and gave her a smoochy kiss on the cheek. "I'll always come back for you, Rocky—no matter what. I'll find you even if you disappear from the earth." He didn't know he was predicting her future. He pointed as if commanding a puppy. "Stay."

She stuck her tongue out, and he walked away.

He headed for the falcon cliffs and immediately got a sinking sensation.

He wished he hadn't said that part about disappearing, because it reminded him of the nightmare of falling madly in love with a beautiful girl—and then losing her and never seeing her again, and waking up crying. You remember that but you don't remember what happened under Gold Lake?

The falcon's nest was a high nick in the cliff, but he never went near, fearing to disturb the family he supposed was growing there. There was no sign of life.

He splashed across the river and saw the grassy clearing of his dream. He fell to his knees and groaned. There were five grave mounds in a circle.

Strange things were coming now: How did you know about these bodies? How did you kill that bear? Or get out of that lake? And why can't you remember everything? For that matter—Had the Indian at the lake been real?

He walked slowly back to where Annabel waited anxiously. She looked scared.

He grabbed her shoulders and shook her gently, "Gotta go... pronto." Bending down he lifted her onto his shoulders. She laughed like he knew she would.

Then he ran up the pine-filled V of the Valoryvale with his little sister on his back. Wondering—Who you gonna tell? What you gonna tell?

There was no answer and—and there was no one to tell.

Beneath a hidden lake he had found a motherlode of gold—maybe *The Motherlode*—and he was about to lose everything.

CHAPTER THREE

GOLD RUINS

1

Dain King killed Indians. That was his sacred duty. He took their horses, beautiful, healthy, well-cared for animals, and kept *his* rifles. That's the way you dealt with Indians. That afternoon he went into the mountains to Point of Rocks, a high cliff overlooking Gold Nation, to wait for a vision, for instructions from god. He was a prophet of god, not the weakling Christian god, his god was Thor.

He severed the thumbs from the Indians to disfigure them so they could never fight again. That was his primitive belief. He was half Shawnee. His mother was the sister of the most powerful warrior who had ever lived: Tecumseh. Dain King was half-red and he would kill any evidence of that fact. He was a Viking warrior returned to earth to destroy the Indians who had wiped out the first American Vikings. Then he would create a new warrior nation in California.

Now he was gathering a race of warrior men that would destroy the two big foolish ideas of America: democracy and equality. What a laugh! The United States was an aberration of history. It wouldn't last. Great war was coming between North and South. A strong man could tear off a hunk of America and keep it for himself. Dain King would be King of California!

Five nights he fasted on Point of Rocks and finally had his great vision. He saw himself and his son in clouds of glory. It surprised him but since it was his sacred vision it must be true.

Petr Valory was handing him a gold crown; Petr helping him create the Gold Nation.

Draw him to you—draw your true son—and together draw the kingdom of gold!

2

Arne Swenson had staked a claim on the North Fork one mile above the Gold Nation diggings. A thirty-foot by thirty-foot square belonged to him. Rain had swelled the river and it sounded like a constant sigh as he worked at the water's edge. He used a rocker, a gold dredging tool that looked like a cradle for a giant infant. The sleeves of his red calico shirt were rolled up because he was sweating from doing the work of three men. Shoveling gravel, sluicing it down the rocker, then raking the gravel. He was a rare man who had refused to work for Dain King. Behind him lay a dozen pines he had felled and peeled, scattered like nine-pins after a strike, which he would cut up for a cabin in the fall. He rocked the cradle by a long board nailed on the side, rock-a-bye-baby. He had a wife in Minnesota and two children. After he made his fortune he would—

"Hey-ya-hey!"

Swenson turned just as a shadow stepped from the cut pines.

It was a scruffy little Indian, wounded or sick, his face looked like it had been ripped up by a wolf. Probably begging for food, and then he'd steal something.

"Get out of here."

Swenson stepped forward but whatever he was going to say next, he never finished. The Indian raised a bow and shot him.

The arrow hit like an axe to the gut, Swenson doubled over, nauseated. When the Indian slung another arrow, Swenson ducked behind the rocker, but then decided to try for the river. He never made it. Something hit him hard in the spine and down he went.

3

Annabel had a job to do. Saturday, June 18th, a week after Petr's birthday—*and* finding the gold lake—*and* killing the grizzly—*and* getting a spoon-beating from Mama for ruining her white dress—Mama wanted her to dispose of something. Early this morning the Valory men had delivered a load of lumber to New Viksburg and then they were back again. Papa sat in the toolshed screeching-away on his beloved Swedish-steel saw, each stroke of the file shaping a sawtooth sounding like metal fingernails scraping across a steel chalkboard.

Petr wasn't around. He had stuffed a sandwich in his pocket and left on foot for Spanish Ranch, a bank for horses and mules, cared for by Mexicans. Miners deposited their animals and went hunting for gold. Sometimes they returned, sometimes they didn't. With Petr gone and Papa busy, it was time to do what Mama ordered. But she didn't want to.

Mama had caught her playing with the golden moon.

Three days ago, petting it, looking at it like the gold heart of the mountains, incredibly heavy, the sound of the pit-saw buzzing back and forth, had lulled her into dreaming about how many horses a gold moon might buy and that's when Mama had sneaked up to the loft and caught her and Mama acted like she was hugging the Devil himself.

She ordered Annabel to dump the gold moon back in the lake.

But right away she got a faraway look in her eyes and gave a tall order: Save a bit for Mama, yes?—handing her a big flour sack and a small flour sack to help her commit the crime. Then Mama got busy. Using the remains of the dress, she turned it into baggy bloomer-pants, colored yellow by the juice of pinenut hulls, which made Annabel look like a small genii. Baggy yellow pants might be better than a white dress for running in the mountains.

But get rid of the gold—and save a slice for Mama? How was she supposed to do that? She sat in the loft combing Miss Daisy's hair. The doll's blue button eyes gazed at her steadily. She hefted the doll, light and innocent. She hefted the gold, heavy and full of guilt.

Tempter Gold, a big golden pie! No matter how many times you saw it—and she'd played with it all week—it was a stunner—like finding a king's crown in your bed. She noticed something had been done to it. There was a flat spot on the rim. Within the last hour—

Somebody had cut off a two-inch piece of pie. Made a withdrawal on the Bank of the Moon? Petr did it? *Why?* And lightning struck: *He's getting me a horse!* She hugged the moon. Good old moon, you will give good things. But Mama wants you back in the lake. Why, Mama? Why get rid of it? Why save a little for you? What are you planning to do?

How was she supposed to do that? The thing was heavy as lead. No way to one-arm it down the ladder as Petr had done. But Mama says—

Down below in the kitchen the crazy woman was singing loud musical scales, a ringing-singing happiness in her voice Annabel had never heard before. Mama's doing Saturday's chore, mending clothes— and singing. Why so happy all of a sudden? You couldn't figure out old people. They were happy or sad for no reason.

Annabel shoved the gold into the big sack, pushed the window open and budged the heavy sack over the sill. Time to commit a crime. She went out, sat, scrunched her feet behind the sack, sprang her legs out, and the sack took off.

Gaining speed, it racketed down the shakes, then swooped off the roof, hitting the ground with a dull thud. She crab-walked down the roof. The gold moon looked like a crashed meteorite. Now it was her turn to fly, her heart began pounding.

Do it now. She leaped from the edge, crying, "Me–meteorite!"

A good jump, better than her first one, maybe even a boy jump, she landed, crumpled, and rolled. Wow! Bloomer pants really worked! A little stinging in her feet, that was all.

The continuous *scree, scree* from the toolshed meant Papa was still busy. Good.

She dragged the sack uphill towards the waterfall. Petr must be very strong to carry heavy gold *and* swim with it, staying under like a turtle, which he hadn't yet explained—and then fight a bear singlehanded. And the very next day he was cutting heavy logs with Papa. True, he carried the gold downhill. And Mama expected Annabel to drag it uphill. Crazy. She'd never make it.

After ten feet she stopped. The lake was two hours away, maybe more. Her arms and legs were already turning into taffy. Dragging the gold back to the lake was out of the question. It probably weighed thirty pounds, half her own lovely weight. What to do? Make a sled? Wait for Petr to bring her a horse and then carry the gold? What would a boy do? He'd do something.

She dragged the sack back down to the middle of the yard. Papa's axe leaned against the chopping block, a big old stump four feet wide used for splitting wood. Why not cut the gold into small chunks? Yes. Cut the gold like Petr had done. How had he done it?

The saw-screeching stopped—and began again. It gave her an idea. Rather than dump it in a lake, why not divide the gold equally among the family? Yes, why not?

She boosted the disk onto the stump and dumped it from the sack. She whispered, "O, moon, forgive me for cutting you."

Well, she would be the second person to commit *that* crime.

She lowered the razor edge of the axe onto the center of the gold, but then stopped. Was dividing it *really* reasonable? She knew from eavesdropping on Papa and Petr that gold was worth sixteen dollars an ounce. A pound wasn't sixteen ounces like Mama used. Rather, it was something called *troy* ounces: only twelve to the golden pound.

She did the math. Twelve ounces times twenty equaled two hundred and forty troy ounces. Times sixteen dollars each, equaled: Three thousand eight-hundred and forty—dollars? Could that really be dollars? She pictured the number: $3,840.

Again referring to conversations overheard between Papa and Petr: Soldiers made ten dollars a month; sailors made twelve. Laborers on the river made two dollars a day but only worked half a year because of winter. So a man's yearly wages were: soldier, one-hundred twenty dollars; sailor, one-hundred forty four dollars; miner, one-hundred fifty dollars—per year.

So—Petr found a fortune in a day! They were rich! Keep it secret? Tell no one? Dump it in a lake? What a laugh.

She cut three lines into the moon, the biggest middle slice for Petr. Then she hammered the lines like a pecking chicken, making a dull clag-clag-clag forming bright dents. They grew deeper very slowly. Had Petr done it this way? She doubted it. He had removed a pound, enough to buy a horse, if that's what he was really doing. Maybe he went to Honey Lake to tell the Rangers about the dead Indians. She looked at the cut Petr made. It was a smooth as butter.

He'd used a hacksaw! Too bad you didn't think of that earlier.

The edge of the axe was now jagged—it was ruined. Papa would hate her. He loved his sharp tools. But no matter what she broke, he never spanked her. That was Mama's job. Anyway she couldn't waltz into his shed asking for a hacksaw. He'd want to know why.

She chopped some more. Make three pieces.

Clag-clag-clag.

The gold didn't break like she expected it to, didn't chop like wood. It flattened. It dented. She was a hen pecking at a giant piece of corn. She made a mental note in her book.

Dear Reader, years passed thanklessly for the dull child growing old chopping gold.

When Papa's saw-sharpening stopped, she didn't notice.

Chop-chop-chop. Beads of sweat trickled down her face; flies buzzed around her head. Chickens heckled each other in the yard. Katie the cow bawled every few minutes. Annabel pictured a convict cracking rocks in the sun but she couldn't stop now. She pictured riding a big Arabian horse, running wild and free in the mountains.

When a shadow passed over her, she didn't notice. She worked steady as a steam engine. When she raised the axe, the axe powerfully lifted from her hands.

"What you do there, lil puddingcakes?"

Papa was smiling, his tongue slurring around in his cheeks, but when he saw the ruined axe, he swore, "Sahtan in hell." She felt a rush of shame. His tools were his precious shining swords. His voice full of wonder, "Where you find this?"

She blurted, "It was by the stump. I don't know why I did it. I'm sorry, Papa."

He planted one foot on the stump and swung her onto his knee but he didn't bounce her. He was staring at the stump with his mouth bobbing open and shut.

He repeated, "Where you find this?"

She explained Mama's orders: Haul the gold back to the lake. Petr found gold in a lake? Yes, it was supposed to be a secret. And now Mama wanted the devil moon destroyed and Annabel wanted it divided among the family. She began shaking. "I ruined your axe."

Papa laughed. "Little honey bee, I fix the trouble." He dropped the axe. He picked up the big dented coin of gold. Still smiling, he said, "You bring the axe."

They walked to the shed and the coin flashed in his glasses so that for one second he had golden eyes.

The shed smelled of Katie the cow and the oxen he used for hauling logs from the forest. In the barn everything was simple and straightforward just like Papa. The meaning of life was: Keep tools sharp. Work like play—play like work. Never get too serious about either.

He reshaped the axe on the grinding wheel, pressing the pedal rhythmically, orange sparks showering from the blade, a hypnotizing grinding rhythm. The disfigured moon lay forgotten on his workbench, a great big stump with two hundred growth rings. Annabel twirled leftover curly pine shavings from a boat carving project. She tossed handfuls into the air, showering herself in fragrance of forest perfume. What happened next was now in Papa's hands. Amazing how quickly control of gold had passed. Petr. Annabel. Mama. Papa. Was that the truth of gold? That shining things turned people into grasping puppets, that gold had a dark side?

In a scream of orange sparks Papa started talking angrily.

"Boy finds gold. Says noth-thing? He does not share? Years I give my sweat of life and his good luck he does not share? What use cutting trees, thinking me a good man on my own land? Who give one damn if John Valory live, die, or go crazy drunk?"

He dunked the axe into a water bucket making a squelching hiss. "Magya don't care! Boy don't care! Nobody care!—may as well get drunk."

"I care, Papa. Please Papa, please don't." But he was off in his own world. He was deciding something big. Sparks reflected off his glasses like flames shooting from his eyes.

"Get rid? I get rid for you, I know fast way!"

She shrank back. Papa was looking and acting crazy.

Raising a big iron hammer over his head, he yelled, "You find big gold and let old papa go back hacking trees? Peel log. Rip plank. Burn stump. Hah!"

He smashed the gold moon. Hit again, again, but it didn't break. It became a metal pancake. Another dozen blows, it became a rumpled shield. He didn't stop. He grabbed the axe he had just sharpened and smashed into the shield. He kept hacking.

The gold shattered into jagged coins.

Swinging the axe, Papa yelled, "Bring down the sack of lightning!"

Annabel stammered, "W-what?"

"You deaf? Get the sack! The sack! Get me the sack!"

Her legs were shaking but she ran to the cabin. When she returned he grabbed the burlap bag and shoveled in chunks, growling, "Yah, yah, Sahtan in Hell—smash the moon to hell."

Annabel stared at him. Who was this man who happily whittled wood, now raging? She asked in a small voice, "What should I tell Mama?"

He looked into the bag and laughed. "What does it matter? Say the thirsty lake got it all."

He was fighting back tears and his voice was breaking. "Run around until she thinks you done it. Then come back and say noth-thing."

She grabbed him around the waist and hugged him. "I love you, Papa."

He hugged her back and then shooed her away.

She ran back to the cabin. Time to think. Get to the loft. Get her doll.

She made it to the ladder when Mama lunged out of nowhere and grabbed her hair. Annabel screamed and Magya yelled, "What's wrong with you? You get rid of it?"

Annabel twisted but couldn't get free. "I got rid of it!—all right?"

Mama's grip tightened. "Just one little sack, you got it. Yes?" A wolf-gleam in her eyes, a look Annabel had never seen before. She stared for a long moment. It dawned on her.

She's really going to do it. She's going to run away. I guess that makes it clear for me. I must go back to the lake. She said, "Have it for you tonight, Mama."

Mama let her go, smiling. "That's my good girl."

Annabel smiled back and said to herself, Not anymore, Magya.

She went up to the loft and retrieved her doll. Then she hopped out the window and without any hesitation threw herself off the roof. Things were becoming clear now. *I'm on my own now.*

Then she sprinted up the lake trail.

After a minute of rough scrambling along the creek she came to the waterfall splashing into a pool where Papa would someday build his sawmill. She looked back at the cabin. Its chimney running beside the gable roof gave a small puff of smoke, all normal enough. Beyond the cabin she saw something that would have been funny at any other time.

Papa was riding old Bumpo, their burro, riding hard north for New Viksburg. The sack of gold was draped over Bumpo's neck.

She gazed into the mountains and sighed and she held her doll at arm's length urging Miss Daisy to understand. "It's no time for little girls. I'll tell you all about it someday, when you're older." The blue button eyes stared back.

Annabel whispered, "I'm going to Gold Lake. I'll get a gold moon. Set things right with Petr." The doll understood nothing, so she continued. "If Petr can do it, so can I—I can do it too." Those were the magic words. *I can do it too.* She hugged the doll hard.

"I'll get a small moon. Maybe get a few gold eggs to play with." She knew she was lying. Gold was no toy. Gold was not fun. She said, "I have to go now, Daisy."

The doll cried out, *I want to go too!*

"We can't hold hands and swim at the same time."

She made a rough solution. She pulled the doll's head off. "Best I can do." She kissed the puffy cloth face. She stuffed the head inside her big bloomer-pocket. She reclined the headless cornshuck body onto a rock where it wouldn't get mussed up. "You can't get wet, Miss Daisy." She patted the torso. "Sometimes heads and bodies go different ways. We'll get back together again soon."

She ran up the valley called the Valoryvale.

If she ran hard enough she could make it to the little lake in an hour or so. Plenty of daylight. *No one will know. Tell no one. Ha, ha. Okay, Petr, I won't.* She dashed twenty feet and looked back at the headless doll by a waterfall—an unforgettable image for her book.

A chill stabbed her stomach because it looked like a warning from the future.

She disappeared up the trail and would never see her family again.

4

Sun blazed the far mountains in gold and it was dawn and she knew she was hurt. Lying in long sweet grass, her heart beating fast, fiery pains in her wing, her own feathers scattered all around her—and she was on the wrong side of the river.

Small birds made darting flights above her giving her the urge to rise and strike. But when she tried she only trembled. She had a flashing memory of wasps stinging her and then her body became a leaf spinning to the ground. Numb and cold. Must get back to the nest.

Her cliff was a sun tower mere wingbeats away, but now flying was impossible. She would walk like a creature of earth. Walk up the cliff.

Lean the head, wobble stiffly forward, thick claws hooking sandy soil, making stubby three-toed tracks, right wing dragging on the ground.

To the fast cold river, feel its breezes. Try the wings but again her right wing failed, bent wrong, burning fire, feather tip missing. To not fly—means death.

A fallen pine leaned across the river. A bridge? She walked to the end of the log and felt low cool air beneath her, not flying air, not exhilarating hot breath air that could lift her high into the other world where she had lived, now a dream world. The end of the log was shredded like feathers ending a single wing-beat from the other side. She gazed up at her silver cliff. Bluejays shrieked at her. Go now.

She jumped and she tumbled upon her broken wing into the water, beating and beating.

Icy jaws shocked her. She flapped and splashed until she reached dry rocks on the other side. Sparrows twittered in the bushes. She stared at them and they flitted away. She looked up. Her ledge was high above her, still. And her legs hurt. And now she had a burning red hole where one of her thick talons had broken from her bright yellow claw.

She found a gentle approach to her cliff. She began picking her way up. What might be watching her from above? Without wings she was no better than a feathered rabbit.

Slowly she hopped higher and higher. Finally she reached her stony nest.

The yolk of her smashed eggs had dried in the sun. Desperate for food, she ate yellow specks until she felt a small flame of energy. Yet nothing was left for her here. And she knew one place where she might find food.

She walked until her legs felt like sticks. The sun fell into the mountains. Darkness came. But she found the feeder pole and something there smelled sweeter than a bee-hole in the side of a tree singing with honey and it loomed just above her. Hunger gripped her. Jump? Climb? Need to rest, just a moment, rest.

Dressing her plumes one by one through her long, hooked beak, remembering the one who thought he was feeding her, the one she felt *warmth* towards, his salty tang scented the feeding pole. And the sweeter scent of the girl. On top was a lump of meat the size of a rabbit. Must climb. Climb and be safe. On the ground she would die. Night creatures with big yellow eyes would come soon.

She clawed her way up.

5

John got rid of the gold. He spent six hours in a whiskey spree, a three-card monte spree. He was at a two-story saloon-hotel cabin with a huge wall tent ballooned in front that held a hardware and dry goods store. Above the lapel-like tent flaps man-high letters shouted in red:

The
Gold Nation

Young women fed him drinks, Lani and Manni, the Sandwich Island girls, black-haired, cinnamon-skinned girls, of coral teeth and almond-eyes, hustling among the miners handing out drinks, and jars of pickles, batteries of oysters, slabs of mackerel in blackened salt and pieces of shredded ham on platters. The Island Girls were pretty whirling blue skirts, tight red blouses, and white headbands. Red, white and blue patriotic girls. He fell in love immediately.

Dain King came in after dark, spoke to the bartender, Mack Karras, who pointed to John Valory and raised his eyebrows. John was very drunk, very surly.

King sauntered over, smiling. "You found the big lightning bolt, John?"

He was having trouble focusing, his mouth making rubbery motions before forming words. "None of your...business...me and Petr...we don't cut no more trees."

King squeezed John's hand hard.

"Petr found the gold, didn't he? We'll partner-up, you and I. You'll have my protection. We'll make things right, brother."

John jerked his hand back whiskey brave and loud. "Leave Petr out of this—and then, *Gunnar Valory*—I won't tell who you are and what you are!"

King folded his arms. He smiled coldly. "It's time for Petr to know who I really am. You've pretended long enough. Shall we get together for a family party?"

John stood and his chair went over backwards. He wavered but he faced the big man. "Petr and me...we cut lumber till your flume is through." He pointed a long boney finger. "Leave Petr alone or I tell everything I know!"

Gunnar Valory was Dain King's real name and he was John Valory's older brother and he was wanted by the U.S Army for stealing rifles. That's what John knew. He staggered away from his brother, whose eyes were black as death.

Very late that night he found his way back to his cabin on the Valoryvale and for some reason Magya was sitting on the floor crying.

King had a room in the hotel above The Gold Nation saloon. He slept a few hours and heard gunfire and thought he was dreaming. When he went downstairs the saloon was empty but that was odd. It was *never* empty.

Outside in the moonlight miners were running around and yelling: "They're all kilt!" And "Get your guns! Make a perimeter!" And "Injuns hit us and maybe coming again!"

And it was worse, much worse than he thought possible.

CHAPTER FOUR

TRY TO GO HOME

I sent my Soul through the Invisible, Some Letter of that Afterlife to spell: And by and by my Soul return'd to me, And answer'd 'I Myself am Heav'n and Hell'.

The Rubaiyat of Omar Khayyam

1

What he did that night was glorious warrior work he would savor the rest of his life. He killed the killers.

He waited for falling deeps of night and rode where the white-eyes did their coyote work of cutting down the sacred groves of pinenuts and making rivers flow into wooden houses. Then he and Talldog climbed a ridge high above the coyote town. There he picketed Talldog, but not driving the stake very deep, for he did not expect to survive this night. Below him the coyote village twinkled like a gathering of fireflies. He made his way onto a prominence of rocks overlooking the valley. He was thinking dark thoughts.

I am a ghost carrying the ashes of my family in the coals of my heart. Now this ghost kills the killers.

The moon was a yellow eye shining over the valley, a ghostly night for killing. Kill them in their sleep just as they had done to my People. He began singing death songs and prepared dream visions of what he would do and how he would do it.

That was when he noticed a strange circle of rocks.

A campfire of rocks ended in a bow-shape. A chill went up his spine. Realizing what he had found he touched the thing hanging from his chest, the black cross, the branding iron.

Here was where the big coyote did his evil spirit work.

He kicked the rocks out of the circle and rubbed ash onto himself. He said, "Now I am Sabbah coated with death."

To his horror he found little bones in the ashes. He picked them up. One of the nubs was much smaller than the others. The Great Spirit told him what they were. He put the bones into his medicine bag. The river inside his heart went dry; no more tears of sorrow.

He took the black cross from his chest and put it where the fire had been. He said, "Now you will know who has returned to kill you."

His rituals were interrupted by a barking gunshot from the valley below. This time of night good human beings were asleep. Only killers were awake at this hour. There he waited while the evil coyotes made their tinkling noises of music and shouts of laughter. Sabbah took his bobcat quiver holding ten red arrows and held each one at a time to the bright eye of the moon. "I hunt as a redman hunts," he said. "I made you a good arrow. I made you with my hands and heart." Then he pictured the arrow doing its work. After he had blessed the arrows he waited for the moon to go down. There was one final, muffled gunshot. He wasn't afraid of noisy guns. He was a silent killer, a wildcat smelling blood.

The moon went down; the town quieted down. Now was the time for quiet murder.

He descended into the town, crooning softly, "Heya, hey, coyote man, a ghost is in your midst, heya hey, coyote man, a bloody ghost haunts you." Then he became quiet.

He was a silent visitor to their rag tents.

It didn't take long. Killing five whitemen using only his knife and his arrows, they were easy to kill. They sat up from their sleeping rags and said, "Who's there?" Then he shot them in the heart. The last one was strong as a grizzly and he silenced his roars by slashing his throat. Now a voice inside him warned: Run Sabbah! Five white deaths are upon you!

Up the mountain he ran, screaming, dancing, exulting in his ghost work.

Talldog was waiting for him. But as he rode away he knew he had not completed his vow. Yes, he had killed coyote men, six counting the one this morning by the river, but—

He said hoarsely, "I must kill a white child soon."

2

Annabel got a lesson in history-making that strange day that ended her life as a little girl.

Ten o'clock Sunday morning, she ran to the strange lake in record time according to her lovely Lover's Watch. Fifty-four minutes. All because of determination and bloomer pants. No tripping, tangling skirts, now she was a modern girl even if Petr insisted calling her "midget".

Now if she was not a boy, she was just as brave as a boy. Time to get another gold moon.

There was the horrible little red lake.

Just go under just like Petr had done. It would be unbearably cold. A white waterfall gushed snowmelt into the far end of the lake.

She ran to the back of the lake onto a slab of old Indian drawings and she wanted to study them but there was no time. Grab a gold moon from the bottom, enough gold to satisfy Mama. Then go.

She climbed up to the rim where Petr had jumped at least fifty feet into the lake, her heart pounding like a drum.

Up here the lake looked like a big blue sugar bowl, not red— very interesting. And maybe by sunset it would turn gold. She leaned forward and imagined a dizzy fall, cold slapping water, maybe instant death. Pull off your boots. Tie them around your waist. Clamp bloomer pouch shut. Pat lump of Miss Daisy's head.

"Here we go. Guess we *have* to win the hold-your-breath game, this time." She made a final entry in her mental Journal of the Valory Family: How do pioneers *do* hard things? Is it because we want to? No—because we *must*. Necessity isn't a strong enough word. Desperation is the word. *Desperation* is the mother of invention.

She said goodbye to the sun. She hesitated. Something was missing, but what?

Petr held a stone over his head before he jumped, a stone to sink him *In-n-n-n*. She looked for a grapefruit-sized rock and hefted it over her head.

Squeeze it, Rocky, like you never squeezed anything in your life.

She closed her eyes and ran three quick steps forward and leaped into the air, screaming. "Ey-eeeiiii! Petr! I love yooo—!" A second later she hit the water.

Water skinned her like a fish, a quick blow with a cold knife. The rock dragged her down headfirst, a hammer going down. And then slowly she was merely a sinking girl sinking to the bottom of ice-cold water. The pressure on her ears mounted and her eyes popped open.

The bottom was honeycombed with pale boulders, large and small, but all dull, nothing gleaming. Where's the gold? This was the Water Pony dream, except she felt like she'd been punched in the head and she couldn't breathe.

Still going down, she clamped the rock to her stomach and sank flat like a leaf, slowing her descent. Good. She began thinking about the bottom and moved the rock to her fanny so she began sinking upright like a genie on a magic carpet. Now the only thing wrong was her lungs which were beginning to buzz like bees in a jar.

She hit bottom like a rug of slimy frogs. She glanced upward. The surface was a mirror shining twenty feet above her.

The only reason she'd made it this far was because of a cold fact— Petr had done it, I can do it. Then a cool reminder: His lungs are bigger than yours. That's how he wins the game.

She was suspended in rigid blue jelly, with icy eyes and crocheting needles driven into her ears. She didn't see any gold and she couldn't do this again. Okay, Petr, where's your gold?

Looking around at creepy green logs and pale boulders, there was nothing shining.

Look harder. There—

Something that made her heart grow cold, beneath the shiny ring of the surface, about ten feet underwater, a big dark line, a ragged rip like a whale's mouth.

Twenty feet of grinning mouth drooling with boulders and gravel as if the mountain had gooshed out its rocky guts. But that wasn't right either. The wide upper lip suggested an equal lower arc. At one time basically a circle, a really big blowhole, a volcano pointed sideways? Ha, ha. She couldn't laugh without gagging on water. But she heard a whispery voice: *That's where he goes when he leaves you.*

Who said that? She was remembering the dream again. Water Pony said that.

Volcano or not, that's where he went when he found gold. You will have to go there. But she couldn't. Her lungs were screaming: *Out of air!*

She dropped her rock and frog-kicked up from the bottom, jettisoning herself towards the mirror that was the bright land of life.

Smashing through, gasping, gulping wonderful breaths of life-fizzy air. Pinwheels danced inside her eyes as she dog-paddled to shore. Climbing, dripping, shivering, she collapsed onto warm red stone touching the Indian drawings, the wiggly lines, the magical life-givers, life-restorers—after all that deadly life-sucking water. She pictured Indian boys doing the very same thing. Brave boys. How could she go back?

Now she must argue herself back into the lake.

She said, "Annabel Rochele Valory, you're a failure." But a kind sweet voice responded, *No you're not. You are a very brave girl. You can do whatever you're brave enough to do.*

She whispered faintly, "I hope love makes you brave because that's all I've got."

The friendly voice was done. She was alone. But she had one friend left.

Searching her bloomer pouch, she pressed the water out of Miss Daisy's head. Something else, something heavy was in the pouch. "Oh, I forgot *something.*"

The pretty watch read twelve o'clock and it was stopped—maybe for good. The Lovers gazed at big water drops. Great, you ruined the watch, lost the gold moon, broke your promise to Petr to Tell no one! And you failed to get Mama that little bit of gold.

She put the watch into a smaller, secret pouch hidden inside the large pocket.

That hole—that volcano mouth—was waiting down there. Who knew where it led? All answers waited inside. Going, was a question of strength, courage, and love. Well—

Are you strong enough, brave enough? Do you love enough? She had to find out.

She climbed the cliff and without hesitation she plunged off headfirst into the air.

For the second time that day Annabel jumped into a lake—and it was really really bad.

3

To the west they traveled on ponies into the land whitemen had stolen to find Sabbah's trading party: Sun Eagle with ten handpicked warriors and three wives to do the cooking—and Minoah was sharing her opinion with her too-gentle father.

"Sabbah wanted to trade horses for rifles, and now we must go searching for him? Won't the white people be glad to see another roving band of Indians?"

Sun Eagle smiled. "Go back, dear daughter. This is warrior work."

"Let you wander among the coyotes? I am here to save you!"

He laughed. She knew he would. He said, "My chattering bluejay, why do I love you so much?"

Three days later they came to a place that told them the trading party had not survived: five grave mounds protruded from the grass. They spent the day uncovering the bodies, then reburying them, and crying. The only question was about Sabbah. He was not here.

The next day they followed tracks of shod and unshod ponies. The tracks led to a coyote town by a fast river and a fenced pen of eighteen Pah Ute ponies. Sun Eagle posted a warrior on the hill overlooking the town.

Then they rode away deep into the mountains.

They traveled high above the river canyon along an old trail few people knew about. Hours later they came to a roaring waterfall pouring into a small green lake. It was high and hidden and peaceful. Here they would make a village for five days, mourn their loved ones, and make smoke signals to call Sabbah to them. If he lived they would get his story and decide what to do. If after five days Sabbah was still missing they would return home to the pale blue lake in the desert and tell their story to war chief Numaga. Sun Eagle sent a lone warrior to inform Numaga of what was going on. Numaga knew all the big whites. He would decide whether to seek justice—or fight.

So the People built round huts they called canees and waited at the end of the long canyon where the blue river turns green after its fall from the mountains, waiting in this place where Sun Eagle knew whitemen were afraid to travel. It was still Indian land.

4

She hit water and immediately began counting like she was playing the hold your breath game. She swam for the arching stone smile inside the mountain, swam into the mouth that quickly narrowed down to the throat of an underwater tunnel.

Oh—goody. I don't think I can do this.

But she swam for ten seconds and discovered an amazing fact. There was light at the end of the tunnel, a dime-sized torch burning a hundred yards away (or maybe a mile) faintly flickering, very golden, very dim...*thirteen-fourteen.* Swim twenty seconds and make a decision.

She frog-kicked each stroke counting as a second.

There was just enough light to keep her skull from scudding along the slimy ceiling. Which she did only once, which felt like a good ol' scalping, and a constant reminder: Swim down! Because she kept rising like a bubble…*eighteen-nineteen.* Just enough light to see the incredibly smooth polished glass ceiling—the only reason she hadn't lost the top of her head…*twenty-two-twenty-three.* Just enough light to keep from going crazy. Just enough light for hope. Just enough….

She decided to keep going. Keep trying.

The water flowed slowly, powerfully, helping her.

After twenty-five seconds the light swelled to the size of a golden quarter. Just how far away was that? Thirty seconds was probably half her underwater range and a voice warned her.

Go back! You'll never make it! She looked back at the murky, grinning entrance.

Do you love Petr—enough? You do know he went this way… don't you?

She was swimming fast and getting truly terrified.

At sixty seconds her lungs felt like buzzing beehives, the light a golden eye the size of a dollar coin tilted slightly. But was it close? Fifteen more seconds? Or was it far? Another sixty seconds? A dead minute? Where was Water Pony when you needed him?

The little-girl inside Annabel cried out: Not gonna make it! *Sixty-eight, sixty-nine!* To which the woman-part answered: I am love, Petr, I'll die loving you! *Seventy-two….*

Love was for keeps and way too deep. Which was a real focuser, a good ol' pioneering thought: You can't go back…you must go forward… *seventy-five-seventy-eight.* Now—

Annabel became a blue-eyed frog swimming for her life.

Arms and legs became dead weights mindlessly stroking as she stared at the golden coin at the end of a tunnel, her mind reduced to a frog-minded will.

At one hundred and eight seconds—

The golden moon, almost there. Go, go, go. *Hundred-eighteen….* Almost—

The moon shattered; her head popped into thin air.

"Su-uuuhh!" Gasping not fresh air but sulfurous, burnt-match air—her lungs flamed, her arms and legs felt like noodles stuck with a million pins, but she dragged herself ashore anyway, where she lay face-down for a long time, gasping, shuddering, crying. When she finally had enough air, she yelled—

"Two minutes? Two minutes underwater!"

What a fool to swim inside a mountain! Now she was warming up on rock that was like a heated stove. She recalled how feverishly warm Petr had been when he emerged from the lake. The shore was deliciously warm as fresh baked bread, and oh that was good after that cold swim. Why was this place warm? She glanced around. The light in the room was dim but a moment later it brightened, or her eyes suddenly adjusted.

What had seemed like a golden eye was really a small pool about twenty feet in diameter.

Where are the gold moons? Care to look around?

She shuddered. "No thanks; not yet." She didn't feel like exploring, not yet. She untied the boots from her waist and poured water out. She squeezed Miss Daisy's head, the yarn dark and soggy, blue button eyes shining bright.

"Spooky in here, isn't it?" It wasn't quiet either. She listened.

A long whispering hush came from somewhere behind her—deeper in—a hush-rush of water. Don't want to know about that, not yet. She allowed herself to become slowly aware of domed walls around the murky lake. Light brightened like the sun coming from behind a cloud and for a moment revealed a glaring fact.

"My God—there's been people in here!"

There certainly had. Annabel tied her boots on tight. Ready or not she must go for a little walk because suddenly she realized the light in this cave room was wavering, pulsing brighter and then dimmer. And she felt and then heard a distant rumble.

5

It was funny how the business went with those two callused old-timers, probably brothers, and four grown sons, the Mexican cowboys. Where had he learned to do what he had just done? Petr Valory the horse-trader? Yet now he was riding down from Spanish Ranch on the finest horse in the mountains: sixteen hands high, powerful shoulders, a gleaming red mare, of soulful blue-brown eyes, seeming to pout for speed. On his test ride he turned her loose, letting her thunder into straight, earth-galloping strides, speed and power rippling beneath him, ripping down the mountain. Did he dare ride this way, no bridle, no saddle? Where had he learned to ride like an Indian (in a dream?). Man-body molded into horseflesh until they became a single being, one burning flesh. He could smell her earthy scent.

The caballeros had all laughed. The Americano was no racer. The horse sprinted away and a hundred yards later she planted her feet, lowered her head and—he went cartwheeling into sun, earth and sky—and then jolted into earth.

The jolt caused lightning to flash inside his head and a strange thought, *I sent my Soul through the Invisible.* It was a line of poetry he had memorized in school, *The Rubaiyat of Omar Khayyam.*

He rolled over smiling up at the horse. "We will call you Rubaiyat because you sent me through the invisible." The big mare stood over him, spluttering, as if to say: Well, what did you expect?

Annabel would call her Ruby for short. But she would definitely need a saddle. He turned his head experimentally finding it still worked. He spoke in reverential, hushed tones, "You ran a hundred yards in five seconds, not counting the distance I flew. You are the mother of speed."

Soon they would need to find a stallion for Ruby. That would make Annabel happy—and keep her out of trouble. The gold moon would bring changes to the Valory valley. This big fast horse was only the beginning of good things.

The afternoon had been magical.

The cowboys showed him twenty horses. Each time he inspected teeth, eyes, hair, the set of the knees, shaking his head each time. The caballeros shrugged, scoffing quietly, offering worn-out saddles to clinch a deal. Then he saw the great red mare.

"I guess I could settle for her. How much?" "No saddle. Hunnert-feefty." "What, dollars?" "No. *Centavos.* What you think?"

He walked away five times. The first trip they yelled, "You got no money! You waste our time!" Petr held up his gold so the tip of the crescent moon flashed in the sun. They followed him laughing, cajoling, slapping his back, praising his fine eyes, glancing at his fist. Bragging: "She's the best in the mountains, a red speedy mother. She gonna make you reech." The old man had no front teeth. Petr walked away from the corral and the price went down. Finally the toothless man cried, "Because my children are hungry and their mother is sick—a hunnert." He spoke seriously. "Amigo, we got horses and burros, more than we know what to do. Miners leave them to graze here for a few dollars. Some don't come back. Horses breed, you know? That's how she comes. The red, she's the best." He pulled Petr aside for a confidence the others must not hear.

"Big man King, he give us feefty a head, tops. I have to sell, but not this one. She's too good for him. She's for you." After a long pause he said, "Ninety?"

Petr shook his rough hand, palming him the gold, letting him know they had a deal. The old man opened his hand and his eyes grew big. "Holy Maria, it's a lot of gold!"

He patted the old man's shoulder and said quietly, "That's what I pay for the best horse. And—" He made a shy smile. "Keep your eyes open. I'll pay for that. I'll come back in a few months. You find me a big stallion worthy of the red one. Okay?"

They shook hands. The old man whistled and his sons brought the red horse forward. Petr took the rope. They hoisted him up onto the horse and they all laughed, he didn't know why.

"You gonna hang on tight, you be all right. Don't go too fast. Ave Maria she's fast! You come back. I'm gonna have a fine saddle ready for you. No charge."

The sun was setting; they asked him to stay. But he was eager to see Annabel's face light up. He'd make a mountain camp tonight with the red beauty, then start at dawn and be home before noon. They fed the horse oats and gave Petr a beef sandwich.

He left them amidst manly cheers and whistles.

After four hours of riding it was dark night and he made a cold camp.

He rubbed her down, and said, "Oh, Ruby, I can't wait for you to meet my little sis."

6

Annabel glanced around at where the light was coming from opposite the side she had arrived in. Light flared and dimmed and she could see things. A channel led away from the lake and into a hole gulping and swallowing water—and shining with the light. So that's where the water went.

The light brightened suddenly and she could see wonderful things.

What glorified the walls of the inner lake made the Indian sketches on the outer slab look like childish scratches. Take this one slow, girl; one thing at a time. She stood up but had to sit immediately as waves of dizziness overcame her. She shuddered at the deep aloneness of the place. But it wasn't quiet or still. Light pulsed brighter and then dimmer; dull roar grew and fell.

Beyond the narrow beach rose walls of moving shadows like troops of dark monkeys, marching down. Rocks swelled with light and then were squeezed by darkness, like big orange and black sponges. Light came and went—golden tides inside a lantern—in and out of the cave. What made lights do that?

She inhaled deeply, made the fiercely-brave face of Princess Lulu, lips pursed, eyes dead: *She who endures terrors and torment.*

It *was* scary down here but you could get used to spookiness. And stop that crap about dark monkeys marching down.

What light revealed was a small water channel draining the lake. No way was she going down that drain. Don't go any farther inside the mountain than necessary. Just get a small gold moon and leave. For now, let your eyes do the walking.

The Water Tunnel, (where she had arrived gasping for air) ended in an underwater trumpet-mouth four feet in diameter, centered, and bugling water into the side of the inner pool, a smooth basin of water about twenty feet in diameter, she could easily throw a rock across.

A series of small caves surrounded the pool, evenly spaced, certainly manmade. But by Indians?—or cavemen? Even more astonishing—

Above each hole was a savage drawing of an animal. Was this a dream? This needed a closer look.

She held out the doll's head. She whispered, "If you're seeing it, Miss Daisy, it must be real." Pausing to let the doll take it all in. "Wait here just in case...." She couldn't explain without sounding exactly like Petr giving a boogie-man sermon. "Since you're a little girl-doll this might be too *adventurous* for you." She propped the dollhead against a rock. "Just see where I...might possibly be going." She looked around.

Twelve dark caves circled the pool like black mouths. She whispered to the doll.

"What's in there? Wildcats? Bears? Snakes? Water Ponies?" She swallowed hard. "I'll be back in five minutes, I promise."

Following the gravel beach, Princess Lulu firmly in charge now, she approached each grotto, reverently touching the beautiful artwork. Her stomach tightened, each time before each cave, waiting for a white claw or fang to slash out her guts like pink yarn. That little blonde girl Annabel was brave, but she could never do this! Princess Lulu's iron stomach and lower lip quivered, but nothing worse. She caressed each drawing feeling she was touching the spirit of some great artist from ten thousand years ago, an artist the world had never known, a savage genius.

Red and white awesome beauty, each animal was outlined in black, figures leaping from stone, graceful and alive. Who drew such magical things? Weren't Indians primitive people?

Who made this place? The cavern was watercarved, then later enhanced by men. Long-ago men. She felt this was the insides of a giant seashell with the stream whispering in the background. But *somebody* made these drawings. And now she felt wild longings to be an artist. This place felt sacred so she whispered, "Let me bring beauty into the world like this!"

The animal above each cave was painted in fine red lines so curved and lifelike they appeared ready to move to higher ground; then a white *outline*; then a black *outline*.

Bear. Fox. Turtle. Buffalo. Her eyes goggled when she saw a strange elephant with big curving tusks and a high domed forehead. Strange!

She whispered, "The Harrisburg circus never had anything like that."

All lines curved perfectly so the animals seemed to be flying over smooth rock.

When she saw the red horse, her jaw dropped. It was a voluptuous thrill she didn't understand. Gasping at its run-carved beauty, its round-muscled strength, something surged through her, urging her forward.

"I want—me into you—you into me." Pressing her stomach to stop the fluttering, she suddenly remembered her pitiful mission. Her voice filled with self-contempt.

"Forget what you came for, did you? Forget Miss Daisy lying sillyfaced on the beach? Forget some good old gold business, did you? Forget Petr? Forget Mama?" Gingerly touching the beautiful horse flying on stone, she stepped sternly back, away.

"There'll be time for the horse, later." She uttered, "Back to work, gold-grubbing girl."

But she felt despair. Her job was impossible.

You swam in here. You'll swim out loaded with gold? Petr had done it, but she'd never make it. Petr's arms were hardened steel; her arms were noodles.

She whispered, "I didn't know it was *this* far in." Not to mention she didn't *see* any gold lying around. Maybe Petr got the last moon in the lake. Was it time to prospect the chuckly old downrunning stream that led down from the pool? She trembled.

She mumbled, "Yeah, I knew this was coming." She walked towards the gurgling mouth.

That's where the water was going. The mountain was swallowing water. The hole was a drain fed by the channel, fed by the outer lake. She noticed it earlier but had tried to ignore it because it seemed leading somewhere *down*, as streams always do. And she really didn't want any more *down*. And it made glugging noises. And she was thinking about what Big Jack said—about all the lost children in the world, their sweet voices sucked down into streams, captured forever, never seen again. She did not want to join the Lost Children of the Stream. But anyway—she looked down.

The light was definitely coming from *there*.

The stream-hole was the source of illumination pulsing and

painting the chamber. At the far end of the pool: a channel, fifteen feet of whispering smooth rock—water funneled through and away—down a water-gulping, golden crack.

"Go on—take a look." Her voice echoed far away into nothingness.

She crawled up close to the water-gulping crack keeping low in case bats might come rattling out of the gap.

Water was rushing in, but what was gushing out was an extra-strong whiff of stench wind. Water went in—stink came out—rotten-egg breeze from the core of something dead. She gagged as she spoke into the guzzling, stink-blowing crack: "Wonder-full place, isn't it?" But—

Orange light pulsing from a hole—did that mean gold gleaming from below?

This place was inhumanly scary. Water gurgled down who knew where. And there was just room enough for a girl to slide down the little splashing stream and....

And something else interesting she had noticed before, but fairly denied.

Another sound, a far-back steady sound, an undertone, running beneath the fine-friendly, bubbly-brightly singing voice of the visible stream, a faraway grumbling, ominously rumbling thunder was coming from below. Squinting down the hole she saw—

Water dancing, prancing, gurgling down stone stairs in foot-wide trilling steps, falling, dappling, light-draining-sluicing inner gizzards of a mountain—falling and swallowing steps. Then leading to what?— another hole—or a big fat mother hen laying yellow death eggs? Or—

Gold moons lying on molten dunes of shiny pirate doubloons?

Wondrous thoughts had the power to draw you deeper *in-n-n.*

What lies below the stream? You sure you want to know? Go deeper and find out! *No.* Don't make that decision yet. Ponder all that this means. It's still early in the game. No reason to rush *into* anything. Petr would think things through. For instance—

What does this strange place *do?* She pictured its workings, its doing.

Snow melted down from mountains. Water rushed into Gold Lake but no water rushed out. That little lake leaked *inward.* As long as enough water filled Gold Lake the grinning mouth just kept swallowing, into the inner pool. Maybe the outer Gold Lake had once been deeper and forced the creation of this hollow chamber of caves. Sounded about right. Water went down into somewhere else—into a heart of gold? The image struck lightning.

Gold Lake has a heart of gold!

That' what Petr found, what he called The Luminah, what must be kept secret: Tell no one! But what was it really? Annabel puzzled aloud, "What do you *suppose* is going on under there? Petr came up with a gold moon!"

She stared at the swallowing suck-hole.

Outer lakes; inner lakes; outer pools; inner pools—it was fairly dizzying. Peering into the chasm, she saw just enough room for a genie-sized girl to walk down the orange hallway of juice colored water. Go to the worlds below, ho, ho, ho, to a lost lake of gold?

Why called The Luminah?

She shrank back. Her next moves required a command performance from Miss Lulu. It was too much for a frightened eight-year-old girl named Annabel. No wonder Petr said, Tell no one. Indians cared nothing about gold. But if miners found this gloryhole—if it took a day, a week, a year—she blurted out: "They'd blast this place apart!"

She had it figured out, sort of. She fell back on her rump, exhausted. Rubbing her eyes, knowing she was wandering and wondering mentally to avoid: *Really doing something.* What now? You wanted a gold moon, not all this scenery. When she opened her eyes she saw something amazing above the stream-hole. She scrambled backwards in awe. "Jesus Christ Holy Mother Mary!"

She didn't mean to yell and her voice echoed for a far, long time.

Mary, mary, mary, mary.

She gazed in wonder. How had she not seen *this* before? Staring down like a winged god—

Was a drawing more brilliant than all others. *By far!* Not lined in red, not double-lined in white and black. This was pure, luminous, eye-blinding gold. *All gold!*

She made little-girl shrieks. Then she whispered, "It's—a gold falcon!"

Poised to plunge downward into earth—a winged flame—flaming down into earth.

Because she was a child she touched everything. She reached up, trembling, hesitating, waiting for instant doom, fingers gliding over warm, glorious beauty.

Gold wings flashed downward upon rock speeding into earth eternally.

Touching the falcon made her suddenly realize what this place was all about.

"A dreaming place, it's where they come to dream, to have spirit visions! It's where gold thoughts enter muddy little minds."

Whoever *they* were: The Indians; the Old Ones.

It was a sacred place, a holy-of-holies, before the whitemen came poking around. She was ashamed and wished she wasn't here. She felt waves of sorrow and tears fell down her face. Suddenly she was crying so hard she was shaking with great wracking sobs of grief and sorrow, followed by shuddering gasps. Pain so intense, it was as if her whole family had died.

Remember everything you can about Indians, things Petr had told her. Gingerly, she touched the falcon again. They believed in sacred animals. Each warrior chose his own animal and it became his luck, his secret, his sacred soul. Bear. Wildcat. Eagle. Horse. They were all here, whispering visions—bestowing powers. She believed it was all true.

She stopped crying and her vision ended. Why think about it? She was unworthy.

"O, falcon! I can't follow your wind-racing path! I just...can't. I guess that's Petr's path. He went down *there*—down the falcon's stream. I know he did—and he's not telling all he knows." Telling it to the falcon calmed her. "No, I'm not ready for you. I'm not big enough for all that...flying around." All that freedom was what she meant.

But of course she knew to what she *was* drawn—the Horse.

Try the horse. Do it now. You can do it now, can't you? What would it hurt?

Really? What about her nagging obligation to Petr, to Mama, to find more gold? She reasoned: "I'll go down your dream just a little way, down the Falcon Stream. I'll find little bits of gold, won't I?" Surely that made sense.

The falcon was *all gold*. No mistaking that message. And it was flying *down*.

But what's the rush? Why not take a peek inside the Horse Cave? See what visions waited for her there. After all, it was Water Pony who had pointed her to the hole in the lake. Shouldn't a girl have visions before going on *her* quest? Or were "Boys Only" allowed these dreams? Anger fueled her legs and arms into motion.

Arms pumping high, Annabel marched back to the pool, saying to the doll in militant tones: "Hold the fort, Daisy-head. I'll be back in ten minutes."

She passed the other caves and reverently approached The Horse.

Wonderfully etched, tall, powerful muscles throbbing, a real glory horse with legs outstretched to leap across a chasm. Thrills raced up her spine. She bowed reverently then rose up. She knew what she was feeling. "Oh, how I love you!" Yes it was love.

She entered the Cave of the Horse and nothing happened.

It was fairly small, a plain gray chamber but she was a little afraid, and filled with awe. This was a *real* holy place, a place where you might actually *do* something—much better than any church. There were drawings sketched on the circular wall. More horses. Not just a ring of horses—a *remuda*. Her imagination painted them into life, spluttering, whinnying, nostrils flaring, legs churning, hooves thundering. Her eyes drowsed closed, and as she dozed—

Horses rolled around her in a happy thunder-nation. Within the dreaming ring of horses, Petr appeared smiling and she smiled back waving as pleasure raced up her spine, swirling into her stomach in rich, glorious gushes of love—

Here he came riding on a beautiful horse, a red horse of love, the beginning of her own beautiful ring of horses—a remuda of love. The dreamy vision swirled around, around, and down inside her heart. She stretched deliciously in love!

A moment later she awakened content, and then she left the cave grinning. She bowed to the picture of the Horse. "Boy, do I feel good. Thanks for that. That's all I ever want."

Her idea about this place was proven. She whispered across the pool to Miss Daisy.

"It's a dreaming place...dreaming your future life."

It was for peace undisturbed by storms of confusion and clouded other-worlds that nagged with cares and tugging considerations. These caves were egg holes for dreamers to fill up with hopes, where hopes grew in the dark—inside dream chambers.

And that cave entrance she feared, the one over which the falcon flew, that way led down into what? *Good question.* A stunning thought hit her: What if The Luminah was the place where Mother Earth placed eggs for storing Earth's future, Earth's memories—

Not to mention gold eggs and gold moons? Was that the truth of this place?

The prod of curiosity begins where necessity ends. She felt a good hard shove of resolve to finish her first mission. She stated it: "I will find gold. I will set things right."

She walked back to the Falcon Stream and felt good and strong, the shakiness all gone. She sat on a rock and retied her bootlaces. She spoke to her doll.

"Well, Miss Daisy, I'll go down the stream. I'll be back in ten minutes—or so."

Or so, was her deciding how many steps to take *down* into the Falcon Stream, if she had the nerve to try it. Five minutes—if she averaged one step per second—was sixty steps times five. That was three hundred steps. Ten minutes meant six hundred steps. Probably never get that far, okay? She stared at the doll. Miss Daisy didn't look right.

One blue eye was missing—the doll looked scared. It was crying, *Please don't leave me here!* Annabel searched the ground, then her pocket. No button. She said, "Miss Daisy, you're falling apart." The doll pleaded, *Where you go, I will go also.* Great, a doll quoting the Bible. Annabel said, "Oh, come on, then." Sometimes the smallest things made all the difference.

Putting Miss Daisy's head inside the bloomer pouch on her chest, then facing the Falcon, gazing up its gold curving wings, she said, "Please don't hurt me. I'm really a nice person."

Then she went into the Falcon Stream, walking in down-running water.

7

There was an undertone. The tunnel was *filled* with metallic grinding sounds.

She bent low counting quick steps down a gloomy orange tube, a narrow version of the Water Tunnel, the ceiling smooth but much lower, like walking down the bore of a cannon.

The Water Tunnel and the Falcon Stream had once been a long, single connected throat. She was sure of that. Only this time she wasn't drowning in water. She wondered if the watery-entrance of the Water Tunnel had once been a test of courage for young Indian braves. *Yes, this place makes you brave.* Now at least she could breathe, the water only six inches deep, the tunnel smooth all around, but the air smelled worse than baby stinkers.

So warm she was sweating, she splashed herself, and the water seemed warmer with every step...*twenty-one-twenty-two.* She was beginning to sense ponderous weight of a mountain weighing on her, waiting to crush her. Deep inside a slimy stinking tube, a wormy girl waiting to be crushed by rocks or sudden explosions. It felt like a deep well and somebody had just put a lid over it. Sweat poured from her body. What she knew for sure was: "You're alone, nobody knows you're here, nobody will ever know what happened." *No body.* Best not to think about that, girl. Concentrate on putting one foot in front of the other...*thirty-seven-thirty-eight.*

Far down the shaft was a winking gold eye. It called her deeper just like the golden gleam in the Water Tunnel had called her. She was learning. Gold has the power to draw you in. *Forty-eight-forty-nine.*

It grew brighter faster, radiating heat like a hot poker. Nothing to get all scared about.

But the grinding metal sound was louder, too. Like pirates dumping treasure chests. *Fifty-three-fifty-fo*– Heat increased, fear gripped her. Walking into a death-trap! Stop!

She squatted in the water, splashing her face. When she opened her eyes something shone in the stream and her hands froze between her boots. The answer to her prayers lay at her feet.

A gold egg—the size of a hen's egg and perfectly round—lay at her feet. The sight of gold was amazing. *Always.*

She picked up an amazingly heavy metal egg, and began laughing quietly, hefting it, holding it to her cheek, the heavy pretty thing. "Gold," she whispered. "I found gold, I'm rich!"

The shockingly bright reality brought realizations. You're deep in earth's belly. There's nobody to share your joy. A thousand dead pirates could tell you: Buried treasure ain't valuable till you get it back to town.

She pocketed the heavy egg inside her belly pouch. But still, she couldn't help screaming.

"Whoo-eee! I'm rich! I found gold!"

She did a rapid blur of math. A pound at least, was two hundred dollars, easy. She leaped into the air and struck her head on the cave ceiling. The pain settled her down.

Get gold. Go home. You're rich.

Ten steps later she found another egg and pocketed it. "Gold!" she cried. "Gold, hee-hee!" And her voice echoed down the stony hallway: *Gold-hee-hee....*

Gold eggs lay every ten or twenty steps, sometimes in globular pairs, sucking her deeper in. At one hundred steps her pockets bulged with small gold balls. She realized she was in danger of losing her bloomer pants. She realized—

"Stupid, why carry gold down, when you have to carry it back up again!"

She unloaded sixteen small eggs and stacked them into a shiny pyramid. Her arms and legs began shaking. They were: exhausted and used up. Oatmeal breakfast and no lunch, she'd run on raw courage and not much else.

She took the crown egg from the pyramid and put it into her belly pouch. There—one egg was all right, just so you know you weren't dreaming—one egg for Mama.

Yes and the nice hefty *heft* of reality she needed so badly right now, and to rest.

She spied a flat shelf rock a foot above the water, a nice dry place for a nap, just a few minutes. The stenchy wind drafted over her, oddly warm and powder dry, as if blown from a desert. She lay down comfy warm and thoughtful.

Petr found a pie-sized moon, not a hen's egg. How much farther to the moon, ha, ha? Do you really want to go to the moon? Well, how long had Petr been *under* that day? How long had she waited by the lake, over an hour? To be exact: An hour and twenty-two minutes. And this place was only part of what Petr found. And it was *tiring* finding what Petr found. And it was just *too far*. And now there was something terrible to think about.

Getting out, how will you get out? Swim out—the long Water Tunnel again? She didn't know if she could do that again. But she did know something for sure about the Falcon Stream. She was done.

"Well, me hearty, don't we worry, we'll not be going any farther *this* way."

That was for sure. Catch a little nap, take a little gold hen egg for Mama, walk out the chuckly little stream for lost boys and girls. Then swim me hearty swim, out the gloomy grinning whale-mouth. Sure would be interesting to see where this stream went. See pirates jumping on treasure chests. Shurrr. But it was bad. Curiosity killed the cat. And she wasn't nearly as strong as Petr.

Warm breezes wafted over her, Rest...juss....rest a minute or so in this grotto of dreamy eggs dreaming. Sleep, and find what Petr found. Yes, dreaming so much easier, so possible in this strangely whispering place, so less messy than galumphing down the stream. She fell asleep, desiring deeply: *Find What Petr Found.*

She dozed and then fell into a very realistic dream.

Walking down the Falcon Stream, farther down, farther down, felt scary because she wasn't sure if she was dreaming or sleepwalking.

Not tired, didn't stumble, and so decided that—*I'm only dreaming.*

She counted just as if she was awake. The stream was now a foot deep and *very* warm. And at Three hundred sixty (which was sixty steps beyond what she would have gone if awake) the light became painfully bright just as the sound of grinding, smacking, crunching became so loud it vibrated her bones. Then something so amazing it had to be a dream.

Falcon Stream rushed *into* a crack six feet tall. *Out* of this crack gushed light, a blinding yellow beam so strong a girl could swing from it. No wonder the Cave Room glowed and the Water Tunnel shined. It was so painfully bright she had to cover her eyes.

She stuck her hand into the beam. It turned gold. *Just like King Midas!* She withdrew it and it returned to normal. Just a dream, so go on, stick your head in. Annabel scrunched her eyes popping her head into the beam and even with her eyes closed—

Cannon blast of light!

"Wow, I'm blind!" But that wasn't true. She saw something. What had she seen?

Amazing images blazed in her brain of what lay beyond—all incredible.

Huge domed crater roared like a circus tent on fire. The circus in Harrisburg was a pokey affair compared to this. This was a three-ring dinger.

Roaring gold arches on fire, calliopes on fire, gold ropes on fire. And the sound! Where did it come from? Go see! But won't molten gold burn your head off?

Stay in the stream. Stay in the dream. See what happens. It's only a dream!

The gold drew her in—she entered eagerly.

But it felt very real. She tripped, slipped and fell spinning into nothingness. Cartwheeling One! Two! Three! She was chicken-flopping in air and then belly-flopping in water of a shallow pool. Rising shakily on dripping hands and knees, her head and heart pounding, this was—

Not bad for a dream!

But her hands and knees *hurt*. She sensed what had happened. She'd fallen from a waterfall and this was a plunge-pool she sat in. She shielded her eyes, and peeked, because there was way too much light! Can't see! But after a moment she did see and blinked in pain.

A floodlighted crater below with an equal dome above, the dome was filled with swirling mists, The Falcon Stream went down another five hundred yards and then exploded into white vapor as it entered something amazing—the star of the show.

A golden bubbling pool spitting gold—Gold Lake.

Pulsing light pierced her eyes and she cried out and splashed water into them. Looking at the Gold Lake was like looking at the sun.

Splash your face and take a quick survey.

The bubbling lake was a cauldron at the bottom of a steep bowl, a crater a hundred yards across, all splattered gold. Stay by the waterfall you might survive here an hour. She was a veteran of Salt Lake but this was much worse. *Need to get out of here.* She looked back at the gushing waterfall.

You fell from there? It'll be tough getting back to the top, maybe thirty vertical feet.

Annabel was getting a real bad feeling about this being a dream.

The stream fell (where she now sat) into a plungepool warm as bath water then raced down the crater. At Gold Lake the stream burst into steam and disappeared. Meaning: hot as hell.

A gurgling metal mouth boiling, bubbling, splashing, gnashing, yellow yelling tongue, tongue-ing up golden waves of heat, *that is Gold Lake.* Grinding, grinning metal screaming—

THE SOUND!

Annabel covered her ears and pressed her eyes shut.

It's a dream place. Why is sweat pouring down my face? No! Wake up. It's too much and I must get going now. Wake up on the Falcon Stream far away from this gold crazy dream. I wanna go home!

She pinched her arm hard, bit her lip, opened her eyes, and it was bad, all bad. She cried, "Ah-ih! Ooo! No-o-o!" She opened her eyes wide, a big mistake.

Gold light stabbed all the way to the back of her head. She clenched her eyes, horrified, because she was not in the Falcon Stream. She was—

"I didn't...I couldn't...it can't be!" But she did, she had, and it was.

Annabel was in the crater of Gold Lake, what Petr called The Luminah. She was really here, not dreaming. This was real.

She hugged herself into a ball. Wormy streamers of sweat poured from her body which felt like a potato boiling in soup. She fought against the golden nightmare, whatever it was.

Stand up, this isn't real. You only dreamed you woke up. You're still dreaming.

A melting girlcandle stood, and she felt herself going into deep shock—deep fear.

"Do something fast," she muttered. "this place is for real," her voice shockingly croaky, a dead mummy voice. She shaded her eyes and glanced around.

There the deep shining crater and the shining high dome, all awful, awful-real. She focused on boiling hell below.

The Falcon Stream raced into exploding fingers of steam, down to *it*. The real Gold Lake! A prodding molten tongue hissed out from the pool showering handfuls of hot coins rattling onto the beach—making the Sound, the awful Sound! She stared at the beach. The beach... littered with coins and eggs and...her eyes goggled. That's where Petr went!

"Look at all those gold moons!"

Hundreds of moons, maybe thousands, scattered around the central lake.

Petr had gone there, *even there?* "Boy-oh-boy, I must go too!"

Dashing thirty steps, counting them, the first moon probably fifty steps away, she'd never make it. Her face began baking like a potato. She remembered Petr's sunburn when he came up from the lake.

Princess Lulu cried within: *Annabel, close your eyes!* And she stuck fists in her eyes but it was too late. "Oh...God," she whispered. But God didn't help bad little girls.

Double moons blazed inside her head and she was blind. Annabel was blind.

She couldn't help it so she screamed like a steam whistle.

"Eeeee-iiiii! Eeeee-iiiii! Eeeee-iiiii!" a shriek dying in the metal roar.

She turned away from the lake, staggered up the stream. Get back. After twenty steps her strength melted. She hugged her knees and bowed her head and sank into warm water. As she passed into wadded-up oblivion her brain switched off and her body went limp.

It was too much. She was done.

She passed out inside The Luminah and it was the end of her little girl life.

8

Dain King admired good killing work, reminding him of his own younger days. Because it took courage to walk into an armed camp and do what this lone Indian had done. You had to not care whether you lived or died. Four arrows, four kills; another killed with a knife. That was cool work. King ordered the arrows and knife removed from the corpses to be stored in a crate with the other arrows gathered from the Pah Ute trading party. As he knew they would, they matched.

The missing Pah Ute had returned for revenge.

The next morning King's Regiment followed the tracks of the deadly visitor. His trail led directly to Point of Rocks where the Indian had apparently spent the night. They found the branding iron.

Tracking was easy after that. The killer snapped a tree branch here and there so he could be followed even by a pack of whitemen. King had an idea where the trail led, and it did: back to the bend in the Feather River where King's men had killed the five Pah Utes.

"Looks like he headed south from here," Tiger said, a small powerful man, King's right hand when it came to trouble. "Maybe hit the Valoryvale next. Do we go on?"

King shook his head. "He's done leading us. We won't find him till he's ready. Round one is done." He circled his finger ordering them back to Gold Nation.

It wasn't over. The mountains would flame with the words "Indian massacre!" That was a fire he could use to his advantage.

King lit a cigar and smiled. His dream was beginning to come true, to take shape. How long before his son returned to him? What he saw in his vision would come true. Together, he and Petr would hammer out the Gold Nation!

9

Dreaming she was dead was nothing like anyone said, not even close.

She was a *boy* herding sheep, wrapped in a thin jacket and baggy pants. His feet looked like small boats until she realized they were wooden shoes. He was shivering cold, hadn't eaten for two days and for some reason she knew he would die in five more hungry years, at age fifteen.

She dreamed other little boys and little girls, familiar as long-lost friends, like short-stories spaced between quiet dashes of sleep, each scene older than the last and further back in time by perhaps two hundred years. None lived very long, dead, after quiet, uneventful lives.

She yawned. Merely dreams.

Part of her knew her latest body slumped on a gold beach far underground, roasting like a duck in an oven. But for the moment this wasn't important. Right now she was having a very beautiful dream she didn't want to leave.

There was a wide blue river beyond which lay endless yellow sand. She was inside a walled city made of stone, inside a temple of pale columns graceful as candles. Inside the gray stillness of the temple women in green robes held petting cats, adored cats, worshiped cats, carried them around like babies. Statues of cats with long necks stood in niches in the wall, along with cat mummies tightly wrapped in cloth. There were no men.

Men were unwelcome as dogs. They were not allowed.

She was young, straight black hair and cinnamon gold skin, astonishingly beautiful, but she had done something very bad and was going to pay for it—and she wasn't sorry. A priestess of Bast-tet, her name was Mirael, and she wore the long impassive face of a woman who knows she is right, certain as a cat is certain—and won't back down. Annabel knew this was the one she called Princess Lulu in her imagination, when she needed courage to go forward completely selfish and strong. What terrible thing she had done Annabel couldn't remember, or refused to recall, but it had to do with betrayal. She smelled fruits and nuts: grapes, bananas, dates, oranges, pomegranates, pecans, cashews, and she was very hungry—and then she awoke, sweating.

The child-lives inside faded. She returned to heat and roaring and showering metal. Curled into a fetal ball, she knew better than to open her eyes.

She uncoiled arms and legs slowly and then splashed herself in warm stream water. Check the egg. Yes, heavy reality in my bloomer pouch, golden egg pressed against belly.

Good. Can you walk out of this gold-belching oven?

She cracked one eye open and saw what she expected—gold haze—nothing else. Swords of pain struck her eyes, hurt like hell.

She was not dreaming, she was actually gold blind, gone on a little golden holiday. With eyes closed all she saw was flaring orange glowing coals. She took a deep breath.

Okay, three hundred sixty steps underground, into The Luminah—the dreaming-center and possibly the remembering-center of the world, I've got a nice golden egg for Mother and I'm really awake now, not dreaming. So what do I do now? I gotta get outta here, pronto!

But get out alive?

With hands outstretched she sloshed forward downhill, the heat increasing like walking towards a furnace. She was growing nauseous.

Definitely not a dream, it's time to turn around and go away.

A wobbly step *away* from the dense heat she felt heat recede. Good. Getting oriented to her little dog-run, the stream was flowing around her ankles, so she walked against the flow. After a few careful steps she stumbled against the streambank and her hands touched hot, dry ground. She cried out, "Don't touch dry ground!"

A few steps later wispy sprays of waterfall cooled her face. What now? Scramble up thirty feet of falls?

A few steps later she was back at the plungepool where she had fallen. Splashing her eyes she got a momentary glimpse of the waterfall rising thirty-feet straight up. Okay. Try it.

She hugged slippery warm rocks and began climbing, but it was too steep. She couldn't hold on, she fell back.

She retreated to plungepool and sat down. She splashed and saw a place beside the waterfall that seemed less steep. She made a run for it, climbing, crawling, and then she screamed in pain. "Hot Jesus, hot-hot!" Her vision faded into orange glow.

She scrambled back to the plungepool and sat in the water, eyes closed, listening, thinking.

The crashing sound louder, the pirates-dumping-treasure-chests roar now a deep, throaty rumble. Like maybe that pool in the crater didn't just bubble. Maybe it blew sky high. Maybe that's how gold reached the ceiling and how eggs blasted up the stream.

Wait long enough you might get blown uphill yourself. So how do you escape?

She splashed her face and drank big swallows of water that tasted like boiled eggs.

Okay, you can't see. But you can feel. What guides people?

Of course the five physical senses, but they weren't doing much good down here. What else? What guides the lame, the halt, the blind, the wayward soul in hell? Greed. Anger. Need. Yes, hungers and emotions. The invisible not-so-good guides most people followed, but guides all the same. What else guides you? The answer returned as a question.

Love? Yes, love, better than gold.

Tears rushed down her face. They dried quickly. She took big swallows of egg water.

Gasping, "I love Petr no matter what...gold or no gold...I will find a way back to you." Tears improved her vision. "Which way, Petr—can you get me back to you?"

His voice whispered inside: *The Indian guided me. He sent me here.*

He guides me still. But his guide is Anger. You must not follow me. You must find your own Way....

His voice trailed off as if it too were lost.

"The Indian?" she asked. She was angry now. "That's not helpful, Petr."

Tired, hot, sweaty, Annabel gathered strength and her thoughts.

So I am Love!—blind, thirsty, hungry Love. Angry Love! A dozen dreams of me live inside of me barely remembered. But once I was a cat-woman who knew what was right. Where is she now? Can cat-woman see in the dark?

Annabel drank ten handfuls of water and waited for inspiration. Blindness was supposed to be dark. Who ever heard of bright blindness and no sense of time?

What was time, especially if the revelations of this place, this *Luminah*, were true—that there was life, and then another life—and then another life, each body a stick of time burning like a candle. Lovely thought except—her present candle was melting rather fast. She waited. Dipping another handful of water, it slowly tasted okay to her. Egg water was reality.

More thoughts came as if her mind was a bright blank page.

This place of outer and inner lakes followed a repeating pattern. What was true of its outer form was true of the inner form. So if the *little* dreaming pool has twelve caves surrounding it, what about this big dreaming pool? Did it have twelve caves surrounding it too? She laughed.

Yelling into the vast cavern, "Who says a blind girl can't see?"

Bet your life on it? Yes. Find a cave, *a tunnel out of here.*

Inspiration flashed: The answer's right behind your eyes. First you dreamwalked into it—then you saw. Then you woke up into it—you saw.

"What I saw was a gold flash."

No. You saw more, now the imperative tones of Princess Lulu bold and unafraid—*Search the gold haze inside your head. See what it contains.*

Something printed by that blast of light on the screen of her mind slowly appeared, something at roughly the same height as the waterfall. She saw something like a golden sketch.

"Another cave, faraway," she said dreamily studying the burnt image—

Twelve caves, yes, twelve dimples in the haze, hard to see, far away, far apart—hidden in washes of light. What these caves might contain she couldn't guess. Hopefully one was the way *out* of this underworld, the way *back* to the world of life and living. Was it foolish to hope for that?

Study the burning image again. This is the creating place of Earth—The Luminah. My brain took a photograph of The Luminah. Tell no one!

Let the golden photograph develop. See that line? It's a trail leading up and out of here—up to the level of the caves. Right? Okay?

Okay, she would bet her life on a vision in her head.

The horrible *aloneness* of the place filled her with despair. She cried hard. A moment later she gave it up because it was a waste of time. *Pioneers have no time for tears.* When she opened her eyes again she could see normally for about a minute.

A trail led up to midpoint between the nearest cave and the waterfall, very faint. Go see the mystery cave.

Her muscles felt stretched like rubber bands, but strength of purpose poured into her small body. She loosened her boots and filled them with water. She soaked the doll's head for a sponge. "Okay, Miss Daisy, let's go."

She climbed a circling rampart of stone, a radiant cowpath carved against the huge crater side. It *felt* like a tall, one-sided hallway, her right hand brushing lightly against warm stone, her left side roasted by hot dragon's breath.

She hurried but the climb took forever, she stumbled every few steps, her knees hitting hot stone, she became so numb with weariness she barely noticed the pain.

Ten minutes brought her to the level of the caves.

A narrow runway—which way to go? Swimming back out through

the Water Tunnel terrified her. No more swimming. She daubed Miss Daisy to her eyes. Her vision cleared.

She dashed away—towards the cave shimmering in the distance—and began counting steps.

At one hundred forty-four she was blind again, but she was there. Her right hand fell into nothingness. She nearly toppled into it. Warm air *inhaled* into the opening. What did it mean?

She was tempted to refresh her vision again but decided to save the moisture in case she needed it later. Blindly tracing her hands around the stone mouth of the cave, it was a foot-wide cleft in the rocks, the top beyond her reach, but she imagined a stone arch high above her.

Yes, it was a cave—hot air sucking into it, must go somewhere. She didn't hesitate.

She went in—to get out.

10

By 9 P.M. the big red horse stood picketed sleeping soundly while Petr lay on his back counting stars. After a while he rolled facedown counting sheep. Thinking about gold, what he found, how he found it, he rolled again facing the star spangled night and made up a song. "Oh, is it—is it she—the Motherlode for me? It is SHE, isn't SHE?"

He wanted to feel excited but something was missing.

Where he should have a memory about finding the gold moon in the gold chamber—was a big blank gap.

Annabel had showed him the watch. He was *under* for one hour and twenty-two minutes, not nearly enough time for what had happened. Annabel thought he was keeping a secret, but he wasn't. He was blanking something out no matter how hard he tried to remember.

He dove into the lake and wasn't afraid because the Indian was guiding him. *Swim into the red mouth of the tunnel and then swim as fast as you can!*

He remembered swimming into an inner pool where a gold falcon marked a trickling stream flowing down. A doorway of memory opened. The Indian whispered, *Follow the falcon down. You will find what you want.* Mentally he walked down the Falcon Stream and a big memory hit: *There is a huge chamber deep within—filled with pharaoh's wildest dreams of gold.* And hellish light burning so bright it turned the mind into yellow jelly. The memory was dazzling, and scary.

He flipped onto his belly again.

You came here for gold. The Indian knew he'd go! But the nagging question was: Why did the Indian want Petr Valory to find gold?

He rolled again facing the gleaming stars. Wind sighed in the pines. It was a night for Indian spirits. But the Indian wasn't talking tonight.

So what really happened under the lake?

He faced cold gravel.

The stream led to a great domed room of gleaming wonders, too bright and too hot. He said out loud, "You passed out in that big gold room of wonders."

Heat, light, stench—what else? There was the gray gap in time. But it was coming now. "You passed out—into somewhere—into *someone* else. Yes?"

Insane. But the fact was—

He remembered returning to Earth like so many lost dreams of finding gold, to find truth about gold. Yes, all forgotten now, covered by black centuries of death. Had he really traveled a strange country of burning sand and gold-faced pharaohs?

It couldn't be real so he had simply blanked it out.

Rubaiyat spluttered awake and Petr startled but stay lying down. The night was cool but Petr began to sweat because he was remembering something else. He had passed out inside a giant furnace chamber of volcanic heat, light, spectacle and stink. And that spectacle had sent him into a jimjam brainfever fit—in other words a dream. He dreamed of hot dusty old Egypt, that's all: A place where things happened that no one could forget, so it was all written down in the Bible. Mama had read it to him. And he dreamed it and a big wild dream was all it was.

Yes, he could believe that.

Except dreams of Egypt opened gates of emotion, whispered from the Invisible:

Egypt! Where are you now, inside me still? Remembered still, your runes, your sandy body, your tears my blood? Am I, You, renewed? Waking in a new land?

He had been walking in burning desert sand until he collapsed and passed out from thirst and exhaustion. Then his mind or soul had flown from him like a bird. It wasn't just any bird. It was a *falcon*. The falcon flew until it found gold. Then the mind switched off the big sad story, the dream territory he still couldn't remember, some long gray *gap*. Some epic failure thousands of years ago that drove him hard even now, something to do with betrayal. He had betrayed someone.

Twelve lives lay dead inside The Luminah! But the last dream— that was his first life. That's the one you're hiding from. He shuddered because he remembered his name.

You are Mahrire, the Falcon Prince.

He sat bolt upright. The horse looked at him. Petr said, "Not sleeping either, eh?" The stars showed the time of midnight. He said, "Let's go on home. There's a girl waiting to meet you."

But he would find he was way too late to get home.

CHAPTER FIVE

LOST AND NOT FOUND

1

He led the horse down the steep slope into the valley of the Valoryvale. It took two hours. Now he was on familiar ground where every boulder and tree was like an old friend. Finally somewhere after 2 A.M. he cantered Rubaiyat into the barnyard. Papa's old burro, Bumpo, stood untethered and snacking on shortgrass. It stuck out its teeth and brayed. "Eee-haww! Eee-haww!"

"Why aren't you in the barn, you bad old boy?"

He heard singing in the cabin and wailing laughter. Not good. He slid from Rubaiyat's back, then stiff-legged his way to the cabin feeling very saddle sore. He pushed open the door.

Inside was bright as Christmas.

Magya sat on the floor in a circle of a dozen lit candles, eyes red and puffy. Papa sprawled beside her, his head in her lap. Petr was flabbergasted. He smelled sickly sweet brandy. The old man raised his arms and Magya pressed them back as he tried to talk.

"Ushh yutta benn darr...."

Petr stepped forward cautiously, his voice flat and dead. "What happened, Mama?"

She began crying a singsong: "He fell... he fell... he fell...."

Papa kicked like an angry child. Petr sighed deeply. He's been to Gold Nation—drinking. Question was, how did he make it home? He saw why Bumpo was loose in the yard. Still, it must have been quite a feat. The Sierras at night were like a walk in a saw factory. He had helped the old man home after dark how many times in Harrisburg when he had gotten bad. But Harrisburg was a stroll in the park compared to this. John's eyes were bright with delirium.

What set you off this time, old Dane? More important, where was Annabel? She wouldn't sleep through this madness.

John Valory glanced around smacking his lips, and then focused on Petr for a moment.

"Lee 'im lone, lee 'im be!" John clawed the air and Magya pressed him down. He cried out, "Gie mi nother trink, willyoo?"

Petr stared at them, shaking his head, then turned away and walked to the door.

"Can't I leave for one day, can't you be decent? Must I monitor you every minute?" He felt old as if he had become the father of his parents.

He returned to them and asked gently, "Where's Annabel?"

Magya rocked John. "Poor old simple head, he done the best he could."

What did that mean? He touched her shoulder, "Mama, where is Annabel?"

He could not know she was not really in *this* room. She changed from joy to sorrow in seconds. What now? She was—

She was holding her beloved husband of twenty summers ago. This young man standing before her was a stranger, but it seemed she *ought* to know him. Anyway he could not be trusted. The circle of candles protected her from the dark evils of men.

She was retreating on musical wings to a happier time when John was a handsome ship's carpenter in the Danish navy. They met at an opera in St. Petersburg where she had performed *Swan Lake*. The handsome man who brought her flowers told her she could out-sing the mockingbirds in mother Russia's mulberries. She fell crazy in love. He resigned from the navy, he returned to marry her, and then he took her to America! Beautiful bride, handsome husband lived in a white house with blue shutters! They would have a baby. They would be happy.

But she had failed. She was barren. Then a child was handed to them.

John's brother Gunnar had abandoned his halfbreed son on his parents' porch. Old Holgar and Martine had raised it for a year then gave it to John and Magya. Magya thought the baby looked dirty, its skin and hair so dark, she felt revolted. But at least they had given the poor thing a Christian upbringing, and naming it.

Magya looked at the handsome young man, whispering, "I did that at least, didn't I?"

The stranger asked her again, "Where's Annabel?"

What had this young man to do with her? It was hard living in Harrisburg. Because of the mixed-blood baby they had moved to the edge of town. Then her bright angel Annabel was born!

Magya looked at the young man coldly. "We must rest now, you know." She seemed to shrink while he waited. Suddenly the storm burst from her.

"Oh, she goes to the lakes, my angel!" She began rocking and moaning. "Get rid of it, I told her!" She pointed at him, repeating, "She goes to the lakes!" Then Magya wobbled unsteadily like a spinning top that has wound down, as he reached out to her. But she made a snort and clapped her cheeks. "So dark, so late, I try to find her. I call, Annabel! My angel is nowhere—nowhere. *You* are not there." She stabbed an accusing finger at Petr. "Then *he* is home sick again." She rapped John's head with her knuckle. "Then *you* are home, stupid-face, empty-hands, all too late, too bad. Oh-too-bad."

A sickening rant, he stepped backwards. Her insanity was not getting better, it was getting worse.

Magya's eyes widened into horror and she punctuated her words with rapid beats of her fists against her temples.

"My *lille* Rochele has blonde hair and blue eyes! You are dirty filthy—and it does not wash off! Dirty Indian boy!" She thrust John Valory off her lap and lashed out at Petr, striking his chest, screaming, "You know that's what you are?"

He gripped her shoulders, pleading, "Mother, stop!" She looked bewildered as he pulled her to her feet, stiff and shaking. He whispered urgently, "Is she gone?"

Magya was suddenly furious again. "She went to *your* lake and she did *not* come back!" He tried to hold her but she lashed out and slapped his face. "Let me go—you Indian bastard!"

He let her go and she nearly collapsed and he caught her just before she fell.

She went ragdoll limp and he held her. "No, Mama, you didn't mean any of it." He carried her to her bed, her ponderous weight staggering him. When he laid her down his spine seemed to float from his back. She laid there trembling as if she was freezing.

Magya sobbed, "She's g-gone! Oh, lost and gone!"

He stroked her face soft and warm; colored from exertion, this woman who never sweated, never smelled of anything except flour, she was unraveling before his eyes.

Petr smiled reassuringly, and felt crazy. "I'll get her back, Mama. You wait and see."

John Valory snorted, deeply asleep and rolled over.

Magya rolled onto her face so he went to see his father.

John looked like a knocked-out boxer. Petr flung an old blanket over him. Flat on the floor, at least he couldn't fall any farther. No wonder Annabel ran off—or whatever she was doing.

Petr scaled the loft and immediately saw his bed was disturbed. He slapped the pillow aside and of course the gold moon was gone. Dented straw showed where it had been. Of course!

He stared out the window at the dark mountains and for the first time realized the power of gold, not in buying horses, or water-wheels, or pianos. Oh, no. It was primitive, simple as the mindless flight of moths into flame—into bright destruction! Papa crazy drunk, Mama wild with despair, Annabel gone—had he started all this in motion?

But he knew. The Indian at the lake started the madness. Why? What for?

He turned to the loft rail. His voice hoarse, unfamiliar, *"Why* are you using me?"

On a sudden mad impulse, he flung himself over the rail, fell ten feet, and landed in the circle of candle flames. Spitting into his palm, he snuffed them all out, one by one. The last flame left a hellish spot on his hand, but he had put out all the lights in the house and could not know how much darkness lay ahead.

2

He grabbed a lantern from the barn. Was it true what Magya said? Terrible words burned in his ears: *Dirty Indian boy! Indian bastard!* His innocent childhood a leaf in a fire: nothing left but black strings, as if innocence never existed. Or was Magya making wild talk because Annabel was gone? Who would tell him the truth? Papa was too drunk to talk.

He lit the lantern. He ran to the waterfall. The splash of light revealed something ominous, a little scary.

On the flat rock above the falls was Annabel's doll—headless. She took the head?

What have you done, little girl? He stuffed the doll-body inside his shirt and left the lantern burning and ran for the lake.

It was dangerous running, hurrying in the mountains at night. He dodged ramrod pines. He hurtled low boulders. Annabel would go to the lake for sure. She knew he found gold. But would she go underwater?

He ran into a tree and fell back in a stunning shock of white-hot stars. He sprang up, made a short dash, and sledge-hammered into a boulder. His knee felt broken, going numb, but he ran again, desperately onward as a deer runs after it is shot.

He was shouting, "I meant to do something good. What *happened?*" The answers were easy as they were unbelievable.

Found gold. Annabel lost. Father drunk. Mother crazy. Was gold a chemical formula that caused the same stunning results each time, with a few tiresome twists? Did the same dreary things happen every time you found gold?

He screamed at the mountains: "Make it stop! She's worth more than gold!" He yelled as loud as he could, "Annabel-Rocky-Rochele! *Where—are—you?*"

Nothing. He cried, "Come back! I don't care about gold anymore!" Then he made a mad dash for the lake.

He plowed into a thicket of manzanita that in moonlight turned into a maze of deer horns. They ripped at his legs as he blundered his way out again.

He gasped hoarsely, "Rocky...please...for god-sakes."

High dark mountains turned everything stark, dreamlike, nightmarish.

A scattering of gray boulders seemed as if ancient tombstones marking old battlefields. The dark mourner trees only yesterday were living beams of light with gleaming green souls were now ghastly gray and solemn. Let me go back to yesterday!

A pine branch swatted him in the face and he fell flat on his back. His chest and legs burned. He began crying and tasted blood. He got up and ran even faster.

"Annabel...show you some pretty waterfalls...some meadows where deer keep their fawns."

Then something good happened, something he had never experienced.

Weariness evaporated, it simply went away. His legs became tireless ramrods of steel, numb as steel. He could run all night into dawn if he had to. He had his second wind.

An hour later he was staring at the black dead lake.

"Anna...bel?"

The moon dipped into clouds as he began searching the rocky banks. How long till dawn, was it another hour? Again he called out, "Annabel!"

Need a better view. Need to get up above the lake.

Climbing the overhanging cliff, he realized just how beat up he was, stinging, aching, throbbing. He stared down at the water and the moon reappeared with its reflection bobbing on blackness like a floating head. A moment later it appeared as if suspended beneath the surface like a prisoner in the lake. He felt desperate. "Annabel?"

Dive in right now!

No, can't dive off a cliff at night. Better wait till dawn. He cursed himself for a coward and hugged his knees, waiting.

The moon crossed the lake slowly. Wind rose in the trees sounding like an oncoming train. He whispered, "Madness is coming for me." The moon shivered in the lake, and disappeared.

"Annabel?"

Here only a few hours ago, alive, excited, sugarplummed in the head and with flower stained hands. Why not now? He yelled into the water, "Give her back to me!"

He pictured her clearly. Blue teardrop eyes, sun blonde hair, honey brown skin. Disappearing into the lake shouting, *Petr, I can do it too!* She seemed so real he groaned.

"Oh, God no, Annabel: Too deep for you, honey—too deep, too cold."

And yet he knew she had done it.

A sharp gust of wind goose-pimpled the lake making him shiver. He muttered, "She's down there right now. All my fault—all my fault." Could she really make it to the inner cave, or was she drowned?

Exhaustion put him asleep sitting up, and there she was: Standing before him in a dream, bright as honey shining in the sun, reminding him of his lost lover.

This time I found you right beside me. I was lost, not you!

But something was wrong.

Hair gooey seaweed, her face green, her smile faded, *Kelpie got me. Get Big Jack. He knows what to do.* Her mouth melted into red smear.

Petr startled awake grasping something soggy on his chest: the doll body with no head.

All around him the morning sun blazed new day. He was at the edge of a cliff. He had slept hard. He looked down. The lake was a round, shiny red coffin lid. He held out his hands. "Please don't let her be dead."

He dragged off his boots sucking big lungfuls of air. Got to get her now, or get her body.

He jumped from the cliff. He knifed into the water that for some reason wasn't cold.

Then he swam deep looking for a girlshape on the bottom. What he saw was pale blue boulders. Good. *If* Annabel came here and *if* she had jumped in—she had survived *this* part.

Now search the *other* part.

3

Water Tunnel was the scariest part because it was cold and dark and you couldn't breathe. That first time his courage buckled and he wasn't sure how he had done it. Now he was remembering. The Indian had *ordered* him to *keep going* or he would *kill him*.

As before the small gold mirror floated in the distance. He swam with otter-confidence, knowing exactly how far it was and how long it would take. He had air to spare.

One minute later he popped into the inner lake like a cork, gasping rotten-smelling air. He swam to shore and sat sucking air, getting accustomed to the stinking smell and yolky light pulsing like yellow blood in a barely beating heart. He looked around the cavern.

"Annabel?"

His eyes roved the small caves surrounding the inner pool, each with its animal painted above it. Deer. Turtle. Beaver. Bear. Otter. Eagle. Snake. Horse. Elk. Fox. Buffalo. And the Elephant—a fur-covered beast with big tusks curving from the ground to the eyes—amazing.

All of it was starting to come back now, along with the questions.

How many years had the Indians kept this place secret, hundreds, thousands? And now you give this secret to a white man? He stared down at the sandy beach and froze.

Little footprints marked the sand, this way and that way—little girlprints.

"Annabel!" His voice echoing far away, he listened hard.

Little footprints led to the downrunning stream. He followed them, spotted a small object in the sand, and picked it up.

It was a blue button.

Annabel couldn't bring her doll so she brought its head, and now it was falling apart. And it proved she was here, she had made it this far. But was she still here? Follow the footprints.

They led to the Horse Cave and the Falcon Stream.

He called to her again.

"Rocky, I'm here now, come out now." His voice echoed: *Out-now-out-now.*

She wasn't here, so what next? Go down the Falcon Stream—see if she's there. Don't pass out. Try not to dream. Go now.

The place below had to do with dreams, remembering the long-lost past, all dizzying and confusing. If a person had other lives, you weren't supposed to remember them. As far as he could tell, that was the trouble: This place beneath the lake the Indians called The Luminah made you remember. Beneath each death, like some bottomless archaeological dig, lay a forgotten life—then another layer of death—then another layer of life. Down, down and down, layers of life and death, all too confusing. It made you crazy, and it made you hesitate. It was very scary. Maybe superhot gold made you remember.

People shouldn't remember what happened a thousand years ago. Today was enough. He was also pretty sure of one other thing.

The Luminah could kill you.

He stood before the outstretched wings of the Falcon. Light pulsed and water disappeared down the hole. Going down into *that place* again? Yes, if Annabel went there, he had to go.

What if she was there right now, too scared to move, remembering all the past?

He jumped into the shallow Falcon Stream and ran in a low crouch and it took only minutes to find something that looked like Annabel's work.

A cannonball pile of gold with the top ball missing: What did that mean?

He yelled down the tunnel, "Annabel?" No answer. Hurry down the stream.

It turned quickly into a watery staircase, and it was getting warmer, like being swallowed by a volcano. One interesting observation: Going deeper didn't require a lantern. Light flickered on walls bright as a fireplace. The next minute the tunnel became dim as a dying star—brighter then dimmer—what did that mean?

Moments later he saw the blaring hole of light and he began shaking. Maybe the brain couldn't remember, but his body sure remembered. This is where the really bad stuff began to happen the first time he came here, the part that was all blacked out. Something pretty horrible must have happened if you could blank out anything this bright. He thought of a grim epigram from his schoolboy years, *Dante's Inferno*. *"Abandon all hope, ye who enter here."*

The cave widened into the smooth bore of a blunderbuss shooting blasts of blinding yellow light. It was starting to come back now and he was stunned his mind was capable of erasing such amazing sights. Beyond this point was a huge cavern where water exploded into steam—into fiery hell. He remembered that now.

Ten paces from the goldblazing mouth he called out, "Anna-bell!"

Squinting hard he poked his head inside the lightbeam. "Ah, God!" He remembered now.

Beyond was a waterfall plunging over a rim of slippery volcanic glass. The blunderbuss *opened* and then—there was a fall. That first time he had been blinded and tumbled into the plungepool thirty feet below. Better not do that again.

He squared himself and squatted—and then duck-walked through the opening like walking into a blowtorch. He remembered something that gave him courage the first time.

The bottom of the fall, behind the churning whitewater, was a hollow space, an undercut behind the fall (that one day would collapse). A man could *get behind* the fall, getting relief from the blast of light and heat. He remembered now that it had save his life the first time.

Climb down the waterfall. Get relief behind the fall. Go!

He slid carefully down the warm, bony rocks. Once down, he hesitated at the plungepool and looked through squeezed fists. It was still there.

Fiery golden hell.

The Gold Chamber roared, boomed, and belched liquid gold.

And Annabel was not there.

His eyes burned, felt liked they'd been rubbed by sandpaper. He splashed his face until he could see again.

Water roared whitely down into the plungepool. Then it made a mad rush down to the crater within a surprisingly shallow trough. The big crater must have been super-heated again and again to produce steel-hard rock. Halfway down, two football fields away, water burst into artillery explosions of steam from a boiling plate of gold.

It was a vast curving crater plain littered with golden debris down to a central churning core—of course Annabel wasn't there. How could she be?

If she was here, she was curled up somewhere. She would stay near the water. The heat demanded it. He studied the waterfall, the plungepool, the sluiceway down to the crater. Nothing living here. He stood up sweating, trembling, incoming waves of weakness and nausea hitting him, and he knew what came next, what happened to the body, any...body...exposed to the blast of The Luminah. Why did the Indians call it that? Was it even an Indian word?

"For god-sakes, Annabel," his voice dry and weak, he took a gulp of warm egg-water.

He cupped his hands: "ANNA BELL! ROW SHELL! COME OUT NOW!"

His words were swallowed in roaring machineries of gold and rasping gases escaping the molten pool in the crater below. Here was the mother source of the stench-wind; the heart of the pounding heat. He squatted again and squinted hard to watch powerful showers of gold erupt like faraway desert thunderstorms. Deep thunder boomed and the ground shook.

He drank again and whispered hoarsely, "Annabel—it's time to go—now."

Go? Who could even be here? He doubted if anyone had ever been here—and survived. The place was deadly. No life was ever *meant* to be here. It struck him: that Indian sent me here to die just like he wanted Stoddard to die. But why not kill me outright? Why show me this?

Big puzzle pieces were missing. And the thunderous spectacle didn't allow thinking.

Far away rose a roar like a cheering crowd followed by a shattering shower of metal. A metal storm gusted over the wide plain below. Then the stench-wind hit.

"Ah, Jesus," he gasped.

Covering his nose didn't help. The god-awful rooster stench was far worse than before, fetid and thick. He pictured a million rotting eggs gumbo-ing a sick soup beneath the earth, a great misery barf from the mouth of Hell. His knees buckled, he staggered back against the cliff from which the Falcon Stream poured. If not for the stink, Petr boy, you'd smell your own goose cooking. He caught a whiff of cooked leather and touched his face. It felt like hardening bread crust, his lips burning and cracking.

Wading into the center of the plungepool he sank to cool depths where water had fallen for untold centuries, the curtain of water splashing just behind him. He let his head go under into the relief of water so great he didn't want to emerge again. He dogpaddled to where he could just touch the bottom with his head visible.

The panorama around him was blazing heaven and hell.

The sunken plain made a wide amphitheater four hundred yards across, easy. No Annabel anywhere. At bottom was a gold-plated crater, funneling to a central bowl—the *real* Gold Lake—thundering, shuddering, heaving, blaring metal. Too bright to stare at it, his mind screaming: *You blanked this out?*

Yes, nearly all of it. A week ago, his birthday, seemed ages ago. Everything had been so shocking he had transformed it to a barely remembered dream. Seen now (as if for the first time) he was thinking: It *is* the Motherlode. It is Hell. It *is* The Luminah of God. Heaven and Hell.

And it *was* shocking.

Black rings surrounded the central core of Gold Lake, which lived in turmoil. Molten snakes writhed and reared glowing mouths, spewing gargoyle faces inlaid with gilded ashen polyps, puckering spewing gas. Hideous growths died back into the abysmal sand only to reappear, again and again. But the central lake was the big show.

Giant flowers bloomed writhing golden rings of birth and death, unstoppable, unending. He heard the rising, roaring cheer and then—

Gold Lake spat forth a great shining tongue.

Big as a golden whale sounding from ecstatic oceans of shining ore bursting floes of crusting, fusing ichors, and then spewing forth its shining sperm. Obscenely belching, booming, bobbing, falling back, crunching, melting—the tongue fell back. Then the sick-wind hit.

Petr staggered back into the waterfall and didn't want to come out again, splashing, drowning the horrible vision.

Passing out—his mind flipped—it wouldn't stop. The view went up, the view went up, the view went up. There was no stopping it.

Go to the hollow behind the waterfall, the undercut. Stay. Don't move—ever again.

He cried her name one last time, "Annabel!"

Staggering forward into the cool watery space, he fell and passed out.

But not for long. Suddenly he was rising like a bird, and maybe this was dying for, as he looked back, he was leaving his body far behind.

He was flying.

4

When she stepped into the cavemouth she heard it faintly, far away. *Annabel....*

Someone calling her from hell? Not possible. Nobody was back *there*. And she wasn't going back *there* to find out.

She was beyond the wild territory blazed into the golden map of her brain.

Ten steps into the cave opening the really bad things subsided: hot, glaring, baking heat, the constant clanking metal machinery of gold madness. All sank into darkness and near silence. She opened her eyes wide, still working but somewhat blurry. Above her was fuzzy brownish haze. Before her was voluminous black ink. She touched her lips which felt like crusts of toast. The greatest irony chose that moment to strike her.

After all that light—the way out—is through darkness?

Just great because—

What lurks in blackness every child knows: snakes and horrible men with yellow eyes! Don't go there—can't go there. Have to go back—can't go back. She shuddered. It was a pickle.

Close your eyes, child. Center yourself. Thus sayeth Lulu.

Thank God—Princess Lulu—made the trip with her through hell. Now she had a chance to feel her face and arms were sunburned, feverish, actually *goldburned*. Her muscles were twangy, snappy rubber bands. She sat rubbing them for long minutes. Princess Lulu was smiling and speaking softly in friendly tones from the Invisible:

Understand darkness...the reason you are here. All gold, all light you think will make you free...it brings you here...to darkness. Follow your darkness.

Just great. Leave light for darkness? It wasn't in the Bible, was it? The other way around, wasn't it? Leaving darkness for light? Maybe Mama hadn't read the part about *follow your darkness*. She sighed, and was very close to crying. She spoke softly.

"I wanted a horse. Not this Belly-of-the-Mountain tour."

Now that she had a chance to think, she remembered the pocket watch. She pulled it out, kissed the dimly seen Lovers. Tears coursed down her hardened cheeks.

Her voice grew stronger, "We wanted love—was that asking too much?"

She felt a faintly repeating *chick-chick* inside the watch. She held it to her ear. Was it ticking? Had the lovely Luminah dried it out? *Chick-chick. Chick-chick.*

"Lover's Time is running again!" A very good sign.

Grinning hurt so bad she instantly stopped smiling. All of this was the price of love, of gold, of light, of darkness, maybe all connected. Also she wondered about Princess Lulu. Annabel wasn't stupid enough *not* to know that Princess Lulu was imaginary. That she had made her an Indian Princess because it bolstered her courage. But was her imaginary friend really *Indian*? Reddish skin, no doubt about that, but—

Another puzzle-piece snapped firmly into place.

Princess Lulu *was* cat-priestess of Bast-tet four thousand years ago, who—

Okay, enough of *that* for a moment. Annabel listened hard but heard no ancient whispers. Princess Lulu was back to her cat temple thousands of years ago—yet here when I need her? The gold chamber of The Luminah evoked some strange fantasies. Maybe being surrounded by molten hot gold produced side-effects. The word *harmonium* entered her. It meant nothing.

Her stomach gave a deep growl of hunger, reminding her it was definitely way past suppertime. Yet there was no way to tell time down here. Her long dreams in The Luminah made her *feel* as if hours had passed, that this might be the same day, or a new day. But there was no way to tell for sure.

Time to make some history: Just what we folks do who have no choice.

Another ten steps into deeper darkness, she risked opening her eyes again.

Gunpowder blackness engulfed her. She called out in a loud, clear voice: "I am Love! You cannot hurt me! Let snakes and men with horrible yellow eyes all run away!"

Ten more steps into blackness, dragging her hands along the sides of the cave although it wasn't necessary, she could *feel* massively solid walls and ceiling as what she could only describe as *pressure* on her head. The tunnel was barely wider than her shoulders. Not straight and smooth like the Falcon Stream or Water Tunnel, it twisted snakelike, sometimes doubling back on itself—but definitely a watercarved, wandering cave. Very different from whatever had caused the straight shafts into The Luminah.

This was bad trouble. This could lead to long darkness, long dark time—long, slow walk into death. But what choice was there? She began counting.

One-hundred fifty-three steps into blackness she felt something palpable in front of her. She touched it but it was not a wall. Her fingers tingled on a stone wedge: a divider blade parting the way into right path, left path. Not only that. To the left felt warm and dry; to the right felt cool and damp. Not only that: I felt this divider before I rammed my face into it. Maybe I'm not as blind as I think. Maybe darkness is only a state of mind, only imaginary.

Princess Lulu whispered: *You can do this, Annabel.*

She cried out, "Are you with me?" Her cat-woman priest finally joined her in person? Annabel spoke to the blackness in front of her: "Okay, Darkness-that-is-not-Darkness. Speak to me. I am Love. Which way do I go?"

There was dead silence. Princess Lulu was being catty: only *there* when she felt like being there. Maybe the idea was to be helpful, but not too helpful.

Reliance on physical fact forced her to make a skulking probe into each pathway. Coal blackness forced her to keep an absolutely tight grip on her mind. "Okay, this is forwards. Okay, that is backwards." After her foray, she returned to the divider and tabulated her results.

"The damp path to the right seems uphill. But no guarantee *up* means *out*. The dry path to the left seems easing down. And I'm tired enough to take the *down*. Maybe it makes no difference. Maybe both paths lead *out*." But really, who could say?

Her feverchilled skin made her feel drawn to the warmer air.

Oddly, Papa's voice broke in: *Just love—you can never go too far wrong.* Yes, he had said that. Good enough for dealing with people, but for choosing your way in the underworld? Petr's voice murmured: *When you're wandering don't give up the high ground.* Yes, he had said that. That felt right. To which she added her crowning logic: You could go down a long time. You can't go up a mountain forever.

Annabel walked to the right, up, and it was the beginning of a very long dark walk.

She should have been afraid of blackness but it was such a relief from the inferno of The Luminah, she didn't mind it. Fear was the idea of the tunnel ending in a blank wall, or funneling into a narrow crevice. That kept her sweating. What gave hope was a faint thrill of slight breeze.

A breeze had to come from somewhere, and go somewhere.

She trudged into the tunnel mountain for hours, days, weeks, years. Way beyond girl-tiredness, she was plumb worn out, numbskull tired; captured in a dread feeling she might be spiraling into endless snailshell of ink. She made up a mantra for sanity.

Get back to Petr. Never lose him again. No more gold—only love.

And her powerful imagination helped. Create bright pictures in blackness!

Here was a life-changing lesson: Hope keeps claws of madness away.

Black centuries passed and there was no change in the cave. It just kept going. Had to lead somewhere, didn't it? Couldn't just snailshell around in crazy blackness forever, could it? Had she chosen wrong? Would she walk into darkness until her legs stopped working?

Slowing down, hands now making mere swimmer's touches on the wall, because her fingertips were raw meat. Ages later she found—

Holes in the wall—hollows shaped like bowls—definitely man-made shapes.

She dabbed her fingers into powdery stuff, then dabbed a pinch onto her tongue. *Food! It was food! Good God!* Explosions of flavor erupted in her mouth.

Nutty, crunchy meal, dry as dust, stone chips no-extra-charge, Annabel scooped small handfuls and chewed a mushy, cruddy cud. Swallowing it, gagging on it, not enough spit to swallow. No water. No hope without water.

Another fun thought: Why haven't mice or rats eaten the meal? Maybe that crunchy part was mouse droppings? She gagged again, grabbed Miss Daisy's head, and squeezed water into her mouth. The nutmeal slid like rust down her throat.

Who put food here? Who on earth expected visitors here? Oh, good ol' Indians, long ago. But didn't they forget something? Like good ol' water? Annabel scooped nutmeal into her pouch until it bulged. But it was useless without water.

She trudged onward, legs like sticks grinding into her hip sockets.

Hours later, as if answering her question, the sides of the cave became slimy damp. She licked her fingers, tasting chalk or something like ground eggshells.

Mmm-yummy, it's almost good as a tall cool glass of milk.

The cave screwthreaded slowly upward, wormed, and then doubled back. Her hands and feet were now coated in slime when she heard a wonderful watery sound. She froze.

Ploink!—Ploink!—Ploink!

Scrambling furiously forward she splashed into a small pool weeping from the ceiling.

Ploink!

She sucked dripping liquid from her fingers. It wasn't good. It wasn't bad either. It was water. It didn't kill her. But she would die anyway without it. Petr had warned her about absorbing food and water too fast—in case they got cooked on the Utah desert—like he knew all about it. She gulped big handfuls of water. Thinking a genuine pioneer thought: You're probably gonna die anyway. She plunged the dollhead into the water and swabbed her face.

"Thar' she is, Miss Daisy," trying to sound like a gristly old pioneer. "We're stopping at this waterhole for the night, or where some-ever this is." She gulped a handful of eggy water, "Yum, she's flavor-full, ain't she?" She curled herself around the small pool.

Now rest, maybe even sleep. But her stomach turned into a hungry monkey banging and scraping an iron spoon inside her gut. Probably just her reaction to the stone grits. It clawed and then magically grew bigger, gnawing into her legs, leaving her hollow and weak. Stop it, stupid. You're just really hungry. She risked another mouthful of nutmeal, followed by painful swallows of water. The monkey quieted down. Thank God the old meal contained some vital life force, just not much. She started shaking, not sure why. Fear came in a rush.

You're so far underground, you're way beyond life. There aren't any creatures down here or this nutmeal would be long gone. And I'm in a bad cave, and nobody knows I'm here.

The scariest part pushed its way out, screaming. *I'm alone, I'm alone, I'm alone! And nobody knows!*

Petr would search for her. Sure. But he would never find this place. She got mad. She fought back. "I'm in the dark, but I'm not lost!" This was true. She could *feel* beyond blackness. Some tunnels might lead darkly who knew where—dead-ending deep inside the belly of the earth. She shivered at the thought. But she knew she was going just right. Felt it in her heart, in her gut. Tiresome ol' tunnel going this way and that, but it would get her *out*. Believe that or go crazy. She had air, water, food. Not so bad. Not so scary like that Water Tunnel. A body shouldn't swim there unless you weren't afraid, unless you were bigger than death, somehow tougher than death—which she wasn't, even with Princess Lulu helping her. She shuddered for Petr.

She said, "Don't do that no more, Petr. We won't be poking around here no more. I don't like gold no more, not after this. We don't need gold no more. Don't tell Papa or Big Jack."

Tell no one. No problem.

But she was way behind on history of the Valory family gold.

She said, "Love Petr. *Love love love*—and everything will come out all right." Imagining a pink cloud surrounding her, and believing it must be nighttime again, she slept.

No way could she know that three days had passed in the real world.

That Petr was only a half-mile away from her—out of his mind in The Luminah.

5

First you fall, then you rise.

He had a *moment* where it felt like he was being thrown from a cliff blindfolded. If that continued Petr knew he would plunge into insanity. But the next moment—just like the first time—the sensation *reversed* and he began rising very fast. Another of the things he had blocked out—sudden sickening falling and rising—a dream that felt very real.

I sent my Soul through the Invisible, some letter of that Afterlife to spell.

Now a gold falcon flying powerfully, flying rhythmically forward, up and up, only a dream so he made a wish: *I want to see Annabel.*

He scanned the crater with magnifying vision, falcon eyes, but he didn't see Annabel. Instead he received a *feeling* that she was safe.

The falcon rose straight up through the crown of the mountain—
and out. Solid rock meant nothing to the falcon soul. Now he was
sailing on cool and pleasant breezes, gaining speed and altitude.

A magnificent panorama lay below.

A pale turquoise lake in a brown desert where the Pah Utes lived;
farther south a deep blue lake known as Tahoe, many miles apart,
joined by a shimmering silver river that made a pretty S-curve between
them like an umbilical cord. The desert lake was pale beauty; the
mountain lake was dark beauty. The higher lake fed the lower lake. It
made him think of outer Gold Lake feeding inner Gold Lake.

Was The Luminah a blueprint for dreams blooming in the garden
of the world?

Now he was moving very fast over the land, heading to the East.

Flying over wrinkled basins and dry red plains, and then flying
over windbrushed yellow prairies and rolling green forests, and then
flying over the low mountains like waves of sea foam, and then he was
flying over the ocean, he was leaving America.

He crossed blue Atlantic in ten seconds.

Before him rose a great stone pyramid capped with gold, and a
big crouching figure he knew was called the Sphinx. He flew past and
continued to the east but much slower now.

Below was endless desert and he saw himself walking across the
sand, the young man named Mahrire, almost dead, but knowing he
must find new goldmines for Pharaoh Horemheb who would then
make him a prince. Not only that, the high priest of the House of Life
had a beautiful daughter named Mirael. She would marry a prince and
Mahrire was merely an artisan who shaped gold figures and medallions
for pharaoh. Pharaoh decreed that twelve young men would roam the
desert and eleven would die and one of them would rise up and find a
new goldmine. A charioteer had dumped him into the desert a week
ago and was supposed to return with food and water in three days.
But he did not return. Mahrire found a low ledge of rocks and crawled
underneath to die. On the seventh day his soul became a falcon. His
eyes pierced dark mountains by the Red Sea and he found gold easily.
His falcon soul flew back to Horemheb, whispering, *My soul has found*

gold. Horemheb ordered the charioteer to fetch Mahrire, realizing he had become that rare thing, a flying prince. He had great military plans for a flying prince. Mahrire easily located the enemy positions at Kadesh. Mahrire was given the beautiful Mirael and many other wishes and many other wives. But one day he awoke and he could no longer fly, no longer see. Mahrire filled his pockets with gold and walked into the Nile and there was the end of his first dream of life.

He fell from the sky and the dream ended, thank God. Intense heat told him he was back inside The Luminah. Now he knew why he feared this place so much and why he blanked it out.

Would he even remember any of this when he got out—if he got out?

But he was barely getting warmed up for even greater shocks inside The Luminah.

CHAPTER SIX

HISTORY IS HELL

1

Somehow he had crawled outside the waterfall where new horrors were forming. He was pretty sure he was awake, but this was so bad it had to be another dream.

He was facedown staring into a bottomless well of blackness now slowly beginning to spin like a whirlpool. This was another part of the memory he had blanked-out, another real reason he was terrified to return here. Now he was being sucked down inside the spiral like it was a magnet and he was a thousand pounds of iron. He couldn't stop sinking.

Layers of life and death were down in the hole, the unedited mystery of human history and not some textbook version of it. The Luminah was making him see the dark past exactly as it happened—which, except for the strongest—was a plunge into insanity.

Why send me here, Tecumseh? Because I was strong enough—or because you wanted to destroy me? Sweat dripped from his body as if he was being barbecued, and he kept going down.

He revisited twelve pitiful lives—and twelve more lay buried beneath that—and twelve more—and....

He strained against unbearable sleeps and deeps of death, its spinning auger-hole making him sick, drawing him *in*. *Grinding* him in. He couldn't take any more Life. Make it stop!

"I'm...sorry for...everything." A rising horror for all the bad things he had done, vast sins innumerable, every error possible, from greed to avarice to murder—he had committed every crime many times. *You lived a hundred lives—only forty-four to go!* Not words but an unmistakable feeling was the voice of The Luminah. Forbidden knowledge, not meant for everyone to know. *Tell no one.*

His body began changing into something else, someone else.

He was able to *completely* view his first life as Mahrire, and he was stunned. Darkly handsome, physically powerful, godlike, no one could resist his charms. He wrote music and poetry effortlessly; sang like an angel. He was in love with himself alone. He mistrusted anyone not adoring him. His second life, he was equally astonished to find himself using his charms to control and hurt people. The next series of lives, showed a fast decline into brutal rage and hatred of mankind—and above all—hatred towards God and the creation itself. The decline continued on the downward spiral in dozens of fearful lives until he was born pitifully degraded and helpless, physically ugly and warped, with no abilities or talents whatever—at the mercy of anyone who cared to kick him further into hell. That was the bottom of the spiral down, the bottom rung of the Fall. From here the soul rose with new desire to serve, to do good, to benefit others. Old anger and hurt cast off, his life seemed to rise. Leaden hate turned into golden love. Now he was Petr Valory, but all good intentions and deeds shone as worthless and ineffectual. He was like a farmer whose hard work has been blighted, drought-out, washed away by storms. He was like Job, yes very Job-like.

How had he made his escape from these memory blasts of The Luminah that first time? How did he break its spell? How did he escape the terrible sucking hole? He found he knew the answer. The Luminah *revealed.* The way out of hell was by remembering good things.

He remembered the good he intended in this life: a saw mill for Papa, a piano for Mama, a beautiful red horse for Annabel. He gasped, "I...tried to love. I am not afraid...of death." Powerful words formed, he cried out: "I Myself am Heaven and Hell. I am the dark and the light of both worlds!"

What did that mean? The Luminah provided instant answers. The unmistakable feeling let him know: If he failed, the *intentions* of the heart were important.

So ask the big question about the meaning of life. What is its purpose? Why are we here?

The great unseen portrait of the human race shows the beginning: Lucifer the Most Beautiful atop a huge V with Christ the Most Loving atop the other beam—the swift descent and rise of the letter V, or interval, as humankind's Life taking 144 attempts of the soul to complete. Once seeing, you realize the Alpha and Omega of the soul—beginning as Lucifer and ending as Christ.

It was stunning news. So this was the heart of The Luminah no mortal knows, where I went to the core of the earth, the pit of death, from where I must return.

Desire saved him from the spinning abyss—the mouth of insanity. Do good works. Go back to the world! Suddenly he was released from dark hole of the past.

Water gushed beside him and he was *back*. He was at the edge of the plunge pool, the life-giving water. He was saved.

He rose shakily on one knee. There was the waterfall, the one way out of The Luminah. He studied the way up the waterfall trying to memorize grip-holds. Too far from the water and fingers would burn; too close and rocks were slippery as butter. He soaked himself thoroughly until water ran down his body—and then he scrambled for the top.

Halfway up, his hands began to burn. Ten more seconds and he made it to the gushing rim of the waterfall. He threw himself into the water and splashed his eyes until he could see again. He turned and looked over the rim. His view was a good one.

Far below lay the great wonder of the underworld.

Great Gold Lake flaming, mesmerizing, hypnotic pool of creation and uncreation! After several minutes he recovered: Wouldn't the miners love to know—

Gold boils below California!

The footstool of heaven, the Motherlode itself, is the heart of a living volcano.

Was it even possible Annabel was here—or was she dead?

His vision flickered. He might be nearing the end of his endurance of heat and strain. He might be nearing the point where he was physically unable to leave. Better hurry now.

He scanned clockwise circles looking for her body. He avoided the central core which seemed increasing almost to the brightness of the sun. Nothing would survive within a hundred yards of that blowhole. Don't look at it. He dunked his head to restore his vision. After ten cooling dunks he had scanned a full circle at the height of the waterfall.

The orbit held faint shadows that *might* be openings, but might not be. It was hard to tell. There was just too much light. Shadows were required for sight. He made a few conclusions.

The Gold Chamber is a magnum version of the little water pool, with its carved caves. Here gold takes the place of water. Openings around the inner pool don't *go* anywhere. They are just hollow chambers. Maybe the gold openings of this grand chamber don't go anywhere either.

He looked until his eyes blurred. There was no dead body in this wretched place.

He forced one last scanning circle, this time counter-clockwise, same result—no body, no footprints. But the blasting light might hide anything.

You can't leave here without being sure.

But he was sure: Annabel is not here, dead or alive.

Possibilities? She came this far, then returned through the Water Tunnel. Then why hadn't she come home? Would he someday find her body along the path to the cabin? No, he'd never believe that. The Gold Falcon indicated she was alive somewhere. Annabel had survived this ordeal. She was somewhere, but not in the Gold Chamber. He would find her or die trying.

Go now! Check those shallow openings around the big rim!

He gulped water, splashed, and squinted at the nearest shadow cave to get his bearings, and then hotfooted for it. He ran feeling like he might catch fire.

After a long sprint across a narrow ledge he fell twice scorching his hands and knees, mentally scolding himself: Don't fall...have to go... have to know.

He reached his goal, bleary-eyed, sweat-soaked, lungs burning, and furious that he had forgotten to count his steps. But this *was* an honest-to-God opening. It was sucking air. That meant something.

He ducked inside wedging himself behind a wall shielded from gold. Blinking—each blink creating a shower of light and horrible pain, his eyes molten hot metal balls—he was blind. He groaned. "Did you make it this far, Annabel?" His body throbbed. He felt for her footprints. He felt *impressions*. His vision improved gradually into blurry smears.

He crawled deeper into the cave a full minute. His eyes made gold showers each time he blinked. He whispered, "Is this what happened to you, Annabel? ANNABEL?"

He yelled her name until he was hoarse. He became overwhelmed with emotion, crying. *The lost lover, I couldn't find her anywhere.* The glare subsided and he blinked alternating showers of gold and blackness. Then he crawled another fifty feet.

"You survived this, Annabel, you probably went insane." Probably find her in here somewhere, drooling and insane.

Hard crying soothed his eyes but now he was enveloped in the total blackness of a tunnel. He crawled another minute into blackness. He halted, his voice a papery rattle, "It's...hopeless."

No one penetrated this sightless madness, certainly not a girl. He sagged to the floor, cold, rugged. His heart and thoughts slowed.

Go home...get food...return with lanterns...search the tunnel...to the end.

It was a decision he would regret for many years to come. He turned around.

He returned to the cavemouth, to the bright dome of gold. Get out of here.

Running hard, he ran back to the life-restoring waterfall. There he drank big hard swallows of water. He shouted into the roaring cavern.

"I searched for you, Annabel! I went crazy again—but I looked!" He turned and began climbing shakily, and did not look back because he was already forming a new plan.

Get help from Dain King. Promise him gold.

Then he ran up the stairway of the Falcon Stream. When he reached the cannonball pile of gold he pocketed two golden balls. That would draw Dain King to his side, the greedy man. He'd want to know where the gold came from. He'd follow Petr.

Something good or bad would happen. Much later he realized the dream of Mahrire was a fine clue to the truth of his father.

2

He climbed from the cold water of the little lake, the so-called Gold Lake and threw himself onto the slab of Indian drawings. He began pounding the stone. He was dead tired and felt insane. He began talking to himself.

"How do I get you back? I don't want to live without you." The barren truth came with an addition. "I'll find you, or kill myself trying." Saying it out loud, his commitment was a relief somehow.

He jumped suddenly and looked around, shouting, "ANNA-BELL!"

Brilliant morning, he felt hopeless, as if days had passed.

Sun glaring across the small lake, sparrows chattering. Nothing had changed but him.

"Wish I never found that rotten hole!" He flung a rock at the water and smashed its calm red stare. Where could she be? Not in the Water Tunnel; not in the Cave Room; not in the Falcon Stream; not in The Luminah. "Where is she?"

She had *been there.* The blue button proved it. The cannonball pile proved it. He yelled at the water: "You cannot have her!" He was numb with weariness, but he got up and got going anyway.

He searched the crater rim and then went up to the cliff crown and then the surrounding stone face, seeking a crack, a hole, a vent—an escape hatch. The tunnel (that Annabel might have used) had to come out *somewhere,* didn't it?

Widening his orbits around the lake, missing nothing, at two hundred yards he found a small opening—a hole big enough for a fox—a fissure filled with rocks like somebody had buried it. He dug the rocks out. He wiggled in, not getting very far. His shoulders wedged. Beyond the first ten feet was deep well darkness. He called out, "Annabel?"

He was trembling with weariness. All of it was too much like the dream of the lost lover.

If Annabel made it through this vent and covered it up, she'd be wandering in the woods, you'll find her any time now. Get back to the cabin. Get rest. Get food.

He felt guilty as if he'd sold Annabel for a piece of gold. He returned to the cabin not knowing he would never see his little sister again.

3

Magya frowned from her big book when he entered the cabin seeing a sunburned boy with puffy lips and red eyes, as if he had been slapped by an explosion.

"You find her?"

He shook his head. "No. Not yet."

A month spent searching for Annabel was the worst month of his life, each day a dark stone sealing her tomb, each day the same: he and Papa ate; Magya watched them go; and every day they headed in opposite directions.

Petr rode Rubaiyat and in the three days covered the forest valley floor of the Valoryvale. At sundown he spent an hour grooming and feeding the beautiful horse, stroking its long neck, pressing its fragrant mane into his face, and crying.

Annabel went missing on Sunday afternoon—that had been June eighteenth. Petr returned from Spanish Ranch on Monday with the red horse. Then he had searched for Annabel under the lake. Tuesday he had wandered all day in shock. Discovering how it felt to be *in* shock—a rising panic, a sinking stomach, jittery weakness as if he had been electrocuted.

But shock did not end there. He suffered mental cloudiness, forgetting to eat or sleep, and then reviewing again and again what he did, or did not do, or should have done. He was a dead man pretending to be alive.

Late Wednesday afternoon of June twenty-first, after three long days of searching, he wandered down the valley to the rivercliffs where they had watched the falcons soar and swoop. Beside the feeder pole lay the thing that darkened his despair.

The falcon, a silver thing not much bigger than a glove—his falcon—was dead.

"Oh—oh, no."

Beneath the pole with one wing splayed back, facing the Valoryvale as if she died waiting for him, her wing had been clawed or shot.

He dug a grave with his fingers. He lowered her gently, carefully smoothing her wing. He placed her in the ground.

"Beautiful," he sobbed. "You were... so beautiful." Tears fell into the grave as he sprinkled pine needles—*over her!* He filled the hole with sand and then a mound of heavy rocks.

Never again be disturbed by this world! Gasping, "Beautiful friend...you did not last long." He had to get away right now. Annabel might last a week alone. He had to get help. But facing Dain King, and probably being laughed at, made him violently angry.

What about Big Jack? Might not his big booming voice help bring her home?

Petr ran back to the corral and saddled up Rubaiyat. He rode to Big Jack's lake.

The man was fishing for trout and when he explained the urgency of his mission, Big Jack threw down his pole. "What can I do, Laddy?"

"Take this horse and keep her. I got it for Annabel but I won't be able to look at her if she doesn't come back."

Jack threw out his hands. "Point me, I'll search for her!"

Petr stabbed in the direction of the burnt Indian village and the hidden valley. "I'm pretty sure she went that way."

Truth was, she was still inside the mountain.

4

The nightmare lasted ten days for John and Magya. Each night John returned to the cabin unable to speak above a whisper, saying the same words, "Maybe tomorrow...yah?"

Magya stopped combing her hair, stopped doing laundry and spent days moaning and rocking in her chair and reading the Bible. When the men returned she stared and shrilled at them like a rusty saw. "Whair *izzz* sheeiii!"

She no longer cooked, she stopped eating, she became thin, and finally took to her bed. She spent days sleeping and looked like she was dying.

The last day of June, Magya Valory disappeared.

5

She scrubbed herself until she felt new and pretty. Packing a bag, she simply walked away from the Valoryvale. North ten miles she found the Beckwourth Trail. There she waited.

Hours later, horses came from the west, five riders carrying rifles, eying her warily and not answering question. "Where you people going?" Two covered wagons followed carrying drab people in faded clothes. The driver of the front wagon had a long beard, like a prophet. Three angry-looking women sat stiffly in the second wagon. Their ages made them grandmother-mother-daughter. But they bore no resemblance. These strange details didn't bother Magya. They were going east and that was all that mattered. Keep going east until she got to Russia, never mind the prophet's owlish eyes and hard mouth. He eyed her inquisitively and halted the wagons.

"We return to Salt Lake. Can you pay?"

She thrust out her chest. "I can work."

Unsmiling, he stared at her a long moment. "We are Mormons. Does that suit you?"

She climbed quickly beside him and looked fiercely into his eyes.

"I'll learn your ways." And she laughed inside: At least until we cross the Salt Flats.

The wagons moved out. The horsemen waited, and now they were riding ahead. She looked back at the other wagon. The women stared flint-eyed. Then she noticed five more horsemen following behind. They all wore long beards. Prophets with rifles. She spoke conversationally to the driver. "Independence Day come soon, yah?"

His lips curled. He had an odd, sneering voice. He said, "*Is* for some."

Three hours later Magya surmised from terse replies that the prophet was traveling *incognito*, that they were returning from Quincy where they had recovered a woman who was a sister of somebody important, who had run away. The wagons rolled east through the dry mouth of Beckwourth Pass and she smiled brightly as they crested the dusty rise and descended into Nevada. Her independence day began just as America celebrated its freedom.

She whispered to the mindless, spinning wagon wheels, "My freedom from men!"

The prophet cut his eyes to her. "What was that, I didn't catch it," gripping her hand and squeezing hard.

6

By the time Magya was in Salt Lake City—John Valory was done searching for his wife, done searching for his daughter, done crying. He had worn out his heart and a good pair of boots. On the way back to the Valoryvale he stopped by Big Jack's cabin where the Scotsman fed him trout and whiskey. The big man Jack Gorgius Frazier related how he had searched for the missing girl and had no luck.

They drank whiskey from tin cups and talked it all out.

"Ten miles all aroond," Jack said, "that gal is harder to find than gold." He shook his big head. "Two weeks is a loong time, and a hard thing to swalloo." Jack's voice was loud, he spoke his thoughts aloud because he had been alone too much. And also he had lost some of his hearing in the Mexican War.

John revealed that life had been hard with the unhappy singing woman. Now she had run off and Annabel was gone. It was time to quit worrying and start drinking.

Jack waggled a finger at him. "You still have a fine son, Petr. And the day is bright and dry. Get Petr to sell his goldmine to King and be done with trouble. Get back to timbering."

That was solid advice. John felt better and fell asleep, knowing. Return home tomorrow.

Yes, return to life.

7

John and Petr seldom met at the cabin anymore because it was too painful. The last time they talked Petr said he was going to ask Dain King for help. John said that was a waste of time because King was finding gold and wild horses couldn't drag him away from gold.

Petr left a note on the kitchen table: *Gone to King for help.* Then he went to the workshed. Fight fire with fire—he would tempt King with a great deal of gold.

Using a sledgehammer he smashed the two gold eggs on the big stump. Amazingly they flattened and spread until he was looking into an oval of mirror-like gold. He looked into it and a face looked back at him that shocked him. It was not his own. Instead it was a man with red hair, satanically handsome and smiling sadly, knowingly. Petr recoiled from the stranger, a past life, but the face caused a word to form in his mind, making him angry, he didn't know why.

Chelleenee. Cellini. A nonsense word.

Petr rolled the mirror into a tube-shape that could hold no more reflections from the past. Then he smashed it into a long strip forming a golden belt. Amazing, you could shape gold into anything.

"I don't want to *remember* anybody else, and I don't want to *be* anybody else. No one should remember anything else." He threw the hammer down. "No more of this!"

He removed Papa's sharp saw from its oilskin wrapper and replaced it with the gold belt. Then he bent the belt around his waist. He would buy King's help.

Get King's twenty men. Find Annabel.

It was a new day. The beautiful falcon was dead. Annabel was lost somewhere, not dead. She couldn't be dead. It was time to get moving again. Find Annabel and return to life.

This life.

CHAPTER SEVEN

FATHERS OF THE SON

1

An hour of walking later the belt chafed his waist so badly he had to stop. He halted at the big edge of a ridge dividing the Valoryvale from Gold Nation. Below flowed emerald waters of the Feather River flashing through green valleys—entering a silver canyon plumed with pines.

Where river curved hard north, the undisturbed beauty ended abruptly.

Craters pockmarked the ground like a battlefield after a day of artillery shelling, the red earth torn, trees flattened like fallen soldiers. Strung along this curve were six smaller battlefields, comprising the Gold Nation diggings. Each camp had its own name but Petr only knew the main one where Dain King was building his great lumber-eating flume: New Viksburg, the central camp of Gold Nation.

The flume hugged a bend in the river and a short distance away on a rise was a wooden tower, 20-feet high, overlooking the diggings, topped by a red flag snapping in the breeze. A man stood at the rail looking down on it all, looking at an amazing valley of activity.

Men were everywhere, men who could search for Annabel, if King ordered them. They wore red shirts and blue pants and at a distance looked like patriotic ants. The *choof-choof* of shovels coughing up dirt could be heard for miles. Red earth was where you found gold. Men scrambled from deep holes with sacks filled with red dirt. Others wheeled red dirt along tiers of shelf-like banks. Some shoveled red dirt into long wooden chutes gushing water. Men dragged rakes through wet gravel, watching sharply for the naked gleam of gold. Wooden chutes shot red water into the river making the nearest edge of the stream seem as if it was flowing with blood. It was a boy's dream of playing in the dirt and looking for treasure.

If men were filled with gold fever—could he get them to stop even for a few days?

If they knew a girl was missing in the mountains while they grubbed the earth for gold crumbs, would they search, would they help him? Pray it was so. Then show them real gold!

He strode into Gold Nation with his arms pumping high. They saw him right away.

The group of miners shoveling gravel into a water-fed chute stared at him warily.

He said, "Where's King? I need to find him. My sister's trapped in a cave."

A short miner, thick and sleek-looking like a muskrat, stopped shoveling while the rest kept working. His voice was loud, and thick with sarcasm. "We heard about that. John Valory was here a week ago. We heard he was missing his wife, too." The three others smirked and continued shoveling and raking wet gravel.

Petr's face grew warm. He spoke softly, "What's your name, mister?"

"Rutherford Gragg. And we know you, boy. You're moping around instead of working. Why don't you get back to cutting boards like you're sposed to, so *men* can make a living?"

Petr's fists tightened. "I *must* find my sister—and I'm willing to pay."

The man chuckled and the others kept on working.

Gragg said, "You're that woodcutter's boy got his sister lost in the woods and made his mama run away. But King figures what happened to the Valory women was, Indians got em."

Petr said, "I don't know that." Suddenly he remembered the grave mounds by the river.

"But we do!" Gragg turned dark red and came within shovel swinging distance. "We buried five good men, killed by arrows. And just the other day somebody found Charlie Swenson sunny-side-up, bellyful of arrows, face like a plate of mashed potatoes. Now you want to send us waltzing in the mountains to do what?"

"I didn't see any...they must be—"

Gragg shoved him hard backwards with the shovel. "You get back to cutting sticks. Men got work to do here."

Gragg stared at him with hatred that shocked Petr. They wouldn't help even for a day? Were all men heartless beasts who worked for King? He couldn't stand to look at their sneering faces another minute. Petr walked away.

A buck-toothed man called after him in a sarcastic voice, "We know all about you, boy. Heard you're a real goldfinder, so why don't you find *us* some gold instead of wandering around in the woods?"

Petr turned abruptly and faced them. "What would you know about *real* goldfinding?"

Gragg said, "Better run, sonnyboy. If King doesn't give you a spanking, I will."

Petr rushed him and Gragg startled and swung the shovel head-high. Petr ducked lashing out a lightning-quick fist that dropped Gragg like a sack of wheat.

Stupid wonderment filled their faces. There was silence, and then the men laughed.

The buck-toothed man said, "We heard you was fast-handed, a grizz-killer for sure." Another added, "Better go. Gragg's gonna be sore when he wakes up. He's pushing hard to be one of them Gold Regiment fellers. King's watching all of this, I guarantee."

Petr asked again, "Where is King?"

"Up in his tower," the bucktooth man said. "And he don't like visitors."

Petr looked at the tower. There was a big man leaning over at the rail wearing a wide-brim, very white hat that made him look like a plantation owner. He was looking through a brass telescope. The big man was watching him. Petr headed for the tower.

The path led sharply downhill. He swung his shoulders, lengthened his stride, and felt the hot stare of the man in the tower.

He passed the yawping tent of the hotel-saloon: *The Gold Nation!* Then passed scatters of shanties and tents and tried to ignore the exposed feeling, as if he was running naked in a dream. He felt the intensity of it—King is watching you!

2

A sharp bend in the river promised riches—and here was the flume, a wooden skeleton grinning in the sun, a strange beast made of Valory lumber. A dozen men worked on a low trestle, the floor of the water-trough that would run a quarter-mile across the L-shaped river-bend. The men sounded like railroad workers clattering and hammering. Except for twenty feet of flooring and caulking, the thing was nearly done.

Petr walked around dwindling stacks of planks which only weeks before were stained by Valory sweat. Men slapped boards into place, then nailed them with a ringing clang of steel and swearing. And the river made its hushing song behind them.

Papa had told him about fluming. When fluming was done the river would be head-dammed, which stopped water from flowing into the bend, and raised it high enough to make it rush into the elevated water-trough and then deposit the water farther downstream—for a time making the river run dry. Once the river was diverted from its bed, these same men would scramble down into the drained curve and rake its guts for nuggets of gold. The quicker they built the flume the longer the harvest. Flumes didn't last long. The spring floods of 1851 and 1852 had snapped three previous flumes like piles of matchsticks.

Forty yards away stood the lookout tower.

Thick pine poles reached twenty feet into the air to support a square platform with heavy railings and heavy canvas awning. Above it flapped a strange flag not of the United States, a gold T shivering in the breeze that fell lazily on a bloody field of red bordered in black.

Petr muttered, "What hell-nation flag is that?"

A broad-shouldered man stood at the rail watching him, arms slabbed across his chest like crossed cannons, a tall man in a billowing white silk shirt and an immaculately white Panama hat. He wore a big black pistol holster but it was empty. Even at a distance Petr could sense the rage in his eyes.

Shouldn't make you nervous, he's only your last hope.

Papa never let Petr meet Dain King, never explained why, but now he saw why: *The man is pure evil.* Petr angled towards the tower under the gun-like stare when a big voice boomed.

"Hey you, boy! Come on up here!" The man leaned over the rail, his reddish copper skin striking against the white suit, looking foreign, exotic somehow. He lit a cigar and put both hands on his hips, but he wasn't mad, he was laughing, his voice booming again.

"Been waiting for you, boy! What took you so long?"

Petr tried to shake the tower, but it was rock solid. He swung lightly onto the platform, fists clenched. King grinned, coming forward, arms outstretched.

"So at last I meet the fine son."

He looked like he could lift a bull but moved with surprisingly graceful speed. Halting a foot away, his grin turned abruptly into anger.

"You and John ever heard of a deal?" His voice jabbed. He poked his cigar at Petr. "You owe me two weeks of lumber. Instead you come here punching my men." His eyes were black, brutally direct artillery fire, radiating menacing power. He smelled of sweet brandy.

Petr said simply, "I came to talk to you."

King backed away as if he'd been insulted. His hand dangled to draw a pistol. Petr had seen a picture of Genghis Khan. This man looked like that—fierce and crazy.

With blurring speed he slapped the holster and then grinned down at his empty hand.

"Guess you got lucky today," he laughed, turning away. "Funny looking belt you're wearing. If you want I could give you real clothes like a man wears. If you're the sort of man I'm looking for you could wear the Gold Regiment uniform," spoken like it was a high honor.

He leaped onto the railing with catlike agility. He brayed at the workmen below, "You mountain bums! Smash those nails, clinch those shiners! Think you're building a piano?" The men were only twenty yards away but King's voice boomed so loudly they flinched as if lashed by a whip. He turned to Petr with a hurt and subdued manner.

"Why do you and John cheat me? Why don't you bring my lumber, boy?"

Petr hid his anger, saying softly, "You know why we stopped working."

King flickered cigar ashes in his face. "My men are out of lumber *tomorrow*. While the Valory men are out mooing in the mountain for their women, that's what I know!"

He made it sound disgraceful. Out of the blue a word arose in Petr's mind: *Bellicose*. Diseased with uncontrollable anger, that's what the man was. And it was contagious. Petr forced himself to look away, gazing at a long table where three platters of food sat untouched and two bottles of brandy, one half empty. There was also a big revolver for the black holster. A repeating rifle leaned against the rail, identical to the one he got on his birthday.

Petr spoke calmly with great effort. "I didn't come to argue about lumber, there will be lots of lumber just as soon as I'm sure about my family."

King jumped down from the railing like a pirate. He lowered his artillery stare onto Petr's strange belt, but made no retort. He removed his clean white hat and carefully placed it on the table. He tapped his broad forehead and pointed at Petr. "I know what *you* want. Do you know what I want?"

Petr was stunned. King's head was bald as bright copper, his eyebrows black scorch marks on a shining dome. And Petr instantly saw what *was* there long ago: a black mane of hair. And he was struck by a resemblance.

The Indian at the lake: Put King in white buckskins and they would be Indian brothers. Petr felt a swirl of dizziness.

King flexed his fingers liked claws. "Beat my hand and I'll do what *you* say—if you really want to find Magya and Annabel," his words puffed smoke in Petr's face.

He knew their names?

Petr gripped King's powerful hand. "I'll make a deal with you!"

King laughed, "Yeah? Like our lumber deal? You can't be trusted."

Can't be trusted? Petr got mad. "I found gold, some place you've never been!"

King puffed smoke calmly, "Oh, where would that be? I heard

you're a real gold finder." He squeezed Petr's hand like a slowly shutting vise.

Petr gasped as pain bolted into his knuckles. "All you care for...is your...damned flume...your gold...not people...not Annabel."

King squeezed even harder. "Now learn about my power, my fine son."

Pressing sideways he began arm-wrestling Petr, twisting and squeezing. Petr resisted until his spine and legs tensed into a bowstring pulled all the way back. His muscles felt as if they were parting from the bone. He had to win this stupid game. Mentally he cried out: *Tecumseh, enter me!*

Ferocious power poured into his blood, into his hand, a thing he'd felt just once—against the grizzly—protecting Annabel. There'd been no time to appreciate the Indian's immense strength. *Tecumseh?* That was his name? And why did he know that now?

King drew closer, grinning happily. "Know me yet, boy?"

Petr shot the bow of Tecumseh's strength into his hand: "Haaarrrh!"

King's knuckles turned white and his face turned red. Big white teeth clenched the cigar and it snapped and fell to the floor. His eyes narrowed, his body shook, and he gasped. When King's cheeks trembled, Petr released him.

King spun away taking convulsive breaths. Amazingly he returned smiling. "I heard you had a bear-killing hand. Got the knife all the way down his throat, did you? I never heard of that before." He laughed like it was just good man-stuff.

Petr's voice was dry rasping, "Corner me...I'm dangerous." He felt he had climbed a mountain, but he wasn't breathing hard. He felt good and dangerous.

For the first time King made a genuine smile, devilish, handsome, charming. Holding out his palm this time they shook hands, man to man. "I respect a strong hand," he said, "even if you got lucky."

Petr squeezed back repeating the words: "Beat my hand, I do what you say."

King flung his hand away and shouted, "I *lied* about that part!"

Swaggering to his chair, he plopped down happy as if it was his right to lie, as if completely satisfied with the demonstration. He replaced the white hat on his head and gestured at the table. "You look hungry as a dog on a desert. Go ahead, eat."

Platters of scrambled eggs, dark slabs of meat, yellow biscuits, a pot of honey, purple bottles of brandy. Petr's mouth watered.

He muttered, "I didn't come here for food."

"Sure, I know, you lost your family." Smiling as if it was an unimportant fact, he nodded in the direction of the big hotel. "Ever had a native girl feed you?" Without warning he flung himself against the railing and bellowed, *"LANI! Come-out-here-now!"*

Petr shrank back. The man knew no normal bounds, no normal range. The hotel was uphill a hundred yards away. Ordinary men didn't expect to communicate beyond twenty or thirty feet, maybe. Petr was struck by a revelation: King dominates everything in sight.

Lani was a woman, Petr knew that much. He reddened, stuttering, "I didn't c-come here—"

"Hey, boy—stand up, you're a man aren't you? Don't tell me what you *didn't* come for." His anger came and went. He studied Petr for the first time with a look of real pleasure. "Hell, you barely fill out your pants." He pulled a fresh cigar from a table box. "You got arms and legs. I guess John and Magya didn't ruin you completely. You dress a little funny. What kind of queer belt is that?"

When Petr didn't answer, he glanced away indifferently. "All right, I guess you'll come to it." He lit his cigar. "How you like the weather?" He puffed his cigar and gazing with interest at a big white cloud bulging slowly over the Sierra crest. A storm was coming for Gold Nation.

"Ever hear the one about the farmer who liked it twice? The farmer said, I think I like the one in the fall, best."

Petr didn't understand. Everything was a test with Dain King—or a joke. Petr removed his stiff belt and straightened it onto the table, but didn't unwrap it. He spoke softly and slowly.

"I have gold—a pureness you've never seen." He let that sink in. "I hire your men for one week to search the mountains for my family. I'll pay whatever amount of gold you're dredging in a week. Maybe more—more than you've ever seen. But I can't show you where it comes from." Knowing how ludicrous that sounded from a boy in rags.

King clasped his fingers behind his head stretching lazily, popping his shirt open, revealing big coppery muscles smooth and hairless. He blew smoke rings. "That would be a lot of gold, my fine son. There's no sunken treasure ship in these mountains. Show me your goldmine, and then we'll talk."

Petr felt his anger rising again. "I've been someplace you've never been."

King laughed. "That's not likely. I chased all over these mountains while you were still in diapers. I crossed your valley when it was just a good place for a bear to squat. I got *here* first," he pointed at the river. "I got here when gold was picked right off the rocks. July of 1850. Two years ago." He pointed upriver a hundred yards. "See that long rib of rock?"

There was a dark hump alongside the river, longer than a football field. King spoke proudly, "That was rotten with gold. We filled buckets all day long with gold. Nobody finds gold like that anymore, that's over. So don't blow smoke through your whistle about finding lots of gold. That talk won't shine in my camp."

Petr unrolled his belt.

There was a sunrise of gold on the table, a golden snake.

King eyes narrowed and he stood over to the table, not touching it. Taking a meat knife, he hesitated, then returned to his chair and began paring his nails. He said, "How long has that girl been gone?"

Petr fought down a fist-swinging urge, then answered huskily, "Sixteen days."

King reamed a thumbnail and made a puffing note of disgust. "That's hopeless. A child can last three, maybe four days in these mountains. Admit your sister's dead and mother Magya ran off. Sooner you swallow that, the better off you'll be."

King was looking for a showdown, a knockout blow. Petr controlled his temper one last time. "I found a gloryhole. You won't have to crawl around on your belly looking for crumbs anymore."

King stood violently. "Bring me that bottle, boy." He lit another cigar.

Petr obeyed, surprised how easily King was manipulated.

King drank noisily, the brandy seeming to ignite his eyes, gazing at the storm clouds pouring over the crest. Suddenly he was raging.

"You come all brightfaced and bragging about gold. You expect me to jump?" He gestured with both the cigar and bottle. "I'll humor you, say you found your so-called source." He paused setting the bottle carefully on the table as if it was the source. "What if it is?" He grabbed the bottle by the neck and smashed it on the rail and held out the jagged glass. Petr jumped back avoiding the splash. King's voice softened, becoming confidential.

"You don't know the...*the contingencies*...of the gold business. One thing is to find gold. Another thing is to keep it. You're no good alone. Look what happened to Charlie Swenson. You need protection. You need Gold Nation."

Distant thunder boomed in the mountains. King poked his cigar towards the darkening crest. He continued in a fatherly tone.

"Your gold's in a lonely spot or I'd know about it. How will you protect yourself from claim-jumpers? Greasers? Chinks?"

Petr held out his hands. "You don't understand what I—"

King shoved him backward and grabbed the rifle. "*Understand?* Understand *this!*" He held it proudly. "Colt Carbine .52 caliber—bang six times and your work's done."

Identical to Petr's rifle, this is where Papa got it.

King sighted on the cloud, the mountain, the workmen. Then he did something crazy. He shot the cloud; he shot the mountain. Then he fired over the men. Screaming at them, "Hurry up before I shoot you to pieces!" He was panting with excitement. Then his breathing slowed visibly and the madness drained away.

"A hundred men carrying these rifles and you've got no problems with claim-jumpers, greasers, Indians—or the U.S. government. Just add a few cannons."

King made a surprisingly boyish smile.

Petr eyed the blue cylinder engraved with a tiny man shooting a tiny lion. He wondered: Papa? Did you make a deal with this crazy devil?

King clasped the rifle against his chest. "Show me your goldmine boy, I'll protect you. We'll partner up." He sat at the table looking very happy. He set the rifle aside and spread his hands in a welcoming gesture as if everything was settled. And suddenly Petr couldn't stand it.

The noon sun magnified the heat pouring into the platform.

Wind rose sharply and the awning flapped and the flag snapped. A great anvil-shaped cloud swallowed the sun and the air chilled abruptly. Petr saw the golden sun swallowed by the mouth of the cloud—over and over again. He looked away, at the miners working on the flume, wavering, flickering like ghosts. He was having a fit. He stabbed his feet apart, didn't want to fall down in front of this man, King, who was gesturing for him to sit. But Petr didn't move and King didn't understand what was wrong.

King flicked a half-smoked cigar over the rail and leaned forward grinning happily. He began eating from the table, pawing meat into his mouth, eating noisily, both hands shoving beef into his mouth and then chugging brandy and then his voice brassy with sarcasm, again the rapid shift of emotion.

"You live on air and water alone, that what John and Magya teach you?" Thumbing a wedge of cornbread sideways into his mouth, he turned away in disgust. Petr swayed from side to side. King leapt at the rail, spitting food, blaring: "Pigsley, back that plank with a sledge so it quits bucking! Tiger, nail it in!" Pounding his knee, he was hammering, "Dammit, Carswell. Get that sledge away from that jackass before he—" A voice below whined dolefully but he cut it off. "Then you do it! Pigsley is better off with a shovel. He can't stand the altitude."

The men laughed because they were only three feet off the ground.

Petr was grateful for the distraction. His dizziness, his fit, went away. The men looked like normal men again, not pulsating ghosts.

He could see—they feared this man—and adored him. They liked his craziness. Petr shook his head to clear it. King ruled with grand arrogance fascinating to watch. Other men were pale and weak beside him, he ruled them easily. And they *wanted* to be ruled by this superior physical and brutal beast.

Lightning arced above the crest, flashing light, and Petr saw something startling.

A brownskinned girl was scurrying lightly as a deer down the hill from the hotel, running towards the tower. Petr knew who she was. She was another reason Papa kept him away from Gold Nation.

King washed his mouth with brandy. "Being a saint, you wouldn't know about women. What else don't you know? Do you even know what day it is?"

King didn't stagger, didn't look drunk, his eyes clear and burning. But he acted drunk every minute. Petr replied angrily, "I know tomorrow is Independence Day."

King waved at the cluster of tents and buildings. "Today we work a half-day. Tonight we shoot, shout, and sing. Don't sleep for three days. Celebrate with us! Go to the hotel and get some good beef, good whiskey, good talk. See what life can be about." Adding, "No mama telling you what to do," he winked as if sharing some great secret of life.

King lit yet another cigar, smoky words trailed from his lips. "Show me your gold, I'll make you a partner in Gold Nation Mining Company. I'll protect you from the greasers and celestials, and that's just for starters." Petr's silence reignited King's temper. "You won't find your mama. One of my men saw her joining a wagonload of Mormons. Your sister is dead for sure. So let's move on."

King let that sink in while Petr blinked. Why believe anything this man said? He puffed smoke like a chimney, like he ran on smoke. He said, "Say I give you a dozen men on horses, you look around for a week, you don't find your sis. What then?"

Petr swallowed hard because that bad thought had never occurred to him. *Never see Annabel again?* King smiled slightly. "Take your time, I want to hear this."

Petr said, "I guess I'd cut wood...or work my claim. I don't...we don't talked much about...after." He stared at the ground and then he saw her—the Island Girl. Coming up the ladder, gazing up at him with a look he didn't understand.

A slender woman, a wave of black hair and cinnamon colored

skin and white shining teeth, a little healthy woman smiling at him. A strange thrill rippled through his belly.

So this is the Island Girl.

3

King ignored the girl's undulations and continued in fatherly tones. "Down the road five years—1860 at the latest—the so-called United States will blow apart because she's tied together with blasting fuses in the middle of a powder keg called slavery. Know about slavery, boy?"

Petr watched graceful arms and legs climbing, advancing, pausing, the way a cat stalks a bird, and he knew his own fuse was being lit. He thought—

I didn't come here for this. Only Annabel matters to me.

King seemed unaware that Petr was riveted by a tawny female presence.

"Either you're master or slave. It's simple as that, a fundament of nature. Partner with me you'll never be a slave." He waved his cigar. "You think I want gold to build fine marble mansions in San Francisco? No. I stay right here. Gathering my men—fighting men."

Petr stared at the girl. She was smiling at Petr, nodding, as King droned on.

"Mexico is mad about losing California. France is interested. Nothing's happened yet, but war is coming." He blew three big smoke rings. "I need gold to build an army. Doesn't have to be big, just dedicated, if you see what the Mormons have done. I'll have cannons soon, I have connections in Mexico." He paused and Petr barely heard him. "I might build a church." Petr looked surprised, and King laughed. "Didn't see that coming did you? Church of America is a *man's* church. The government leaves churches alone, if you see the beauty of that."

The girl-woman climbed level with the platform. Now he saw her clearly. Beautiful, long and athletic, with no female softness, she stood at the rail staring at Petr. He stared back at her. Finally King noticed her and frowned.

"Lani, hop over here. Man's insulting your biscuits."

She brushed against Petr shoving his shoulder. "You don't like my *bis-coot?*" Her head was under his chin and her voice held a curious cooing quality.

From the trestle somebody called, "Colonel King, it's half past noon."

King gazed down the valley where the thunderhead made three thick columns of rain, steadily marching forward. "All right, goddamn you, go celebrate. Go celebrate to hell." Folding his big arms he gave an iron smile. Then, fatherly to Petr: "Eat first, then business. Make it a rule; make fewer bad decisions that way. Go on, son. Make her happy, eat her biscuits. She won't bite, not in the daytime anyway. I think she likes you."

Wind blew making the canvas awning buck, the storm minutes away.

Hunger needles stung Petr's jaw as Lani buttered biscuits dabbed with honey, and then held one under his mouth. She fed him bits, moist and tangy, and bared her teeth and laughed.

My God, what a mouth of pearls, pink lips, pink as seashells, eyes like whiskey fire.

She laughed, nodding happily as he ate three more yellow lumps, forcing his eyes away from the remaining two. He thought he heard King laugh.

Nearby pine boughs swayed like wings as the canyon began to fill with storm music, singing, *rain-on-the-way.*

"Thanks, very much." Petr nodded but she didn't leave. He added, "You can go now." Maybe she didn't understand English. Her eyes radiated laughter and birdlike hunger.

Lani whispered, "I *like* you. You *like* me?" Pulling her shoulders back, revealing prominent woman-charms. She pounced and began rubbing his chest in rapid circular motions, nodding and smiling at him. King continued the droning monotone.

"My first was a Delaware Indian woman...named Tamaris. She expected me to marry her. But I was settling a score with my old man. She had her baby right on his porch—a boy. Know who that boy was, Petr Valory?" The monotone voice paused for a long moment.

"Then I went fighting Seminoles in Florida."

Petr barely heard him. The girl kneaded his shoulders like bread and the sore muscles in his spine and then his hips ached for more of the same. King's voice droned on the rising wind.

"By sixteen I was a ship's cook. The Fairweather got shot with so many holes I'd been safer floating on a log. I fought Indians wherever I found them, war or no war." There was another long pause. "I lived with the Mandans on the Missouri River. That was 1840-something. Don't remember...I went a little crazy then."

Petr would remember this strange story, but only much later.

Lani now worked her way down and Petr clamped her eager hands, shaking his head. She smiled, whispering urgently, "You like me too?"

Petr stopped resisting.

"I joined the army in 1846 with Braxton Bragg and rolled artillery into Matamoros, then Cerro Gordo, then Mexico City. Cannons make the difference, boy. Remember that. The more the merrier."

Petr would understand later why King was telling him this. Lani slid down, he couldn't stop her, she was moaning in pain. How had he hurt her?

But she whispered, "I like you *very* much."

King finished up. "After we returned to Fort Snellen, Minnesota, I took the rifles and I can't tell you about that part. Ended up striking gold right here. Two years ago in 1850."

The valley darkened and midnight came at noon.

4

Wind bucked the platform and the awning flew away like a gray bird. Thunder boomed into the valley like a giant drum and a minute later they would all be drenched. Lani jumped the rail, giggling, and flung herself down the ladder and raced away.

King laughed. "Sahtan on horseback, I bet you're thirsty now."

Petr froze. "What?—who says the devil's name...*that way?*" Answer was: *John Valory.*

King gazed at the storm cloud and he was smiling.

Petr was incredulous. He choked, "So it's true. You...John Valory... are brothers."

King slapped the table. "Who told you that? I'll rip him apart. Sahtan in hell!" King began pacing like a horse in a short stall. "My goody half-brother talks too much. Maybe it *is* time you knew the rotten truth."

Lightning exploded nearby and the top of a pine burst into flames. King laughed as Petr backed away, crouching beside the table, again sensing raw animal power of the man. He asked, "Don't you know lightning can kill you?"

King flung his hands at the sky. "Can't kill *me!* So learn from me, what I'm trying to tell you. I'm two days from fluming. And here comes my fine young jack, wanting to go merry-go-round in the mountains. Think I care about your little boy problems? It's time to be a man."

Petr regretted coming here, all of it a waste of time.

King towered over him, shaking the tower like an ape in a cage. "Show me your mine! We'll search for Annabel. I promise, five men, five days. You have my word."

Petr squeezed his eyes shut, tired now. "Like I said—I can't show you the mine. It's on sacred Indian ground."

King shook him roughly. "There's *nothing* sacred in this world! You want proof? I'll tell you a dirty little secret. John and Magya aren't your ma and pa."

Petr stared at him and blinked. His world tilted like he was on a ship going down, he felt sick, he mumbled, "My God....it's all true?" King held onto him as big splatters of rain hit, forerunners of a deluge to come. King spoke sternly like he was dispensing necessary medicine.

"You grow up I'll tell you everything. I had a ma and pa once and they didn't like me. I say leave mothers and brothers and sisters. Leave them—then do what you want to do!"

Petr didn't see it coming. King pulled him in by the shirt and slapped him hard in the face, yelling, "You need a man to tell you what to do, and I'm that man!"

Petr wiped blood from his mouth and stared at it. He clinched his chin downward, his voice thick. "Like I said—King—I'm looking for my sis and ma." He twisted away and went to the table. He rolled up his gold belt and curled it around his waist. "I found more gold in a day than you'll scratch in your whole miserable life. Even with that troop of roosters scratching after you."

The rain started—and stopped again.

King roared, "Mama's boy! And that so-called father of yours!"

Petr shivered like he might vomit but nothing came out. He said, "Maybe I am. But I'll never be your son. I'll find my family without your help."

King grabbed the repeating rifle and pointed it at Petr. It looked like a toy in his hands. Then he jerked around and fired it into the flume where yellow splinters flew away.

"Don't leave me, boy! Please!"

Lightning flashed. Suddenly rain fell in straight gray sheets.

King raised the rifle with both hands and bellowed, "Strike me dead if I'm wrong! Petr Valory is my son, and he belongs to me, heart and soul!" He stabbed the rifle into the air, daring the sky to strike him.

Petr backed away from the big man, a crazy man playing with lightning.

It came brilliantly. Lightning exploded and Petr fell temporarily blinded, smelling burnt cloth, and King's flag smoldered on the pole. King pumped the rifle up and down, laughing.

"The sky answered me: You belong to me!"

Petr looked down the long curve of the river where another shock was coming. A familiar figure toiled through rain and mud carrying the heavy buffalo rifle. Couldn't be, but it was.

It was John Valory coming for his son.

5

Running through gray downpour, gasping for breath, he yelled, "Leave...my boy...alone. Come here...Petr...come home."

King held Petr with a big strong arm. "He's mine now. He's home *now*."

Petr ducked out of his grip and John raised the buffalo rifle at King. With it, John had killed buffalo and deer at well over two hundred yards.

John said, "You need killing…long time ago. So here it is."

King shook with roaring laughter, "You kill me? Go ahead. Try! I can't be killed!"

The rifle made a dull clanking sound. The powder was wet. John threw it down, yelling, "I don't need to kill you. I tell the Army where you are. They want you all the time—alive—so they can kill you."

King stopped laughing. "What would you know about that?"

Now it was John's turn to grin. "I know…every-*ting!* I tell about your rifles—and your Indian mother—and your men will laugh at you."

Rain poured down turning all of them into gray ghosts. King stared at John for a long time.

John finished his threat, "Leave my boy alone—I shut up. Leave him be, I leave you alone!"

King grabbed his repeating rifle and clicked the hammer back, aiming at John's heart.

Petr leaped forward and grabbed both ends of the rifle and twisted. Whether the repeater would fire in the rain he didn't know, and didn't want to know.

"Please, let him go."

King's eyes reddened with rage and he twisted the rifle as Petr's arms coiled against what felt like an immense iron wheel. The rifle turned as hard reserves of strength massed against him and Petr smelled sour sweat like moldy grain. Petr held on, barely. But something happened. The Indian's mighty power surged into him. *Tecumseh.* And the words: *I will be with you when you need me.* The barrel twisted back—the other way—his way.

The big man let the rifle go and Petr felt as if his spine floated from his back.

King grabbed the rail and blinked at the rain, a new look in his eyes. He spoke quietly. "Good son, all right now. Go on now."

Petr shoved the rifle back at him and went down the ladder where

John was on his knees in the mud, pounding the buffalo gun, crying, "Oh, why can't I kill him?"

Petr helped him to his feet. They stumbled away.

Something had shifted and Petr wasn't sure what, only that he would find out soon. And that it was big.

He wondered about Tecumseh. Who on earth was Tecumseh? And how did he give you power? Was it all just a fantasy? Wasn't it simply desperation that gave you power when you needed it?

6

Booming rain ended abruptly, followed by brilliant sunshine. Empty white clouds scudded south as big double rainbows arched over Beckwourth Pass. The forest glistened all around as John and Petr staggered home. The boy was quiet, deep in thought, and he wondered if they could get past these bad days. Could he tell Petr the sad story of the Valorys—everything?

Let him decide: *who* is your real father.

That's what he had to do. Tell him tonight.

The so-called "Dain King" wouldn't last in California. The regiment at Honey Lake was only a day's ride north where Captain Weatherlow had sixty rangers. Just whistle and they would come looking for the man who stole Federal rifles and maybe hang King from the nearest tree. Dain King had created his own noose and he didn't even know it.

Back at the Valoryvale Petr stoked up the fireplace and began frying potatoes, onions and bacon for supper. John felt better. Everything would be all right after supper, after they talked.

7

Mack Karras was with King from Mexico to Fort Snellen in Minnesota—and now deep in the Sierras they were making a bank of gold. Why not relax? Enjoy life's good fortune? But Gunnar, now known as Dain King

(Mack had shortened his own name from Karrasopoulis) had decided gold wasn't enough. King wanted his own *Country* for god-sakes.

Mack paid the miners seven ounces of gold a week, over a hundred dollars in San Francisco at sixteen dollars an ounce. His Island Girls served the men whiskey, food and charm, and got most of the gold back. Lani had returned just before the storm hit with a big smile on her face. Now she was wearing her favorite green silk dress, her ladyskins. Her sister Mani would be drunk by the time they waited tables. They would be busy today, eve of Fourth of July.

By late afternoon Gold Nation was roaring with miners, Americans, French, English, Italians, Swedes, Greeks, Irish, Germans—all celebrating independence. Mack and the girls were exhausted well before midnight. But eating, drinking and dancing would continue for the next three days. Shooting pistols and rifles into the air was tolerated as long as it was done outside. By dusk all of the miners were loud, drunk, and happy.

For one man it was a perfect night for murder.

8

Dain King counted on it. He stretched out on his bed in his room over the tavern. The men would drink all night. It was perfect. Tonight he would shut up his brother permanently. John Valory cutting boards was one thing. But John Valory drunk and shooting off his mouth was another story. How he ended up in the next valley after he hadn't seen him for twenty years—that was a mystery. But it didn't matter. His wife and little girl had disappeared, and that simplified things. Just make sure Petr didn't get killed. The boy was important, his own flesh and blood.

Below in the tavern, men laughed, yelled, drank, and played cards. Music to his ears, the way men had enjoyed themselves for centuries.

Dain King stopped being Gunnar Valory when the U.S. Army put a $5,000 reward on that name. Nobody knew that name except John and Mack. John needed killing. Mack would never tell about

Gunnar Valory. What mattered now was that Petr Valory was the son of Gunnar Valory. The boy needed to learn that, and respect that. Petr Valory had found gold—that's what mattered. He needed to share that with his real father.

And John Valory needed to die tonight.

Nobody would notice a little extra shooting and shouting. Then Petr would see things clearly. Together with his beautiful son they would create a new nation—Gold Nation. The United States wasn't going to last. Any fool could see that.

Forget the United States. The so-called "Union" was an illusion. The cold North was wedded to the hot tropic bride of the South—slavery. Everybody loved the stink of money. But the North was confused about loving freedom while still allowing slavery. Why couldn't they just leave it alone? But they wouldn't. The North was self-righteous about slavery when the world had been running on slavery for thousands of years.

Long dirty war was coming.

Gold Nation would hold no illusions of democracy. Gold Nation would be a warrior society. In Gold Nation—

Men began as slaves, would become warriors, remaining a warrior until age twenty-one. After successfully serving as a slave, a warrior, then and only then, becoming a man, getting his freedom: land and a woman and as much land and as many women as he can handle. That was the true life of a real man.

Real men—warriors—would flock to Gold Nation!

Real men knew the way the world was meant to be before the dream-peddlers brought their illusions of freedom and equality. Washington. Jefferson. Paine. Franklin. Madison. They were all great tricksters. Along with their great sideshow, the Lamb-god, to keep their 'free people' meek and mild. What a laugh. The god that mattered was The Hammer God—Thor.

Thor would smash them all. Why the flag of Gold Nation was blood red with a gold T.

Gunnar Valory now Dain King had a vision while he was up on Point of Rocks: He saw the future of America.

North and South would attack each other like rabid dogs biting and spinning in circles. They would exhaust themselves while Gold Nation grew stronger and stronger every day.

West shall rule East—and California wears the golden crown. His vision was vivid.

Dain King shall line the stern face of the Sierra Nevada with cannon—the face of The Gold Nation. Let the Union armies come! The East will break upon the Western wall! Let them cross dry weary desert. Cannons will defeat the red-white-and-blue—leaving the Union in ruins.

His vision was hard, angry, certain. Looking west he saw—

The Sierras sloping gently into huge salver valleys of the California bellyland, producing ransoms of grain and fruit—all harvested by slaves of Gold Nation. New towns called *viks,* would spring up along great western sweeps of the new nation that ended abruptly in the sea. His smile broadened, picturing the hard western face of Gold Nation. The overlooking palisades were tactically perfect for cannons that would perforate any pathetic flock of wooden ships. He laughed. Thor's hammer? Thor's hammer was cannons!

The god asked: What do you need now, Dain King, mighty ruler of Gold Nation?

What he needed was hundreds of cannons and thousands of men.

For that—the King of California—needed much gold.

Despite laughing, singing, bellowing men below, he fell deep into sleep, deep into dreams, dreaming the Old Dream.

Three dragon ships skimmed ice-chipped northern waters prowling far beyond the Greenland floes. Viking! His men all fire and ice berserkers, smiling stiffly in freezing breezes, salt spray white on their reddened cheeks, ice stars in their beards, long-limbed Viking warriors, blue-eyed lions of the sea, iron-armed men of war and will. Two weeks of sailing brought them to a coastline of endless trees. Ashore, redmen greeted them as gods from the sea. That night the redmen attacked them in their sleep with knives.

King awoke gasping feeling blood dripping down his face and

arms. But it was only sweat. Only a dream! King grabbed his pocket watch. Four o'clock. Time for blood.

From his closet he retrieved the small crate of arrows. He smiled. By sunrise John Valory would be dead.

9

The Fourth of July began on the Third. It would blaze three days, three nights, until men were too drunk to dance, sing, or even sit up. Tonight they'd sober up enough to shoot their guns, maybe blow a few kegs of gunpowder. King opened the crate and found two dozen red arrows nested with five short bows, one small enough for a boy, Pah Ute weapons from Sabbah's band, plus the arrows recovered from lone Indian's killing spree.

At 6 A.M. King went down into the saloon and picked four men from the regiment who had helped with the Pah Ute trouble. These men could be trusted to do anything he asked, and they were still sober. Tiger. Gragg. Ruble. Pigsley. One would not survive the raid on the Valory cabin. He ordered them to leave the saloon separately and told them where to meet and when.

"Sleep all day. And then get some coffee in you. I'll give you the plan tonight."

They did as they were told.

By 7 P.M. darkness the five had slept and then departed New Viksburg by separate paths. They met again on the wagon path to the Valoryvale. A mule carried the crate and four lanterns—and four repeating rifles just in case things went wrong. King told them they were his chosen lieutenants, and in all of his plans, sworn to secrecy.

Tonight was the real beginning of his kingdom. The false father of Petr Valory would die and King would get his son back—the bringer of gold.

King explained his plan for tonight and his men nodded silently. Then Blackie Ruble said, "What about the boy?"

"Don't let the boy see you. Leave him alone." And again, "Don't hurt the boy."

They set out in fading light for the Valoryvale.

CHAPTER EIGHT

THE VALORY MASSACRE

1

Petr was upset. Why wouldn't he be? John wasn't his real father. That's what Dain King said. What should he call John now—the old man? John sat at the table rocking back and forth, pale as marble, the cabin heavy with silence. They had avoided each other all afternoon. Now the sun was going down, the sunset filling the cabin with crimson light. Petr warmed a can of beans along with leftover potatoes and bacon, anything to keep busy, anything to keep from talking. He shook the pan back and forth on the iron grate, thinking, He's not my pa. Yes, let's have a bite to eat. John and King are brothers!

He muttered aloud, "How can that be?"

John stood abruptly and glanced outside. "Bad things are coming... you need to know. Stuff I didn't want to tell you."

Petr smelled potatoes burning. He flicked the skillet, banged it down. His voice was loud, "Dain King told me—you're *brothers*. Not only that—"

John spoke quickly. "I tell you every *ting*. My brother rur...ruh—I can't say it—raped a Delaware squaw. She h-had a baby. She...you—"

Petr knifed a hand through the air. "King told me the whole charming story. How he made some woman have the baby on his father's porch. Who was she?"

John looked away. "She wasn't just any woman. Did he tell you who the baby was?"

Petr stabbed the meat with a fork and sat down holding his head. Whatever this was, it would be bad. "Let it all out," he said.

For ten minutes he heard the terrible story of his life—and about his real father Gunnar Valory. The masks were coming off—the whole rotten story—told by the man he loved most.

Petr sat stiffly in a chair and felt like he didn't dare move, like his head was passing between two moving blades: John grimly pushing the one, Gunnar pushing the other. Blades of truth sawing his head, and down the sides of his chest, down his legs. Finally the floor was cut beneath him. What Petr Valory really was, stripped bare like a piece of wood.

John stared straight ahead cutting away Petr's false childhood, replacing it with a secret child, with a secret history, hidden for so long.

The red and white baby was himself. That knowledge, not of mind but of blood, made hair rise on his neck, like lightning might strike where he sat. Move!

He sprang to the fireplace and thrust fat slabs of pine, one after another, until the hearth choked with wood. John stuffed his hands in his pockets and went silent, his face sad as corn shucks. Petr stood over him and stared at the man who was his father and now was not his father.

"How *could* you keep all this rot inside you? How do you *do* that? How do you not *tell* someone?"

John stared down at his gnarled fingers clasping and unclasping. He started talking like an automaton, a cuckoo-bird popping out of a clock. And he was crying. How charming.

"Holgar and Martine Valory, they were your grandparents. They were too old to raise you. Magya, she miscarried twice, two dead babies. So we took you. She removed one letter from your name—to save ink. She save every penny so she can go to San Francisco—to sing."

Petr went back to the fireplace, now a churning mouth of smoke. For a moment the small orbit between the fire and his chair seemed the only safe path left for him on earth. He set the frying pan aside and rammed a poker into the coals jugging the logs up and down. John's details of the Valory history joined with what the man in the tower had told him only hours before.

Dain King—the brutal man—was his real father.

Faraway he heard John saying, "You are my son, always my son!"

154

The churning smoke in the fireplace burst into flames and Petr felt himself disappearing up the chimney along with the smoke. He slumped to the floor. He stared at the frying pan.

What was he now? Warmed-up leftovers? He spoke aloud his new-formed person.

"From my halfbreed father, Gunnar—I am one-quarter Shawnee and one-quarter Dane. From my real mother Tamaris—I am half Delaware." He arranged the burnt potatoes in the pan into three rough portions. "So, that's me." He shoved the pan away. He gripped his hair. "Indian hair...?" He made a hysterical laugh. "I'm scrambled meat!"

The fireplace belched big red flames. He stared into the roaring mouth, trying to hold his head together. But it felt like it would explode. The flipping-fit ripped into his head.

The fire went *up*. The fire went *up*. The fire went *up*.

He began trembling. Wildly his teeth chattered. He gripped his head. "Make it stop...make it stop." He clenched his eyes. Let this life go, let it burn.

He whispered, "I'm...going now...I'm...passing away."

When he opened his eyes he stared at long dark Indian fingers. "From out of a red belly." And Magya knew all along! All good white milk he had vaguely imagined drinking from those great bursting breasts, evaporated. As if an angry baby, he began drinking milk from mysterious dark breasts. Each new simple breath performed strange miracles.

His whiteness shrank and his redness expanded.

"Ah—*me!* Ah—*me!*"

When he stared into the fire the Indian was calmly smiling at him. It was Tecumseh. And another puzzle-piece fell flatly into place.

So that's why you gave me the lake!

When he could finally speak, he asked John, "What happened to my real mother?"

John gazed out the window as if waiting for something. "She went back to the Lani Lanape. Back to the river...back to the Delaware. Alone, I guess."

Petr choked. "You guess?" He filled with explosive anger. "Why does no one tell you the truth in this world?" He began laughing. "Fourth of July is to celebrate freedom; what a laugh."

Staring at his new hands, he walked out of the cabin.

2

As he walked away from the cabin into warm July evening, the mountain peaks seemed like ragged black teeth. He stood out in the yard looking up at the first kindling stars.

He whispered, "Fourth of July—and I am an Indian." He heard far away pistol shots snapping and the heavier boom of rifles. "Should I be glad to know what I am?"

A twig snapped sharply in the forest.

Was it a deer? His vision quickened into hunter's eyes—Indian eyes. Is that what you meant when you said you would be with me, Tecumseh? His eyes roved milky hollows of twilight. *Something* was out there beneath the settling light. A hundred yards away at the tree-line—

There was a man holding a lantern.

That wasn't possible. But the rosy lantern flare showed a man, definitely a man. Lighting something, but what? What was he doing there? Petr frowned. Suddenly there were four men, no, five—a Fourth of July scene of revelers lighting fuses on fireworks. No. That could not be.

A comet flashed into the sky dripping a trail of sparks sailing gracefully over the cabin. *Whisss!* Was it Fourth of July antics? Petr cut his voice to the cabin door: "Papa!"

One lantern had become five men walking quickly towards the cabin. Petr suddenly knew what they were doing. "Papa, get the rifle, hurry!" But there was no response.

Another comet launched from beyond the barn flying flatly at him. "Ahhh!"

Light roared at his head thumping into the cabin wall. A feathered shaft blazed against the wall sending yellow tongues brooming fire up fuzzy logs. Move!

He leaped at the arrow and snapped it off. A rag burned at the tip. He smelled lamp oil. A third comet thunked into the wall and immediately began crackling. He slapped it down and then he ran inside.

John stood against the wall as if nailed to a cross. He was whimpering, "Oh no God, no!"

Petr peered back into the forest and saw the men clearly.

Whitemen, not Indians, in the gloaming light they fanned out into a semi-circle drifting steadily towards the cabin. They paused to light arrows—and shot them at the cabin.

Thunk! Thunk! Thunk!

John threw himself into a chair and folded his hands as if praying. "No God!" But they were beyond prayer.

Thunk! Thunk! Thunk!

Petr sprang outside and snapped off the arrows and flung them towards the creek. Two blazed on the roof and there was no time. He raced inside and slammed the door.

Run? No, they want us to run!

"Papa, cap the rifle! Burning arrows, the cabin's on fire!"

Smoke drifted into the room. John's voice was quavery high: "Is it *him?*"

Petr lunged at the mantle grabbing the Hawken buffalo gun. John got the powder horn and sack of half-inch balls and the cap box, clamping everything tight to his chest. John was breathing hard, shocked, his forehead arched like slash-grain wood.

Petr said, "It's a scare, that's all. He wouldn't he kill us?"

John flung the ammunition onto the floor. "No—it's real. Watch what I do now." He picked up the powder horn and pulled the cork with his teeth and poured two-seconds worth of powder into the rifle. With his jackknife he cut a cloth patch and placed it—and a lead ball—onto the end of the upraised barrel and thumbed it in.

"He wants you," John said. "This is it." Ram-rodding the ball down the barrel, John said, "The ball goes *tight* on the powder." He glanced out the window. "I ever tell you how your grandpa Holgar filled our heads with Viking stories?"

"Papa, this is crazy!"

John slipped a firing cap onto the nipple where the hammer would strike powder. He raised the hammer to half-cock and pulled his clay pipe from his pocket, poking it upside down in his mouth. He nodded closing his eyes. "Light my pipe, son. Watch me work."

Petr struck a match into the downturned pipe. John sucked in draughts of smoke.

"Never forget I was your father." He took a deep drag. "Now then—the first one's the hardest." He leaned the heavy barrel against the window frame. He snicked the hammer to full cock. He pulled the back trigger that would make the forward trigger go off at a touch.

John sang softly, "Come, my comets, come, come come—come my beauties of light. Now blow the stars from off your helms returning you to *night*."

The barrel roared and fifty yards away a man screamed. That lantern stopped but four others came bouncing along on the run, coming fast.

John sounded tired. "Load, son, your hands are quicker than mine. You'll learn all there is to know about killing in a hell-made minute." Petr wanted to say he didn't know if he could but John turned away and Petr heard vomiting and then came the sour-milk smell.

Petr reloaded glancing out the window. Magically, lanterns appeared and disappeared. His hands moved mechanically. You put the powder in? Or is the ball jammed in the barrel like a dead plug, no way to get out? Yes, he put the powder in. Move! How much—enough to burst the barrel? And where was his fine repeating rifle? Hidden under a tree, forgotten through all these days of trouble. He glanced out again.

The bouncing lights spread into the barnyard.

"They're coming," Petr said, surprised at his own calmness.

Out in the yard the wounded man screamed, "Gawd…help me!"

John began sighing wildly for breath. Petr stuck the rifle out the window, aiming at the closest man. He curled his finger tight around the trigger. It froze. He felt disbelief.

"Can't…do it?" Then realizing he had squeezed the back-trigger. John eased the rifle away from him, nudging him aside. "Don't do it, son. It's so dirty. They should never have come." Two arrows hit either side of the window—*thunk! thunk!* John crawled to the other window. "I should not have threatened him. He cannot stand the truth."

John sighted—paused—and the Hawken roared again.

A man yelped but didn't go down, cursed and ran away. Two down, three to go, Petr thought, scanning the darkness. Flames crackled on the roof. But the wounded man returned carrying a long slender box. The rain of arrows stopped and there was loud arguing.

"Help me with this, let's get that bastard!" A big voice roared back: "JUST SHUT-UP!"

Petr recognized the first man as the miner he had knocked-out. The big voice was definitely King, definitely close by—at the work shed. There was long silence. Then—

Flat cracking rifle-fire opened up. Three rifles. Lead bees hummed into the windows smacking the walls. Petr flattened onto the floor and John crouched below the window, cursing.

"We're in for a hailstorm of lead now."

Shots came in very fast. Repeating rifles.

Petr was amazed at the destruction. The cabin filled with flying spittle of wood, curtains danced, bottle ships exploded crashing to the floor. The frying pan clanged spewing food. The ricochet hit Petr in the leg like a hot poker, making him gasp.

John screamed at the window, "I see you, Gunnar, you dirty devil!"

Petr said, "They want us to run."

"We can't! We gotta knock them from their game!"

John fired and Petr loaded. Killing was extreme. Killing happened for an extreme reason. What was it? Why was John such a threat to Gunnar?

King's big voice yelled from the shed: "Come out, John. We won't hurt the boy."

John grimaced and tears welled from his eyes. "Load that rifle and say you love me. That's all was ever going on here."

Petr gripped John's arms. "We've got to—" He stood and ran to the door. "I'll stop this!"

John reached out a second too late, "Petr!"

Petr Valory flung the door open and stepped into the yard.

The yard was lit-up by a dozen arrows stuck in the ground like blazing torches. Heat from the flames crinkled his hair. He felt sharp wolves-eyes cutting into him. He squinted and took a deep breath, waiting for the stunning blow that would end it all. Unseen rifles felt like hot spikes probing his chest. His heart hammering, he called out, "Don't shoot."

Remembering a dead rabbit he found in the snow, eyes popped out like red buttons, guts stringing from its rear, as if it had exploded from fear. He was afraid like that right now, but he was mad too. Speak now or forever hold your peace. Speak the deadly wedding.

His voice commanded, "Let John go. He'll go back to Pennsylvania." He waited a long moment, listening. Far off like a distant theater, Gold Nation snapped, banged and laughed.

He had only one card to play, but it was a big one.

"I'll show you the mine. I know you don't believe me but just give me one more day. You'll see it's big. You'll buy your hundred cannons. Just let John go."

King couldn't refuse that, could he? The man was hungry for cannons.

A hammer clicked nearby and Petr closed his eyes, then a voice surprisingly close.

"Don't move, son." Another voice grumbled, "That old bastard shot me like a dog!"

Petr opened his eyes and spoke the magic words. "I'll partner-up with you, Dain King. Do anything you say. John didn't mean any of this." But Petr could *not* see the terrible thing.

John stood behind him with the Hawken rifle.

A pair of shadows moved across the yard stealthy as wolves, then became men with rifles. Two more fanned to either side forming a killing triangle. Petr's legs turned to jelly and he guessed his shaking legs meant he was a coward.

Then came the angry voice of Rutherford Gragg, "Plan's gone to hell. Shall I shoot?"

Gragg was leaning across the chopping block, his shoulder smeared red, aiming a rifle.

King strode forward pointing an antique-looking musket, an old Indian trade gun, his voice commanding, "We got a deal: Petr stays and John goes."

Then something bad happened.

Suddenly John leaped in front of Petr, protecting his body, and brandishing the Hawken, pointing it at King. "He's my son! You can't have him!"

Petr began pulling him backward when the rifle by the stump boomed.

Father and son were swept off their feet by a smashing hammer of lead.

Another explosion rang hard, like breaking metal, all wrong. A man cried out in pain.

Someone yelled, "PETR!" But he couldn't move, couldn't breathe. Lightning had struck his heart and John lay sprawled across him. The world went gray and then black.

3

King watched a fan of blood spread across John's shirt. He rolled him off. There—a seeping hole in Petr's chest, a hole directly over the heart. King sighed heavily. He had seen death before. No taking it back. He pointed the Indian musket at John's chest and sighed again.

"It all ends so badly." The musket roared and John jerked. "Now, that is for sure."

Petr's eyes were sprung wide, dull looking, obviously seeing nothing.

King sighed again. He flung the old Indian trade musket away, disgusted. Then he walked over to Gragg. Something very wrong with Gragg: jaw gone; red strings hanging down where his teeth had been. King cursed him. "You damn fool. You forgot to pack the rifle cylinders with grease." The cylinders had chain-fired and the rifle lay in pieces. The man with no jaw made mewling, keening noises.

King shook his head, "Killed my brother and my son with one

shot. Why did you do that?" Shaking with rage, holding his big pistol to Gragg's head, but he didn't fire.

Tiger and Pigsley approached slowly from either side, rifles ready. Rubel was not with them.

King yelled, "No more shooting! Now we make the Bloody Eagle fly!" Signaling to his lieutenants who looked startled and uncomprehending, King ordered, "God damn you! Stretch him on that stump."

Tiger and Pigsley pinned Gragg's arms back. He was a bloody horror to look at.

King went to the box from which he had drawn the arrows. He returned with a sinister axe, tarnished silver, something from a different age of mankind, very old, a Viking war axe gleaming in the firelight.

King yelled madly, "Behold the axe of god!"

Gragg was losing blood fast from his severed jaw. His body began to shake.

King pulled out a small whetstone and made smooth strokes, brightening the axe like flame, shrieking like a woman singing a single brilliant note. Gragg's eyes glazed into circles of horror as King balanced the axe on his chest, his voice a hoarse whisper.

"Gragg, you killed my boy."

Sliding the blade along the sweat-soaked shirt, buttons popped revealing a boxy, bony chest. Gragg blinked rapidly. Explain—he could explain—but he had no mouth.

King yelled, *"Go to hell!"*

He swung the blade—again-again-again—and the chest split in two. Suddenly King gripped deep inside the gore of broken bones and winged his elbows out—

Pulling the chest apart there was an ungodly gurgling scream as King jumped back in a triumph of blood spraying joy, yelling, "Behold the bloody eagle *fly!*"

Petr's eyes were frozen, but he saw everything, a scene from a nightmare.

The obscenity on Gragg's chest rose and fell: red bladders, pumping lungs, beating like wings. Gragg's eyes rolled whitely, and he died.

Blood formed two dark pools around him. Tiger and Pigsley drew closer to view the gruesome wreckage of "The Bloody Eagle".

A man with his lungs pulled out was an unforgettable sight.

4

Petr couldn't *stop* seeing. King was doing something unimaginable, a scene from Hell. Maybe this *was* Hell because the flames and heat sure felt like it.

His chest and his right hand burned; a hole in his chest and hand? Why? He couldn't think why. Blackbirds had begun flapping inside his head, and he was weak and nauseous, and he was trying not to vomit. *Where are you Papa?*

John Valory was on his back, blood spurting from his chest, big man standing over him saying words that made no sense."Sahtan's hell is finished." What the big man did next was also unimaginable. He pushed two arrows into John's chest. Then he pulled a long knife from his belt and made a long slashing cut on John's right thigh.

Petr knew that's how Indian's marked their victims. He tried to scream but instead passed out again.

5

Jack Gorgius Frazier was gripping the tail of his little burro towing him up the ridge that divided Gold Nation from his big lake he called *Loch Loong*. Once to the top, he heard gunshots and yelling celebrations. The burro was carrying a barleybag, a gallon jug of whiskey, two empty kegs, a rifle, a pannier with clothes—and her master's bagpipe. Big Jack was exhausted because he was six-foot-four and weighed nearly three hundred pounds.

Sunset painted the world red and he felt he had just enough time to reach the celebration before pitch dark. More gunshots sounded like a man snapping a newspaper. But these were coming from the Valoryvale two miles below to the east. How could that be? They wouldn't be celebrating there. He turned east and saw the Valoryvale.

A bonfire of witch's hair was blazing to the sky. Now came rapid shooting.

"Aihh God...the Valorys are on fire...and oonder fire!"

He gripped the burro's nose looking into big dark eyes. He spoke a deep highland brogue.

"Those sad men would'na be celebrating. Something's wroong there, Tamsen. Can you make it? The Valory's are burning down. Lord, that canna be!"

He pulled the rope and dainty hooves clattered in a tight circle, reversing her to southeast, away from Gold Nation. Tamsen butted him in the belly but it did no good.

"Little clootie! No nonsense now. Shake a leg, little wife."

They returned to the big blue lake that reminded him of the lochs of the Inbhir-Mis, so far away. From there he followed the stream that led for an hour of walking to Valoryvale.

His strong *taisch* was that he was needed badly and also that he was a wee bit late.

6

In a dream, John was rowing a silver boat talking about Gunnar. *Old man Holgar was easy on me, but hard on Gunnar; I think it made Gunnar snap.* The boat retreating now from Petr: *Remember I always loved you, my dear son. I was always your pa.* John rowed away but after a minute he stopped and stood. Shining holes in his chest poured out silver light. He waved goodbye, and he was crying. *Every ting is gone...all gone!* The boat rising. But something—a silver chain—was holding it back. It tied him to the ground.

Petr wanted to wave goodbye but couldn't. His heart was barely beating. It felt like a damp sponge cover with rags, stuffed inside his chest.

And suddenly he was lifted up by someone with great strength.

The big man carried him away from the smoke and heat and laid him on the ground and checked his pulse and Petr heard him swear under his breath, strange guttural words.

7

Such weak pulse was hopeless, his skin cool as wax, his eyes like dead bees. King had seen death many times. Such big plans for you! How can it be all over?

Best for my son to have a Viking's funeral.

Tiger and Pigsley closed in to stare at the boy and he whirled on them. "Get away from me!" They backed off. He yelled after them, "Carry John twenty feet, don't drag him. Then make some footprints, barefoot. Then drag Gragg and Rubel out of here."

Rubel gut-shot by John, was now dead.

"What should we *do* with their bodies?" asked Pigsley.

"You notice all the deep holes around Gold Nation? Use one."

Gragg's stupidity killed his son. He wished he hadn't killed Gragg so quickly. He wanted to kill him again and again, over and over, hacking, burning—then impale him on a stake.

But it was all over. Time to take care of my son's body.

8

Petr was aware of his surroundings, but couldn't move. The big man carried him downhill and laid him on hard gravel. Strong hands tilted his head sideways making a tear drain down his cheek, pooling against his nose. He took one slow shallow breath, with no strong urge to take another. Sleep now. Good. He was falling asleep. He heard faint, ringing noises. Probably just the brain *not* filled with the *busyness* of living. He felt something cold on his face.

Now he understood, now he identified the sound. King had carried him down to the creek. The big man was carefully washing Petr's face and hands and feet. King sighed heavily and said nothing and then combed Petr's hair gently to the sides, parting it in the middle.

The tenderness surprised him.

But it no longer really mattered. If you were dead nothing mattered.

Petr inventoried his body like a store clerk checking shelves. He was faintly amused for still wanting to do this as most of his hardware seemed crated for shipping. Head to toe wasn't much to take stock of. Numb, a faint heartbeat, he had a strange feeling of dreamy peacefulness like going to sleep.

Death was sad, but not so bad. Why did people fear it?

The big man carried him uphill again and he sounded childishly angry.

"We would have *ruled* together! Did you know my plans for you?" He rambled about things that didn't make much sense or any difference to Petr. Must have him confused for someone else, he sounded so pained. Petr wished he could tell him so he wouldn't be so distraught. Then the man spoke harshly. He said, "Now the funeral."

Petr was lifted powerfully and his arms dangled like broken wings. Air gushed into his lungs. Oxygen sparkled his eyes. Tears drained, vision cleared, smooth as lake water. For the first time he noticed the moon gazing down on him: the great moon-watch, the great timekeeper trapped in a golden ball, the face of eternity smiling down on all. For just one moment he knew.

The moon rules us all.

He saw where the big man was taking him—back to the cabin. It was still on fire and hot as an oven.

Petr's head swung so close to the burning door jamb that his eyebrows singed, he felt them crinkle. Then enter a smoky orange theater of dancing flames. Sap drooling, flames dripping from rafters steady as yellow heartbeats. Hard to believe the Valory abode, in its death, could produce so much light. Purple drapes dripping fire wouldn't last another minute. The roof sounded as if dirt clods were pelting down on it.

Petr was carefully lowered onto the kitchen table.

The short drop caused another sharp intake of breath, wonderful cedar smell of sharpened pencils, the shingles burning. The good smells reminded him of Magya baking cakes and bread, smells associated with love. Her beautiful Bible somewhere burning with all the Valory names: Holgar. Martine. Gunnar. John. Magya. Petr. Annabel—all burning together. And a big blue Shakespeare book he had loved, that too would be no more, would end in flames. But did it matter? He no longer belonged to this world.

For some reason the ringing subsided in his head and he could hear again. There was fierce crackling on the roof. Pillows of heat pressed his face like a smothering of warm feathers. Yes, he could *feel* his face again, if that mattered. Papa's work was burning up, that caused a sharp twinge of regret. For some reason he could see John rowing his shining boat down the valley not very far away. Next (and now he realized it was a vision) Magya was in a stagecoach crossing wide yellow prairies and she looked very angry. But death gave him an even greater wonder: he saw Annabel was in a cave with holes of light pouring from a ceiling.

She was still alive.

That comfort made him want to live. He tried to talk: *Don't kill me, Viking father. Don't give me Viking funeral, I'm alive. I can't die; I have to find her!* But nothing came out.

The big man made a crazy laugh. "You never *knew* the life I could give you! We Vikings returned to set things right, to take America back for warriors. Now death steals you away from me. Now take the last part: All Vikings end in flames!"

Petr willed himself to move but again nothing happened. His mind screamed but nothing came out.

King tilted Petr's chin into a proud attitude; folded his limp hands together on his chest. The big man hugged him, kissed his cheeks, and shuddered giving an anguished look of sorrow and then brushed Petr's eyes closed. "All done now," he said. "Return to the sky on wings of flame!" And then he left.

Petr was left alone in the burning cabin. The Valoryvale and all it meant, was burning up, and it was just too bad.

9

Jack began towing Tamsen down the valley—because now she smelled smoke and she didn't want to go. He was wheezing badly by the time he saw the big bonfire in the central V of the valley that was indeed the Valory cabin burning down. He fired his rifle into the sky and he was furious. "Fly ya madmen from me! Ah plug my whinger in'ta yoor mirkhearts!"

He reloaded his rifle and holstered it on the burro. Then he took up his pride and joy—his bagpipe. Biting the blowhole he marched forward blatting a skirling pibroch tune.

He took a deep roaring breath, "Harrrh! Let banshees take no souls tonight!"

The last half mile Jack's war music preceded him, along with Tamsen's bawling refrain, clearing the way spiritually. The terrible sight was plain now—

The Valory cabin was a carcass of leaping flames rising into the air.

"Tamsen, hurry up!" He tried dragging her but she had planted her hooves solidly.

Big Jack fell to his knees, sobbing. Tamsen was right. Why hurry? What had happened was over. He was winded, his heart pounding, lungs aching, mouth tasting like pennies on fire, he was blown. He had not run so far or fast since he was a nonny lad, remembering old Ian MacClain's hounds snapping at his boy-legs as he ran throwing stolen carrots at them. He had been a starving boy.

A moment later Tamsen passed by him. She towed Jack the rest of the way to the cabin. She was an unpredictable little wife.

10

Petr's funeral was eye-popping hot, a devil's den of leaping yellow flames. The walls held Papa's tiny ships sailing in blackened bottles on boiling seas. Papa's world was burning up.

Must save Papa's ships! Must get water! It was very important.

When the powderhorn exploded Petr jerked violently. He fell from the table onto the floor causing another big breath of air. Must get out right now! Suddenly he could move again.

He had no strength but he crawled on his hands and knees, out of the cabin—

His father's body lay in the yard. He glanced at it, didn't want to remember him that way.

He crawled to the drop-off above the creek where the earth grew cooler. Before he went down he glanced back at the cabin.

John was still hovering over the cabin, sitting in the shining boat, reading a shining book.

Petr whispered, "Come back...to the creek...dear father," gesturing for him to follow. John pointed a graceful finger into a great gold book and traced as he read. *Says here you become a famous man.* Then stepping from the boat he walked away west, his head bent, his movements somehow musical, and he was still reading.

"Wait for me," Petr whispered, "I want to go, too." He began weeping, "It's not fair."

Below him the creek sounded as always like water ringing quietly through hollow glass tubes. A cool breeze blew into his nostrils and for one moment he felt he glimpsed the mystery of man. *Man is fire and water commingling strangely.*

He heard a childish giggle, a rattling birdsong. *Hee-ee-eee!* Then a singsonging, *Petr cay-n't fi-nd me!* He rose on one elbow peering down at the stream and called, "Rocky?"

There! Dancing in dark water, a luminous, twisting, turning, phantasmagorical figment of a girl, her arms outstretched like waving fronds. *I see-eee yoo, Petr!*

"Hold still, Rocky, I'll get you."

She bubbled, gurgling slowly underwater, teeth and eyes—going under—smiling, trusting him to save her as her words gurgled: *H-gee, h-gee—water kelpie got me!*

"No!" He tumbled down a quick second and was slapped by cold brilliant water.

For a moment he was thrashing inside liquid ice, and then he swam.

A moment later his chest and arms grounded into a sandy shoal and he dragged himself half out of water. My God it was ice blue cold. But he was still alive. And of course Annabel wasn't there. Why would she be? When would this hellish fantasy end?

"God, I loved her! I loved them all! Why did you let them die?"

But was she dead? He lay down wishing cold water could wash away his heart.

11

The Scotsman lumbered towards the crackling, withering flames rising from the cabin's blackened carcass. A body lay sprawled in the yard. The burro halted fifty feet away, and then ran off kicking and braying, overcome by insane fear. John Valory—one leg crooked under him, a hand on his chest clutching two red arrows, his face frozen in horror— was an awful sight.

Big Jack stood helplessly over the body clenching his fists. He gazed into the blazing cabin and then back out at the yard. Where was the boy Petr? Hoping he was dead—not captured by Indians. A moment later he made a gory discovery out in the yard by the workshed—

A bloody chopping block like somebody had been beheaded. My God, what has happened here? He entered the shed. It was empty. Reluctantly he returned to the cabin.

Leading up to the cabin more dripping blood, and it led inside. *Don't go there.* But he had to. He took a deep breath, covered his mouth, and ducked inside.

Scanning quickly—he saw no bodies. The roof blazed, the loft would collapse any minute. He lowered himself beneath red waves of heat and stinging smoke and looked again. No *body* inside. A big black book sat on a rocking chair. He picked it up and ran out of the cabin. At least I saved something.

Outside, not knowing what to do, he carefully laid the book on

John's chest right below the arrows. Now for an awful thing—he dragged the body by the boots away from the yard and left it beside a nearby boulder. That big gray stone would be John's monument.

Jack sat still for a moment but he couldn't stand doing nothing and his mind was racing.

Go to the creek, get water, stop the flames. He ran to the drop-off, realizing: What was the point? He looked back at the cabin and said, "Canna get her out with a few hatfuls of water." Yes, but you must do *something.*

He muttered seldom-used oaths and turned away from the creek. He was fire-blinded to things in shadows. What he didn't see straight below him was a body lying in the shallows with water flowing over it. He walked back to the barnyard.

Hurrying into the gloomy barn, he ran his hands over dim shapes on the wall, found a peg-toothed rake, then trotted back to the cabin where he began scraping pine needles away from the perimeter. At least keep the Valory forest from burning down. After a few minutes of fierce heat he mopped his face and neck with his pocket rag, which came away soaked, and he discovered his face was hard as leather. He leaned forward on the rake, panting. He looked at the inert body of John Valory.

Poor old man. Dead eyes stared far off at a finger of smoke hurrying north like an accusing spirit—and Big Jack believed in signs and wonders. The smoke pointed at Gold Nation. Jack knelt beside the corpse.

"What happened, John? Who done you this way, man?" He brushed the dead eyes shut realizing what he had to do. The arrows had to come out. "Aihh, God."

He braced himself over the corpse as if to lift it by the belt. With a shuddering heave he pulled the stubborn arrows. It was worse than unhooking a fish. They held like thorns and made a grisly popping noise as the barbs jerked out with flecks of meat. The big mountain man bent over and threw-up trout supper—and then his trout lunch. Tamsen stood a good distance away.

Wiping his mouth, Jack went over to the burro and undid the

pack and found the big gallon jug. He drank head-walloping swallows of whiskey until tears streamed down his face. He set the jug down, sighed, and slapped his cheeks loudly, and then petted Tamsen's nose.

"Whew! Whiskey is my doctor. Tis the only way to get tru this life, little wife. Aih, how else do we do it?"

July had become a horrible month. Worse than June, when Petr came to him with the sad story of their lost women, now they were all gone. But was that true—was Petr Valory really gone? The lad so full of life; he could not imagine him dead. Move on! Find him!

He walked widening circles around the Valory freehold until he was panting like a dog, until he was certain the boy wasn't within crawling distance. Maybe he had escaped. Maybe he was away when the Indians struck.

Jack returned to the body and stood over it protectively. He knew what he had to do. Have to hold a vigil tonight. He took a deep breath and held it, calming himself. Then he saw something awful, it made him scramble back, screaming.

John Valory raised his head.

Silver hair lifted from the ground, and then fell stiffly back—and didn't move again.

"Holy Mother Mary protect me!" He crawled to the burro, recovered the jug, and draped his arm across the animal for support. He drank until his eyes bulged. Then he stood panting, gasping, "Man, get a grip a yourself!" Remembering terrible things of war, dead bodies at Cerro Gordo—moving. What else could dead bodies do?

Fling an arm. Kick the feet. Another memorable corpse turned its head slowly looking at Jack—hours after death. They were deadman's tricks.

He took another long, burning drink. Ghosts in the air, goblins in the forest, kelpies under water, Jack believed in them all. He drank whiskey and waited. When nothing happened, he cradled the jug like a baby and trudged back to the body.

He picked up the arrows, Pah Ute for sure, points like black claws of a small bear, cruel, beautiful little things. The authorities would want to see them. A regiment would get after this. But how could it be Pah Utes? He knew them very well. They were peaceful Indians far across the hot Nevada floor. They came here to trade with the local Indians, the Mahdoos. They did some deer hunting, a little gambling, fishing and feasting. Big Jack sighed heavily and took another solid wallop of whiskey. *Man o man!*

Pah Utes would'na do anything like this!—unless terribly provoked. He sounded a long loud, "Haa-ooohh," which was his thinking sound.

He spoke to the burro. "Tamsen, we must watch all night. We must hold a vigil."

Cropping nearby grass, she brayed when she heard her name. Big Jack knew she wanted her rubdown and barley. He walked over and fondly squeezed her long ears. "You doon yoor part today. Let's get yoor little packee off. My little brindle bride, my love-sick slave."

The familiar hand and thumping laugh was a soothing drum easing weariness from her wide back. She was a jenny ass, tall as she was long, like a fat sullen deer, a comically small beast of burden for such a big man. But surprisingly strong—she would one day save his life.

Jack Gorgius Frazier put a barley bag on her tan snout, and then rubbed her round body. "My tan-face Tamsen. You eat no matter what, does nothing bother you?" Drying her sweat with a rag, his voice unusually subdued, "What goes into your body, that's the truth of your life, that's your real religion, whether 'tis pure—or something brutal."

He rubbed her rough forehead. "We hold a wake for poor old John Valory. Thank lord his wife and cubs are not here. What a terrible ending for a man."

Jack had witnesses hundreds of such bloody endings in Mexico. Now he hungered for peace and quiet with plenty of food—maybe even a real wife instead of a donkey. But he had little hope for such a hopeful future. He was getting old. He was thirty-five.

He sat on the big boulder by the corpse gazing out at the dark forest. Probably very near midnight. He hoped he didn't see a bogle. If the Soul-eater was trumpeting around tonight—It—would strike at the witching hours past midnight.

Suddenly the cabin roof collapsed in a wracking, crashing shower of sparks. Jack jumped back wildly looking around. All of the forest was gunpowder black.

An hour later the cabin walls flamed out and ember eyes glowed at him from the ruin. Nothing a man could do—but this. He fetched his bagpipe, and then slouching against the boulder, he wailed and blatted noisily, he blew every piper's tune he knew. Then he drank.

Then he made mournful piping dirges that were such good ones he cried, knowing he'd never remember them in the morning. Then he drank.

He heard a long howl, the Ancient Animal, keening for flesh in the night.

"Keep yoor distance, Black Donald, ya ald clootie, this soul you shall not have!"

✖✖

At dawn Jack stared red-eyed and fierce, throat and tongue parched stiff, whiskey gone, mouth sour, the cabin smoldering gravely, and the vigilante himself stiff as the corpse he was guarding. Beyond midnight (by the stars he guessed 3 A.M.) he had gone into a staring trance peering into the infinity of space. John, if he was meant for it, was certainly halfway to Heaven by now. As first rays of dawn pierced his bloodshot eyes, Big Jack collapsed onto his windbag making it sigh.

"Aihh God, I'm too auld for all this. Be blethering like a new-bairn babe when I wakie."

Then he slumped over his bagpipe and slept like a dead man for five hours.

12

The night lasted a thousand years as the icy Sierra stream rushed over his life reducing his heart to a delicately beating wing. But another life-saving effect had occurred. The cold shrank the bullet hole above his heart to the size of a pea, stopping the flow of blood. Before he passed out he took a last look at the sky and instantly regretted it.

Impossibly, the stars were *black* dots, the sky a silver sheet, and not only that—

From one of the distant black stars a pale strand of silver descended directly *to him*. He closed his eyes and began dreaming the stream had reversed itself, flowing uphill into the mountain of The Luminah where it was warm, warm, warm. He needed to imagine that—because he was freezing to death in the stream. Everything he looked at was all silver, the color of reflection: memory, mirrors, old photographs, death.

He saw his history as a baby born to an Indian woman and the date was: June 12, 1835, his birthday. Two old people raised the baby (but only for a few months) and then a handsome couple he recognized as younger versions of John and Magya, took him in—where the boy grew quickly, and he loved the nearby woods, and he loved books. When he was seven, a little sister named Annabel joined them and he loved her more than sunshine. He sped through his young life until he came to the lake and the Indian—*and he saw a red spirit bolting into him*. The vision ended, he slept, and then slowly it began again, but a very different life.

This time he was a knight in polished silver armor swinging a spiked iron ball on a chain, attacking a knight in dark red armor, denting him with terrific clanging blows. The dream ended abruptly; and he became a handsome red-haired youth in a small room carving glorious gold figurines, a boy prodigy, a gold master with terrible temper. His name was Benvenuto Cellini.

Next he saw a huge windmill perched at the edge of a windy lake and inside the mill a short, thick-shouldered man scooped grain into the path of a massive grinding wheel. He smoked a small white pipe and was smiling even though his back was throbbing with pain as if hit repeatedly by an iron ball.

When he dreamed again he saw a young woman arranging red flowers in a white vase. She was black-haired, solemn, and very particular about the placing of the flowers because her sweetheart had gone to war and would return any day now. But the flowers wilted and she replaced them again and again—for forty years. And she died alone.

Next he saw endless sand with nothing beyond it. Here the golden falcon flew like magic from his body, leading to his dream of drowning in the Nile. He knew that was his first life—and he must never return to it—never destroy his own life again.

Then all dreams ended.

13

Jack heard hemp rope sawing back and forth through a wooden crate— then realized he was snoring. A pair of deer listened, and resumed dipping their black muzzles into the creek.

When he sat up, they ran away.

He stretched and groaned, and saw the smoking cabin, and John Valory's wax-like body, plain in the ten o'clock sun. Time to bury that poor man. He got a shovel from the barn and spent the next hour digging a hole beside the boulder until sweat ran down his face.

After lowering John Valory into the ground, he picked up the big Bible he had save from the cabin—the Valory family Bible. He held it over the body as he spoke.

"Lord, here lies a good man, laying his broken bones down. Give him good rest, Lord." He hugged the Bible to his chest in silence. What to do with it? He loaded it into a pannier bag on the burro. Then he buried John with earth and then stacked rocks on top until he had a foot-high mound. Under a cairn of stones no wolves can get you. Best he could do.

All right, that was that. He staggered towards the creek thinking how good it would be to flop down into that cold water. At the drop-off he saw something awful, and he groaned.

Another corpse shining in the morning sun, a body white as marble lying in the water—it was the boy. "Oh my lordy-lord: Please no more of this."

14

He draped the cold boy onto Tamsen's back and lashed him down and covered him with a poncho. He was still alive and it would be a muckle job getting him up to Long Lake. He was lively as a fish, jerking in his sleep, talking gibberish: mirael and horemebb and some such blather. How to keep the boy from slipping all agley and leading the burro at the same time? Would he waken with a broken brain? That seemed most likely.

The trip was two long hours but they made steady progress up the steep valley.

Big Jack ached as if he had wimpled up a stone-clogged creek all day. Finally they came to the high gray cliff that walled the high-side of his lake. Here was blue water much like a Scottish loch, deep and cold, full of sweet and lordly trout. Here was his wee cabin beneath the towering Sierra cliffs.

Inside the cabin Jack placed Petr on a soft rabbit robe and then got the fireplace crackling hot. The lad's breathing was steady now, and the tom-tom of the heart beating strong and true. This swankie lad had a chance. But how long before he woke up? And what to tell him?

Was it Indians? Was it a bushwhacked claim? Maybe the miners wanted to believe it was Indians. Redskins were handy for that. If Petr Valory knew everything that happened (and Big Jack supposed he did) he might not want to wake up at all. When he does coom roaring up, how is auld Jack going to keep him from going unco wild? More importantly, What to do now to keep the boy alive?

He must keep a chilled body warm.

Big Jack whispered, "Lordy. He looks just like a prince."

Petr opened his eyes, and said: "Mirael...Mahrire...Horemheb." Then lay still again.

Jack clutched his beard, wondering what such nonsense meant. Maybe the brains were scrambled. Maybe it would be better if this one just faded away and died.

CHAPTER NINE

ANNABEL'S SIXTEEN DAYS

1

She was dead when she found it. But it saved her life. It was a survival cave. Whoever made it had set up for a long siege underground. What it *was* was a roomful of the same tasty nut-stuff, this time in sealed clay pots; also many pots of deer jerky, enough for an army, which was to say, a tribe. Also there was dripping water, a seep, much fresher than that first one. Due to her weakness, this cave had taken much time to discover. Rather, many periods of consciousness. One thing you realized underground: Time didn't exist down here—only consciousness and unconsciousness.

She wasn't mad at her body. She had walked until muscles turned into jelly and then crawled on her knees until they became burning knobs. She guessed this had taken four days, but no sure way to tell. The estimate was based entirely on the way her body *felt*. Petr told her you could live five days without food and water. Then you died. Thirst was the worst part. The body did not function after five days without water. Her throat felt like a stick of chalk had been used to draw four coarse lines inside it—and was beginning a fifth.

She wasn't mad at her mind. Why wasn't she skunk-bit crazy after so much total blackness? The Time-of-Gloom had been a total eclipse of the brain. How had she survived? Simple. She repeated her mantra over and over: *I am love. I cannot be hurt. I am love.* Then aloud, and more sensibly, she had repeated: "This is what it's like to be blind. I'm a blind girl."

That flat statement had really helped her survive mentally. The discovery of the cave meant she would survive and it also meant she was close to a way *out*.

And the first thing that really kind of perked her up (in a snailish sort of way) was, after she felt she just couldn't go on, there was a faint baby whisper of breeze. *Fresh air!* Crawl, worm, shrug herself forward, whipping her rubber-noodle-body with a cat-o-nine tails of will.

Telling herself: Where there's a breeze, there's a world. Keep going!

About twenty thousand miles later, she smelled faint pine-smell, then loamy smell, welling from the left hand side (her good hand), a loaminess *not* to explore. What was that, pinesap fertilizer? Maybe I've finally cracked up.

Shrugging forward, she emerged through an opening she felt was a hollow room. She *felt* big empty space, a little frightening after what seemed like years of confinement in a worm tube. She crawled forward into moving air, staying close to the wall for security because the floor slanted way to the right, to some unknown depth. Bearing to the left because that was the hand with skin left on it, feeling her way along until she actually *smelled* water.

This time it wasn't just *ploinking* down, it was actually *drizzling* into a fresh pool of water from some unknown source. The pool was a foot wide, six inches deep, and pleasantly cool. She drank slowly, dipping and licking her fingers. She waited a minute then tried a few more rusty swallows. When her stomach gurgled (and nothing worse), she took a few more gulps. It was delicious mountain water.

What she really wanted was to stick her face into the pool and glurp like a horse. But she'd learned a thing or two about restraint in her fine old age.

Next she slept for what seemed like three thousand years.

When she awakened, she actually had to pee. Annabel giggled because this hadn't happened for a really long *while*.

Now she recommenced her slow exploration around the perimeter of the hollow space, her new world.

Creeping like an inchworm (a wounded one) putting an arm out, then humping her legs forward. About ten years later she came upon a rounded shape and knew by running her fingers around it, what it was: a clay jar, capped. She opened it and found ground up pinenuts. The next jar contained the intoxicating aroma of dried meat. She didn't have enough strength to chew on meat jerky, although she might have sucked it, or eventually figured out it needed soaking.

She ate a single handful of nutmeal and awaited her stomach's approval.

God in a bottle! Never had she felt so vitally the transforming of food into strength igniting her body with a spark of energy. If in her previous life as a little girl in the green world, her normal bounty of vitality was ten sparks, and if in the long blackspell of the tunnel her strength had guttered down to a single spark (maybe even a half-spark) she now felt: Two sparks, maybe even three!

She rested, protecting her flicker of energy like a cave-girl kindling a tiny fire. The food jug was small, the size of a nail keg but not nearly as heavy, because *somebody* had cradled it into this hollow cave. Carefully stretching her hand into the darkness she felt another clay roundness and then another—twenty jars. The last one startled her. It was open—and half empty.

She called out, "Anybody here?" No answer. Annabel laughed and began feeling pink waves of joy rising from her tummy to her fingertips. She whispered, "Mine, all mine."

Protectively she cradled the god-bottle into herself and log-rolled back to the waterpool. The first time she made the trip the distance was vast and listless. Now because it was a known thing, and because she counted, it was a short happy journey of thirty-two seconds. If ever she got back on her feet, she reckoned the distance between the jars and the water pool would be a careless stroll of ten seconds. The expression, Back on your feet, seemed enormously funny.

Reclining by the pool, Annabel slowly ate nutmeal and slowly drank water. Then she again slept soundly. Again she was awakened by her new peeing ritual. Realizing, you didn't know how important that was, until it stopped.

Thus began the rosy dawn of Annabel's first exploration of the Real Way Out.

It didn't begin quickly because, like a cat thrown down a well, she was deeply hurt. She had to think like a cat. The first order of business was lying around and restoring her dried-up body. The gurgle in her stomach, the food and water factories working cheerfully again, that was all. Gurgling meant she wasn't permanently damaged. Wait for the spark-factories to crank up four, maybe five sparks. Some while later she had very good news from the boiler room. She had her first golden moment.

A thing the girl of the green world had despised when it meant going out to some offal smelling outhouse. Whether Harrisburg or Valoryvale, little girls weren't allowed to poop in the woods like boys if even the rudest crapper was nearby. Wind, rain or shine, doing her business was unpleasant. Now it was her joy.

She rolled all the way back to the tube hole she had emerged from (several centuries ago) and poked her nose inside. It was sucking air just like a chimney. Momentarily she got the sensation that the mountain was alive—living, breathing alive—digesting things. That was so unpleasant she immediately stopped thinking it.

She rolled on because she had an urgent reason; rolling because, in the luxury of this roomy space, it was the least painful way to travel; because her hands and knees and legs were islands of throbbing pain that probably looked like red flippers. Good she couldn't see them right now because she might throw-up, a thing she could ill afford.

She found a spot far away from the food and water.

It felt like giving birth to a clay pigeon. It hurt, but she felt joy of a new mother. Proof she had survived the ordeal of darkness—and that she could go on surviving—if she chose. Surviving down in this black hole was a big deal. And she would need some sanitary engineering if she would stay here a while. The thought came to her forcefully. *No, don't be silly.*

She realized something that should have been obvious right away.

Many others had lived here before. A little exploring, a little sniffing, she could find their potty arrangements. Annabel sensed this had been a hidey-hole for twenty or thirty Indians. Why she knew it she didn't know. She just did. Women, children, old people had hidden here during attacks from other tribes, especially the white tribe. Then another really good realization—

I can't be that far underground!

But she would find that, sometimes, an inch is a mile.

Annabel rolled around like a crazy girl until she gained sensorial knowledge of every nook and cranny. She got the overall quality and layout of the place just like Petr would have done. The room wasn't very big. Nor was it round. Nor was it flat. Mostly it was a ravine with huge boulders roofing it over, making a lumpy ceiling. The long periphery ledge was scraped away by handwork, she was sure of that—that's where the jars sat on level lips. Ten jars of nuts. Ten jars of jerky. Debris from this work had been kicked down to fill the V of the ravine. Here the Indians had made a central floor; a living room and sleeping place. She found black-ended sticks that had been torches. But no cooking fires. This was a survival room. Yes indeed.

She had food and water galore. Now find the tribe's squatting place.

Following her nose (now working superbly) she found a faint pine scent, and beneath it, very faint, loamy earthen smell. This came from the tube hole out of which she had emerged. The strong breeze had stopped. Why was that? For another thing—and this was really crazy—she thought she could almost see. Like the slate blackness was turning bottom-of-the-ocean gray. She decided to ignore this. Possibly the gold glare in her head was healing slightly. Never mind. Explore the piney loamy place.

She found it easily and remembered passing it on her way to the survival cave. It was an offshoot cave on the way back to The Luminah. No thank you, very much.

She groped along until she felt a grotto where you could lean back against the wall and squat over a falling-away depression. Beside it was a trove of pine needles for clean up. Good work. The place she had passed because she had no use for it. Now something smelled a little too fresh, too recent. But she dismissed this idea as way too creepy.

Food, water, relief: these were the rewards of her first great exploration. But she was used up. Her sparks of energy were sapped. Returning to the water pool and nut jar, she drank, ate, and slept.

When she awoke, she got a nice shock. She could see again.

"My—goodness."

Five shafts of golden light pealed like music from the crude lumpen ceiling.

She washed her eyes, grateful it wasn't any brighter, not sure she could *take* full strength sunlight. It might knock her eyes out. After much blinking she realized what she was seeing.

Whispering, "I entered this cavern at nighttime of the real world. Now this is daytime of the real world. Sunshine leaks through these gaps in the boulders." And—

"And I am not very far underground!" She had almost ceased to believe sunshine still existed. But here was positive proof. "Daytime in the real world and I am nearly out."

But there was no time to savor her joy—she had awakened something.

A figure scrambled in the shadows then crouched in the dark, gathering things unto itself. It grunted, "Heya-hey!"

2

After the shock of realizing—this must be an Indian! (maybe a caretaker of sorts) Annabel managed to speak: "I'm sorry, sir, please don't run."

There was thrilling silence. Be still. Be gentle. This Indian person... will help you out.

A strange cadence, a hard guttural voice, "What are—*you? You—* rock girl?"

Annabel pointed behind her. "I got lost and came out...*here.* I didn't mean to...break *in.* I just need to—get *out.*"

Heavy silence. Then sudden energy. He turned away, small and quick, walking through three shafts of buttery light, flickering like a ghost.

Annabel got a ten-spark surge and chased after him, running for the first time in days, and falling, and running. He was digging at something and suddenly there was a huge burst of light, a hole in the cave. She screamed, "Please, let me out, sir!"

The little man whirled and his face was an eclipse of darkness, a bright halo all around. Annabel blinked and fought the urge to cover her nose. He didn't just stink—

He was skunk, garbage can, and month-old corpse, all rolled into one.

Growling at her, "*You* rock girl, *you* stay in mountain!" Shoving her backward with fierce easy power, she felt like a rag doll. She decided to stay away from him. The little man was dynamite. And she was down to about half a spark, she merely raised her head. Now as he crawled into the narrowing beam she saw his bow and quiver slung over his shoulders. Now he was—*Outside!* He grunted. "Huh." Then black rocks stoppered up the light.

He was outside! He had blocked up the hole! He had left her in darkness!

Annabel gave in to girlhood. For the first time in a long time, she cried.

Crying was good, yes it was. But was anything else good? She crawled into one of the big shafts of light and studied herself. Dirty scratchy hands, dirty raggy bloomers, dirty bloody knees, dirty slick-pink seashell ankles—the picture of a nasty peasant child who would eat rotten potatoes and make a toothless smile. "And steal gold moons that don't belong to her."

She reached into her pocket and got another shock. The big gold egg was gone.

Gone after all this?

Cold sickness spread out from her stomach inhabiting her completely with frogskinned despair, all of this suffering for nothing. She whispered as if the creepy Indian was still nearby.

"At least you still have the pocket watch...don't you?" Pulling out the Lover's Watch, holding it beneath a beam of sunlight, brushing off soggy flower petals, the blue enameled case radiating light from the center—from the Lovers—to the gold-rimmed bezel. The Lovers inhabited a perfectly-never-changing world, never growing old, always lovingly longing for each other. She kissed them, especially mushing her lips across the pale boy as she spoke to him.

"That's the way it always should be." She pushed the knob. It popped open. On the white face slender sunburst hands pointed to the twelve. She clicked the case shut and twisted the knob until it wound tight. She shook it and looked again. Time had stopped. She burst out angrily.

"Make time run, make more time! Must never lose lover's time, never, never!" She gazed at the Lovers. Wasn't it strange Mama owned such a thing? Lovers looking at each other reluctantly, afraid to touch, afraid to believe in love, afraid to believe in each other—so instead they harvested wheat. She opened the watch again. The gold hands poised at twelve, always midnight. Beads of water were *under* the glass. Oh. She saw.

It was going to be midnight for a very long time.

The only reason the watch had survived was because Annabel had sewn a small pocket for secret things just behind the big pouch. She turned the pouch inside out and found a mush of flowers that fell out in a yellow wad. She returned the watch to its secret pocket.

"If you would have put your gold egg in there you would not have lost it. If something is important, you must take the trouble to safeguard it. It is possible to have big losses in life." The first time she'd ever had that *thought*. Not just knowing it in her head, but in her flesh.

A staggering realization came: You can have serious losses that last forever.

3

She began counting days by the coming and going of the light, and time passed, real time. She drank, ate, did her sanitary business, and she healed. Each time the light appeared she placed a stone and she decided to make circles of seven stones for each week. The thought of weeks made her shudder. Yet she needed time to get well. At each stone-placing time she inspected herself. She was healing. Hands, elbows and ankles were slowly becoming smooth again.

After five stone-days she was running on ten sparks all day. Deer jerky was easier to digest the longer it soaked and, although she preferred nutmeal, the meat really boosted her energy. Then she got back her anger. She began yelling.

"I am love and I am pissed off!" Screaming at the blocked entrance, "No Indian can block me in a mountain, rock girl or not!" With a mallet-sized stone she attacked the pumpkin-shaped boulder clogging the entranceway. *Clack! Clack! Clack!* Didn't matter how long it took, she had plenty of food and water, which equaled time. "I'll pound my way out. And if that Indian comes back, I'll knock *him* out, too." Once she thought about it, she was a *rock girl*. She liked it. Yelling again, "I came out of a mountain! I *am* a rock girl!"

Of course she wasn't quite *out*.

Each day gave new strength; each day she attacked the stone door *harder*.

"Rocks cannot stop rock girl." Realizing: Papa and Petr called her Rocky, which had truly become her name.

More importantly: If that stinking Indian ever returns—she must be ready. Likely he would return for nutmeal and jerky when he got tired of eating dead skunks.

Beneath the second light-shaft, Annabel made a pile of rocks resembling a curled-up girl. Close enough anyway. She wondered if she could actually hit the Indian. After all, she didn't hate him. He was just some confused and superstition-filled savage who thought she was a rock spirit. Why wouldn't an Indian be crazy? How many years had they been chased, hunted, and killed? Even a girl heard about such things. Forced to run, forced to hide underground. Were caves such as this common? She supposed they were. Much as she loved Papa's sweet smelling log cabin, it could easily burn down. A stone fortress was a great idea. If she lived long enough, she'd build a stone house where no one could hurt her. She could stay hidden, and secret.

Indians kept lots of secrets because they had to. The smelly Indian probably had plenty of secrets. If she had to, she'd knock him out a little bit, even if it wasn't fair—if he came back.

4

By the seventh day, Annabel knew the Indian had placed four rocks between her and freedom. One plugged the narrow crevice. Three more formed a triangle atop the plug. She knew this because the plug lay shattered in crumbs at her feet leaving a triangular kiss of light where the three outer rocks converged. Now she geared herself mentally to spend all summer knock-knock-knocking on the rock, if that's what it took.

Her rockgirl body had cycles of weakness and strength with positive swings towards greater strength. She no longer felt like a girl, never wondered if she was pretty—or even if she was human. The mountain had molded her, squeezing her, extruding her into a new being.

A ring of seven stones sat in the far shaft of sunlight. One week in the survival cave. Any normal girl would feel helplessly depressed stuck underground for so long. Maybe even crazy. But she wasn't. She was healing and *gaining* every day, smiling. *Fortitude:* that was the word. The green world was a mere three stones away, the closest she had been in what was possibly ten days after leaving The Luminah. Just guessing but it felt right.

She found a smooth brown stone like a duck's egg. That would serve as a weapon.

A dozen times a day when she tired of hammering, she practiced crouching at the entrance and swooping down with her egg. Practice hitting swiftly but not too hard. No need to kill him. Then back to work widening the kiss of light. But she couldn't get a good swing at the narrow area and her fingers were getting a beating.

Two days short of another week she'd smashed all of her fingers and knuckles one way or another with glancing blows. She'd learned to work with her right hand until it ached, then her left, on and on. A smashed finger hurt. But what really hurt was smashing a smashed finger the *second* time. That throbbed so bad the pain traveled down her legs, coiled back into her stomach, and then rose up her throat to the verge of vomit.

When she hit her left thumb the *third* time, she crumpled into a fetal ball of agony, cradling the dying thumb in her bloomer pouch. She made stifled *"Mimmm...mmiiimmm"* noises—and tried not to vomit.

That's when he came back.

5

First she heard a grunt and then a boney rattle of rocks being rolled away. She flung herself against the side of the hole barely escaping the blast of light. She forgot her throbbing thumb. She planned for this. She knew what to do. He would enter on hands and knees. She palmed her special rock in a hand that felt big as a ball glove.

He called from outside the hole: "Heyah-hey! Little rock girl, you come out!"

All wrong. What was he trying to do? Why not come get me? She didn't move though the beautiful light called like a song. Play the waiting game—win the game.

Thirty seconds, then she heard him—no—she smelled him.

His dark blunt head poked inside the opening, below her knees, gazing stupidly at the circle of rocks and then at the pile of sleeping-girl-rocks. Annabel coiled to strike.

Suddenly his black leather face turned grinning up at her, crooning, "Heh-heh. Little rock girl trickster." He chortled, "Sabbah let you go home now. Okay?"

She gagged because of the dead-blood stink and forgot about hitting him. How did he know she was there? Did she stink, too? He backed away from her grinning like a dog. He was outside. The hole of light was open—*the way out!*

She didn't hesitate. She pocketed her rock and scrambled madly for the light.

She popped out from the hole like a newborn thing.

Right away discovering her eyes weren't healed, she stood blinking in piercing waves of radiance, stabbed by silver peaks, roaring green pines, and the smashing ball of the sun.

Stumbling shakily forward—*I'm out, out, out!*

When Sabbah grabbed her his stink engulfed her and she began struggling like a cat. Twisting, kicking, she caught gasping breaths and blinking sights of him. The odor was awful; the sight was worse. His face carved into crudely hacked little mouths—welts—his monstrous face only inches away from her, she tried to scream, but what came out was, "Nuhh!"

He chuckled. "Shush, little cub, soon you see."

Her cat strength evaporated until she was squirming like a worm on a hook. She blurted: "Petr will give you a hundred ponies! Don't hurt me!" Her fingers drifting to her pouch, to the goose-egg stone.

The Indian grinned. He was covered with cakes of black blood but he had big white teeth. Not a happy sight. She stuttered, "D-d-doh–"

"Shush-shush, I am Sabbah, your friend," She felt him hiccupping, laughing soundlessly. Then he stopped and her vision healed too quickly because now she saw the bloody brown yolks of eyes. Fiend's eyes laughing at her!

His voice darkened: "I take you where you see what happen to your family. Then you be ghost—like me."

Now!

Swinging with all her might, it was enough. He gasped and collapsed like a sack. Annabel scrambled free, screaming, "Eeeeeiiiiiii!"

Her mind crying, *Free! Free! Free!*

And then she ran like she was on fire.

6

As she scrambled through long manzanita mazes red-armed branches tore at her legs. Her mind whirled: Knocked him out, didn't I?

She ran twenty yards and then glanced back.

He was flat out cold, his brown body like a finger pointing where she had been held—for twelve days? She could see now the uniqueness of the location.

A big gray ravine capped-over with five boulders, big as barns, with shrubs filling in the cracks between them, the entrance was disguised by leaves and shadows. If you didn't know right where to look, you'd never notice the opening. The Indians were very good at hiding things.

She ran wildly away and knew when she was going to fall before she fell. And it was *nothing*. Sunlight world was easy world, wonderful world! Nothing mattered but distance and time between Annabel and the cave of the crazy Indian. Her eyes hurt like vinegar-filled cuts, but she laughed and she was crying because now she could see almost normally.

She followed the shortcut back to the Valoryvale. She passed the slab where the Indians had ground-up all of the nutmeal—thank God for Indians and nut-grinding. She passed the burnt smudges that had been their dwellings—what happened she would never know. They were called Mahdoos and they had saved her life. That's all she knew.

Oh God, I'm out! Yet she felt ashamed and sorry.

Mama would be worried sick. Annabel wanted to sit down and cry, but that would take time and she was in a hurry. Get home, Annabel Rochele. Tell Mama everything. Everything's okay.

She plunged through a dead manzanita thicket that looked like a maze of deerhorns, a twisting maze leading nowhere. She squatted down to rest. She was well hidden. Fresh wind kissed her face. Breathe cool clean air. *Out, out, out!* She would tell Petr how sorry she was. She practiced her speech.

"I didn't mean to be gone so long—how long was I gone?" And put on a pathetic peasant-face when you say: "If I wrecked your secret place I'm sorry. Beat me with the ugly stick every day. I'll even turn the other cheek." She would try for just the right mixture of dread, self-scorn, and stupefied vexation.

These thoughts were the last forward momentum of her childhood. The cave had changed her. She was something new—not quite human: A rock girl. She was *not* aware she was suffering from shock or that it was about to get much worse. Out of these feelings came an urgent inner command: Get home, girl. It's later than you think. The dark cave had given her the ability, not to see the future, but to *feel* it.

She escaped the manzanita maze. She could feel her way out. It was easy. It was nothing.

Ten minutes later she found familiar landmarks that meant she was nearing home.

Most prominent was a stately Jeffrey pine growing from the heart of a granite slab. Amazing tenacity for life! Be like that, always. Tenacious Annabel.

She staggered down the mountain the way a wounded soldierboy from a lost battle would wobble, head held high and proud, weary as hell, dying from a wound he couldn't reach, somewhere in the chest, a wound only urgent desire could overcome. Where did such strange feelings come from? But of course she was thinking of Petr.

Unknown to her, she was glimpsing her brother's future, preconceiving it, pre-acting it.

"Go home now, soldierboy. Run!"

Annabel broke into a shambling run down the mountain, sprinting a hundred steps, then resting, then running another hundred steps—just the way Petr would do.

Ten minutes later the pine-filled valley of the Valoryvale lay before her interspersed with sunny glades of wild greenery.

She gobbled mouthfuls of lettuce that Petr called miner's lettuce and topped it off with handfuls of grass, all sweet and good and full of life pouring into her greenstarved limbs.

Yes, I'll be all right now. Really believing it was true.

7

Thirty minutes later she stared at the ruined Valory cabin. It wore an expression of scalped surprise, the roof hacked off by black hatchets and walls worn by years of black wind. The tops of the windows were gone.

A few steps from the cabin there was a stone pile, the length of a man.

Unnatural stillness surrounded the cabin.

Her voice was small and hollow, "Mama? Papa? Petr?"

How to know? Dig it up? No! I would rather die than see the corpse of someone I love.

The burnt cabin was horror enough.

The charred wreck stood like a sacrificial animal gazing mutely at the forest; a stark reminder to future settlers of the dangers of wandering too far from the herd.

Hands at her sides, she entered quietly wanting to reach out, but there was nothing to reach. She skirted charcoal walls, avoiding touching anything, avoiding the old table with new black spots, not wanting to know.

She made a circle path of ash footsteps like small dropped photographs. Looking everywhere, everything she knew about the cabin was gone into self-absorbed silence, the quietness of ash and death.

Slowly she began to dance.

This was very important, she knew not why.

Stepping quickly, one two three! Sideways now, then turning, arms curving to the sky, a sweet pirouette. For just one moment—

Flames leaped around her, yellow ghostflames, and she in a white dress with garlands of green, and white flowers in her hair, and she was beautiful and she was dancing and she was going to marry soon, and she was the most beautiful woman in the world.

Someone moaned a steady moan coming from her throat.

She was automata, something she had once seen, a little wooden clock; a little wooden man came out and struck a bell. She smiled cheerily, bowing, saying "It's time... to go now...."

She left the cabin. She did not look back at the footsteps in the ash that would dissolve at the first rainfall. What horror next?—

Mama's garden overgrown with weeds, what did it mean? She walked among shriveled potatoes and carrots where she heard a little girl asking, "How much time has passed?" Tears came brimming now with memories of Papa making bottle boats and Mama reading Bible and Petr promising a red horse. All gone to ashes now.

Annabel began skipping. First lift one knee—hop!—slide the back-foot forward. Her knee-joint popped and she wondered, Have I lived... for this?

Picking imaginary flowers, dancing with an invisible lover, tears fell down her cheeks.

She had been brave in the cave and now what she really wanted was Miss Lulu to take over the job. Bravery was overrated and tiresome. What she needed, like her doll, was a new head—one without memories. She whispered, "Can you *empty* my head, please?"

Nothing seemed real. Numb now, unaware she was descending into fatal realms of shock, the image of the automata replayed helplessly swinging at the bell. But now the bell was gone. Now she belonged to the clockmaker of fate unable to escape mindless turnings of cogs and wheels. Walk the weedy path to the workshed and there was the chopping block—and more black spots. She poked her head into the toolshed and then the barn, not knowing why, calling in a childish voice.

"Mama?—Papa?—Petr?"

Her orbit ended back at the ruined cabin.

She thought, Sheepherders must have lived here long ago in some forgotten time.

She faced the pile of gray stones that certainly must be a grave, her voice barely a whisper, "Mama?—Papa?—Petr?"

Then she uttered the long hard cry she had been holding in during all the darkness. She cried until her filthy shirt was soaked with tears. Could tears wash you clean, wash away memory? We must try. She got an idea.

She staggered down to the creek and sat in cold water. Coldness of death, let me die, let me not remember anything. She urgently desired to blank everything out.

No mother. No father. No brother.

She sat drinking cold water—and crying—with some vague idea this might eventually wash the life out of her. She drank and drank, and cried and cried. The newspaper story would read: *Child cries to death after family dies in blaze!*

193

Thinking later that drinking too much water was the only reason the stinking Indian was able to sneak up on her like that.

He grabbed her and when she twisted she was looking into a face carved with hate.

He squeezed her neck until her world turned gray. Her mouth opened but nothing came out. And like a bubble of air, her last thought popped into her brain—

Thank...you...Sabbah.

CHAPTER TEN

TELL NO ONE

1

Dawn stretched a pink finger across Long Lake pointing to a cabin on a rocky shelf above the gray water. The cabin was big enough for a bed, a fireplace, a table and not much else. Moments later the pink light pierced into the front window.

Jack startled awake facing the body.

The boy, Petr Valory, lay stone still on the rabbit robe.

Third day. Did he make it? Touching his patient's neck, Jack felt thin rapid heartbeats, and then watched slow breaths so shallow they were hard to see. Jack shook his head. This one showed less signs of life than a trout in a pail. Would he ever gab or laugh again? He spoke softly to the body. "Save you, laddy, what will I have: a man or a potted tomato?"

Jack crawled to the fireplace and stirred the embers and then threw on a couple slats of pine and the fire reignited. If only the lad would reignite so easily.

Keep him warm. If Jack was sweating, that was about right. First week of July, that was easy. But was he doing the right thing? He thought back on his doctoring of the boy.

First he had pulled a lead ball from Petr's chest. It hadn't pierced the heart but it had *thumped* the heart. The hole would heal but the lad was in shock. His right hand had a strange fragment of metal, not a bullet, right in the palm. Jack had extracted it and wrapped the hand. These were the bare physical considerations. Now he went back to worrying about possibilities.

What if the lad never woke again—but went on living? Or woke but with somebody else's soul—or some-*thing* else's soul? *A clootie.* Chilling, fearful thoughts and Jack had slept poorly that first night, only in snatches, then startling awake, checking his patient.

The second day, Petr trembled, jerked, sweated, and occasionally cried out nonsense.

The second night was a vigil and Jack hadn't slept at all.

Now was the third day and his patient was a zombie. Maybe the boy *should* die. Was it wrong to think that? He felt ashamed to admit it. He looked at the pinetrees that were more of his doctoring work.

Jack had placed a bucket on either side of Petr Valory, holding warm water and a sapling pine tree, boiled to release their healing fragrance, glistening, and exuding a sugary scent. Petr Valory wasn't responding to the cure.

Jack clutched a pillow and crouched over the boy. He held the pillow out and then he froze, dripping, sweating like a butcher. The swankie lad was handsome as if charcoaled by an artist of great skill. But was his soul gone? Would it be better to do away with him?

He gibbered, "What monster moves you, Jack Frazier? Love—or fear?"

Looking into the dream-lost face, he felt love for its youthful beauty. But he feared the shadowfilled eyes might flare awake with hellish light. He pulled the pillow sharply back.

"I canna do it! Whotever you are, laddy, I canna take you. God must do it on his own." Imploring with raised hands, "God, ya havta take him back."

Jack felt a little better. No more thinking about murder. He threw the pillow aside and yawned. "Just rest yoor bones, lad. I have more doctor work to do." He put on his hat which looked like a beaver sitting on his head. He grabbed two tin pails. "Back in a jiffy."

The morning was fresh with sugar pine and the pleasing tang of woodsmoke. He hurried down the granite slab to the big blue lake and Tamsen followed like a five hundred pound dog. She was upset. He could tell by her morose silence. She was used to sleeping in the cabin but that was all over now.

Jack swept up two pails of crystal cold water and returned up the path.

The lad still hadn't moved. Jack whispered, "Having yoorself a fine big sleep, are ya now?" But three days out of the world was a long time, what did it mean?

Jack yawned loudly and poured water into a big copper boiler suspended over the fire. Then he grabbed his hatchet and went outside but there was an obstruction.

Tamsen brayed blocking the doorway and Jack had to push his way past her.

"Oh, my dear little wife, it's only a while longer! Can't have you trampling my patient."

He walked behind the cabin to a cluster of pine saplings and harvested a fragrant stem.

Tamsen sulked in the yard while Jack went back inside and dunked the pine in the tub and left it to steep over the fire. His stomach rumbled. Aihh God, no rest for a doctor. Jack hung a smaller kettle of water over the fire and grabbed his fishing pole. It was time to catch breakfast.

Where limbs overhung deep blue water he tried some new flies he had tied last night. He quickly landed five trout and threw them into the pail. "By the lochs of Inbhir Mis, I do know my troutwork, I certainly do."

He hurried back to the cabin, the donkey trailing behind. "If he wakes and finds me gone, what then? He does na know where he is."

The cabin was sweltering in pine sweat. Jack began cleaning trout by the fireplace. Living alone for three years had turned him into a man who talked to every*thing*. The narrow fish-faces looked like surprised old men. He told them, "Time to be soup, old trooters. No sense fighting it. Time makes soup of us all."

He slid the fillets into the small kettle and minutes later added potatoes.

Then returning to doctoring, he removed the dressing from the chest wound revealing a small puffy volcano. He dripped whiskey into the hole and the boy flinched, straightened, and relaxed. Yes, still some fireworks going on there. Jack cried out joyfully, "The deaf man always hears the clink o' the coin! Are you in there, boy?"

The handsome face remained as graven stone.

Jack inventoried the boy's wounds. They were strange wounds. A long, fiery scratch ran down his shoulder. Three punctures marred his right hand, all old wounds, pink and healing. He had heard of the grizzly bear fight. If true, this boy was one tough piece of leather. He might survive a thump to the heart. Jack put on fresh dressings. He sponged water onto the parched, cracked lips.

Jack smiled at him. "Where are you off to, lad? Having some sweet dreams?"

An hour later he dabbed soup broth into his patient, just a few drops. The long finely drawn face remained stolid and immobile. Jack shyly touched the dark fuzz of Petr's chin. Was he eighteen? He whispered sadly, "So young for dying, why not coom back to the world?"

God was he ever handsome!

He patted the pony mane of honey-colored hair, brushing aside forelocks from darkly hollow eyes. The beard, eyelashes and long straight eyebrows were jet black strokes. That gave him the sketched look, as if the artist had meant to emphasize the eye ridge, the cheekbones, the cut of the jaw—with dark shadows. Jack wondered aloud, "Is man or beast so nobly good as he looks? Or ugly like me—bad as he looks?" He scratched his head.

He laughed. "That theory makes me pretty bad."

Petr Valory was the opposite end of the horse from Jack, in looks. They could still become thick friends couldn't they? Jack figured himself for a lumpy bear with the stuffing sagged into wrong places. This lad was Arabian horse for sure—streamlined, radiating electric quickness, magnetic pulse, a golden grace. Jack feared imposing his ideas even on a sleeping man but he had to try *something*. "We could be friends!" he whispered. "Coom back to the land of the living. There's muckle we could do tagither."

There was no response.

Jack snatched a hand in front of his face as if throwing something away. "Come back, darling boy. Catch fire if you can."

Jack stirred stew and hunks of fish chased each other followed by the slower potatoes. Without looking at Petr, he made his pitch.

"We could be partners, ya know? I found me a good bend in the crick." Glancing around as if someone might be listening, "Gold, ya know. I'm looking for a partner who can keep his mooth shut and you seem fairly tight-lipped."

Jack glanced shyly. "I never had no friend as fine as you before. My pals been mostly the rough sort. Outcasts." He slopped a rag into the boiler containing the pine tree and sponged Petr's forehead. "If that fever does na break, I guess you're soon joining your pa and sis anyway." Jack looked out the window.

When he pulled the body from the creek, it was pale as frozen canvas. Now his skin blushed ripe as strawberry with a pure sheen a girl would keen for. He had gone from dead gray to rosy ripe in three days. The skin told of fine progress, and Jack marveled.

"Lad, you're prettier than most lassies." He laughed. "Wall, I have not actually seen one for two years, excepting yoor little sissy. God praise her. Where did you get that pretty noggin, laddy bucks? Sure it was not from your ma and pa." Wondering if the boy had any idea how handsome he was, he guessed not. He pictured old man Valory's tired old face. And Magya of the black brooding eyes shining from a yellowish oval face, always looking like someone expecting to be turned out of the food line, and always ready to fight for her place. Ah well, maybe she'd been a sweet girl. Certainly she had swell big bosoms—what big bobbins!

Jack gripped his beard. "Forgive me mither, I'm a fool. Teach me to love God's flowers and leave the lassies alone. Only a mither's love lasts forever." He stirred soup and because of that, did not see Petr move.

The eyebrows wiggled, the shoulders shrugged, and he whispered disjointed words.

"Walk...the other side...the river." He shuddered and became dead again.

Jack stirred and talked to his prospective partner. "The cannons blew out most of my hearing at Cerro Gordo." He shook his head, humming and puttering his lips, "All long ago. Now I hear waterfalls rushing in my head all the time."

Jack spoke over his shoulder. "I was never sick more than a day in my life. The way I was raised, Molly Frazier, that's me mither, she cured fever with hot towels all over, and hops tea spiked with whusky, a guaranteed *womit*-producer. She'd cure you right now. Need not be sick to get the cure, either. We got used to her healthing us up, packing things on, poking things in whether we were sick or no. Now I think that's poor economy. Now I think a man should burn his energy *out*. That keeps good juices flowing. Good food and good work, that's the ticket, not hiding behind a cloud of herbs."

He bobbed the pinesapling in its boiling tub and glanced at Petr. "Course, herbs are needful *oncet* in awhile." Jack laughed at his memoir. Work was easy to find for a big man. Getting a full belly was not. He added, "There are no fat men in Scotland."

He threw out his hands. "I got my own lake in America! Can you believe it? Here in California, I get enough to eat." He went over to the sleeping boy.

"It's time to bake the other side of the bun." He gently cupped the head so it didn't flop. He removed the rag diaper fashioned from an old shirt, noting it was barely damp. Looking at the rump, he clucked his tongue.

"Lordy boy, you sure gonna break them lady hearts. Coom back to health now, at least for their sakes, you hear?" He laughed so loud a chunk of soot fell from the chimney and exploded into flames.

Jack placed the third pine bucket with the other two, making a grotto around the sleeper.

"You got the devil's own skin, maybe from the fever, maybe not. Maybe just the way you are, eh?" Jack sighed. "Aihh God, please say he hasn't flown the basket. I need someone to blather at. There's Tamsen, but she's not much for a chat, you know? Leastways not for *diskissions*. She can answer yes or no questions like: Do ya think we belonged in Mexico? Or was it Mr. Polk's War? Are ya for slavery? Are ya glad California was made a free state, not slave? But she's no good for asking: What do ya think of taxing Chinamen's mining claims to pay the sheriff's salary? Or: How bout hanging that Spanish woman at Downieville?"

That was old news. The hanging of Juanita had taken place July 5th, 1851. That was a year ago. But that wasn't the point. Nobody tired of debating if the mob should have hanged a *woman*—even though she killed a man. That dumb donkey stood there blinking at such promising conversation.

"Ah, how we're gwointa gab." Jack removed his beaver-hat. A mound of hair fell to his waist. Jack had more hair than most women. He yawned loudly. It was time for a nap.

2

If a redman stayed away from land easy and beautiful to white men's eyes, *if* he kept out of sight from those pale eyes—*then* a redman was safe. Sun Eagle knew this when he situated his camp above a wild river canyon far beyond the white man's eyes and trails. Each day the women gathered pinenuts, berries, roots and tended camp, one man staying behind to guard the women and catch fish in the river. Six others hunted for Sabbah and were careful not to be observed.

Each morning Sun Eagle and Minoah walked to a high ridge where Minoah made a fire with twigs. When it blazed she covered it with heavy grass. Sun Eagle threw a wet blanket over the grass and after a moment pulled it away.

A smoke puff rose steadily into clear blue sky. It drew no response.

3

Sabbah no longer slept soundly as a good man sleeps. He had a strange dream. A red boat was coming down the river towards a big waterfall. The boat got caught in the rocks when Sabbah found it. Inside was a giant red heart lashed down by leather thongs, beating wildly to be set free. He woke up sad.

Each morning he considered freeing the little girl. Each day his heart hardened. He thought of his murdered son, Nojomud. Get revenge. The coyote people needed killing.

When he saw a smoke cloud high in an otherwise empty sky, he knew what it was because he had been expecting it. But he had no wish to be helped, this was spirit work. The girl ran away but he had recaptured her easily. And now something strange was happening with the whites. They were killing their own people.

The big white-hat coyote burned the hut where the little girl dwelled. Sabbah had seen a wounded man taken to another hut by the big lake. Sabbah knew the beaver-hat man was Big Jack, who had been a friend to the Pah Utes long ago.

The Great Spirit was showing him these things for a reason. Spirit would show him how to use them. His eyes had opened with his successes of the last few days. Realizing if you attacked the whites in great numbers, you were doomed. Big fights were their strength. But if you attacked them one at a time, stealthily, you could kill them all.

The great thing was he had decided to kill the white-hat coyote. Torment him first, and then give him a long excruciating death.

He would leave Big Jack alone. Maybe count coo on him, and knock him in the head. He was mystified by the wounded boy, the one attacked by his own people. Maybe he was useful medicine helpful for killing whites. He would see. That boy and girl were brother and sister. That would be useful somehow. The girl was a wildcat. He wouldn't kill her. Let her life be tormented like his. Now she was back inside the squaw cave. She would be useful.

Sabbah decided about the smoke signal. My People will not support my purpose. I will stay hidden until it is time to show them my great deeds. The smoke cloud disappeared.

Sabbah looked at the thing he had shaped for several days now. It was a scalping knife.

Now it was evening and she would be expecting him. He rolled the heavy stones aside and entered the cave warily. He liked this girl. He expected what came next.

She swung a rock and he cuffed her aside and she grunted.

Then he grabbed her hair and swung his knife.

4

Petr awoke like a blind baby inside an oven. His eyes were pine-sapped shut. It was death and it was taking way too long and it was too painful, his chest felt sledge-hammered. And the same hot sap was dripping a hole into his chest. And his right hand was on fire. And there was a rhythmic sawing noise close by—snoring—like maybe he was inside a bear cave.

But whatever this place was it smelled wonderful—like pinesap perfume. Not only that the warmth pressed all around him like a nest. Not bad. He wanted to pry an eye open but his fingers weren't working. Something wrong with his right hand, when he held it up it wobbled like a rock on a stick. He couldn't see or move very well, but his ears were working just fine.

A ripsaw bucked back and forth, long easy strokes through a log close to his head, very thick, very long strokes, soothing really. It halted for a moment and he heard something even less glamorous, a low trumpeting fart, and then a soggy hay smell.

Petr laughed. This was definitely not Heaven and he didn't believe in Hell, but maybe it was time to begin. He was roasting and sweating profusely. Why so hot? He spooned an eye open with two fingers making a kiss-smacking sound.

A few feet away a funny-looking fireplace belched out heat, but why? Wasn't this July? The room was small, a gloomy bear's den, and the big bear was only two feet away, his belly going up and down, snoring on the floor. Monsterous.

Petr shrank back instinctively making all his wounds scream. This was too strange. The bear wore a plaid skirt over cannon-shaped legs. Green and orange socks ran to the knees, huge wrinkled elephant knees, smudged with dirt. He knew the man. It was Big Jack Frazier, but how did he get here? Had he put out the fire? Was there a fire? *The Valory cabin was burning.* No, that was impossible. He was having a very bad dream and this big man was part of it.

He was very close to the big man in a very small room. Jack filled the room. If he went berserk he could snap you like a twig, throw you

203

over his shoulder with one hand, and drink a tanker of beer with the other. His leather shirt rose and fell with a bellows-like leathery squeak. His dark beard and his top hair fanned out around a head big as a nail keg. He was solidly asleep.

Petr's voice rasped horribly, "Why...you...here?" But Big Jack was deeply asleep.

An explosion of memory hit, not a dream: *Fire. Arrows. John. Dead?*

He tried to get up but his arms and legs shook. He had no strength. He remembered an old circus giraffe, swaying and staggering. When the circus came to Harrisburg he had proudly carried his little sister, but his young arms failed and he dropped Annabel and Mama yelled, You dropped the baby! Suddenly he remembered lots of bad things.

"My God, don't wake me up any more." But he was sitting up wide awake now.

A bandage wound around his chest with a wet red spot. When he tried to touch it he saw his right hand was wrapped like a mummy. No wonder he couldn't use it. A whole memory flashed into his brain like lightning. Petr grabbed his stomach sick with fear. He saw—

John Valory dead with two arrows in his chest.

Suddenly he remembered lying cold and wet in a creek.

He scooted backwards and bumped into something scratchy, strange, and completely unexpected. He whirled crying out, "Holy Jesus *Christ!*"

Green children, three of them, stood glistening wet and listening.

"Back!" Then they became small pinetrees standing in buckets of water.

What sort of madhouse was this? His clothes were sprinkled wet as if ready for ironing. He gripped his knees to his chest but was stopped by explosions of sharp, deep pain.

He made a cry of despair. "Jack...what is going on here?"

But Big Jack sprawled like a boxer caught by a ripping uppercut, his dark brown hair fanned behind his blocky, tremendous shoulders, he was out.

The miners had many names for him: Big Jack; Gorgeous Jack;

Unlucky Jack—because he never found any gold. That was his story: hard luck all the way.

Jack snorted in his sleep making Petr laugh and he was rewarded with another burst of pain. Next Jack smacked his lips, mumbling, "Stop-pit Tamsen…tickles," then returned to snoring. Petr marveled at his size. He was a fallen giant. If Jack ever married he would need a three hundred pound bride to keep from smothering her at night.

The fireplace whispered with red flames and good smells roiled from the stewpot. His stomach knotted. His jaws stung with sharp hunger. Get your bearings, Petr Valory. He guided his head with his hands and made mental pictures. The floor was packed dirt and scattered straw. A scrap of paper posted at floor level read: "Rats and mouse stay away from this house. Run to the mill and take your fill."

Windows on either side of the door formed twin pools of light. He guessed, "That's east." And, "I've been here all night."

He panned his head upwards.

The cabin was a crude lean-to, with a high-side over the front door. The backwall was low; a child would have to stoop. There the fireplace radiated solid wallops of heat. So rustic was the workmanship, Petr smiled. A stick and mud chimney rose from a stone hearth. The mantel was a plank covered with smashed flat tincans and perched upon it was an iron skillet and a miner's pan. He followed the rise of the front wall.

Jack had built a loft right over his front door—and there was his bed high in the air. A bed over a door—what kind of a Scottish apartment was this? The sleeping area was a high balcony with a thick ladder running up. Well, heat runs uphill doesn't it? He saw the brilliance. Jack stays warm on cold Sierra nights. Petr began to appreciate the heavy-handed, beaver carpentry work. All boards hacked and butted together, not quite Papa's dovetail constructions. But still—the man knew how to survive. Petr stood again, which wasn't a good idea. "Oh…god."

Dizzy wobbly, he clung to a rough table with both hands, resting for a moment. The smell of fish and potatoes was wonderful. Jets of saliva stabbed his jaw and he was suddenly savagely hungry, his stomach rumbling with desire.

He gazed into the kettle. Smooth white goo and iridescent chunks bubbled up and down. Hazy gray steam filled his nostrils and his mouth opened and he was drooling. He felt guilty. The man who caught trout, peeled spuds, chopped wood, made fire—and wore a skirt—was exhausted. He was a fine man who kept a clean cabin and clean dressings on your wound.

Head, arms and legs, all would heal. This man saved your life. You owe a life in return.

Losing Annabel had taught him it was life's *hidden* wounds could hack your heart to pieces, keep you flat down with no will to move, and then keep you on the prod all day, every day.

A braying cry made Petr jump like a thief caught in a spotlight. He turned to the door but it was a bad idea: the room carouselled in a dizzy circle. He tipped away from the fireplace. But his feet tangled and he was tripping, falling—tripping on what? What thing?

A three-legged stool appeared and he grabbed the table but that was suddenly tipping and falling and it went over with him on his way down. There was a loud crash.

Jack sat up big-eyed and awake. "Holy Mary and Joe, yoor alive and rambling aboot!"

5

The youth righted the table but acted like he was drunk, reeling backwards grabbing his chest. Jack's voice filled the room, "My God, my good doctoring has worked!"

Petr righted the stool, bracing himself against the table, staring at the big man, suddenly out of breath.

Jack stood on the other side of the table and said helpfully, "Yoor having a big sleep. Yoor—" He flipped through bad memories like cards: burning cabin, the body of John Valory. What to tell and not to tell? "Yoor out cold when I—" Jack flushed.

The young man had wolf-eyes the color of whiskey. Why didn't he speak?

Jack stammered, "I t-tended you... since you were suh... I c-can't s-say it—since you were sick." Trailing off miserably, staring, hard not to stare at the young man's eyes. Jack pulled his kilt straight and held out his big hands and felt foolish. "Lad, I'm a friend, no harm cooms for you here." There. That was good.

Petr Valory glanced around and firelight illumined his face. Jack took a sharp breath. *There.* What's about his right eye? *Look at that!* Jack shrank back. "It's true what they say, ain't it!" His hands reached out, he realized what he was doing, and snapped them back.

A tiny gold star glimmered in the right eye.

Haunted eye! Supernatural power—but for what: good or evil? Jack stepped back from the table. "Need a minute, laddy. Got to warm up. Then I'll make breakfast."

Jack pressed his knees and straightened his back and then swung his arms around like an athlete readying himself for a contest and savagely broke wind sounding like a rail spike ripped from oak: *Rarrrt!*

Jack turned rosy red; even his globed knees blushed pink.

"There might be drawbacks to my companionship, but many good points." He turned away, coiled his hair into his beaver hat and covered his head. "I'll get coffee bubbling."

Petr sat on the stool and watched Jack moving, nimble and athletic.

Jack got his coffee-fixings going, thumped his wide belly and gestured at the kettle. "I'm hungry as a billygoat on Sunday, how about you? You're welcome to it."

Petr nodded as Jack placed two big bowls and then filled them with bubbling gray soup. Delicious aromas filled the room. Jack sat on a log-round. "I have but one stool—and no spoons." Jack hoisted his bowl and Petr did the same. He drank greedily, his hands trembling.

"Take her slow, lad. Everything she falls into place, you give her time."

Petr sucked on soup and couldn't help muttering, "Never-never-never."

Jack stared at him hoping his next words would make sense. "You nary-nary what?"

Petr drank, cleared his throat several times, and then said, "Nary... tasted better."

Jack laughed and slapped his knee. "Wahl now, I'm sure your mither cooked ya bitter."

Petr said, "She was bitter, all right."

Jack laughed. Laddy was coming around and he had returned with his heart and soul intact. They ate in silence and a few minutes later Jack poured coffee into tin cups. Petr looked sternly at Jack and said in a husky tone, "Did you...get them?"

Jack stiffened and Petr spoke again. "My pa, did you fetch him too?"

Jack pushed his bowl away, took a big gulp of coffee and said, "I buried him by the cabin." After a long pause: "I did na *get* them." He stared into his thick palms. "I was too late."

Petr sighed heavily. "Do you know what I have to do now? Don't you *know?*" The fury burst. "Do you think I *want* to?" He groaned, trembling, his voice wracked with emotion. "Why didn't you just let me die, Jack? It would all be over. I wouldn't have to go back." He gripped the table so hard his knuckles turned white.

Jack didn't like what he was seeing. Was Petr turning out a demon?

Jack said, "Petr—me lad—Petr." Then nothing came next. His hands knotted and folded. Finally Jack *harroomed* several times and then explained all he had done: burying his pa; finding Petr in the creek, the shock of it; and wrapping him up. And then carrying him to this cabin and tending him; fever and delirium for three days.

The lad looked with incredulous eyes. The gold spot in his right eye glowed like an ember. He said, *"I've been here three days?"*

Jack smiled shyly. "Yea—and mumbling about sand and fary-ohs, We got the fary-ohs in Scotland—and broonies too. Faeries are contrary but broonies are good."

Petr looked horrified. "Jack! Did you get *any* of them, Jack? Did you?" His voice rose in a hysteric curve—"Didjajack? didja?didja? Did ya gettum, Jack?" He stood abruptly pointing himself at the door but he was wobbly and talking wildly.

"Magya and Annabel are gone. Papa is gone now too. And King... he thinks I'm dead! I've got to kill King."

Jack stood. "King? Did he— Was he—" The next words almost convinced Jack that the lad had returned as a demon.

"Why shouldn't I kill my father? Can you tell me?"

Petr headed for the door but Jack caught him with surprising speed and held onto him, thrashing and wouldn't quit, obviously out of his mind. This newly awakened Petr was not all right. He had no choice. Jack mauled up a fist and swung. Petr fell hard, knocked out again.

Jack clucked, "Oooch, I am *such* a bad doctor."

6

Petr awoke with a sore jaw and with Jack talking as if he had never stopped.

"Me cooking and eating I do sitting down." Pronounced "kickn and ittin".

Fur tickled Petr's nose. On the floor, back inside the rabbit robe, the room getting darker not brighter. How long was he knocked out this time?

Jack was saying, "Heat travels up to the ceiling to my loft. I get cozy in my bunk with a candle and a book. I have Tom Paine, Bin Franklin, 'Imerson and Thro'. All good leather covers, no cheap stuff for Jack, see?"

His voice rich and tender, words rolled from his tongue as if someone enjoying the aftertaste of a good sandwich, a fine melodious voice. Petr turned over onto his stomach listening to the warbling song of the man.

"I ken it's a wee odd bunk, but that's where all the heat swoops off. And to boot, anybody tries to sneak in, why ol' Jack's got the drop on em right away, see?" Making looping gestures with his powerful arms he crouched into a spine-cracking hug. He looked pleased with himself.

Petr suddenly felt old; the strength of his voice startled the big man.

"Jack—what if they storm your place with fire and shoot you when you come out—what then, Jack?" Petr stood and felt very dizzy, and dead tired.

Jack smiled. "There you are, back in the world again. I thought you had left for the night. I was crazy with worry, you being my first patient and all." He handed Petr a cup of cold water. "Go easy now and listen to some great news. When we strike gold, know what we're gonna do?"

Petr understood this; Jack was trying to occupy him with happy talk.

"Here's what we'll do. We open the biggest hotel you iver seen, right after I open the biggest restaurant. Right then we get enough to eat, see? Call it *Jack's Place*. She takes up a whole city block with a saloon *and* a theater." He stretched out his arms and rubbed his belly.

Petr played along. "So where's this dream place to be?"

"San Franciscoo! That's where all the lordy rich people are."

Petr could have been charmed by this plan last year, but not now. His memories were like grinning corpses: Annabel underwater; Magya runaway; John dead under cold gravel: and Dain King grinning with satisfaction. Petr said, "Sounds like a smart plan."

Jack looked at him shrewdly stroking his beard. "Listen, you clabbered onto me at just the right time. I need a partner. Don't tell a soul, but I found me a small gloryhole last fall, just right for two men. We could get rich together, see?"

Petr answered heavily, "Was it at the bottom of a lake?"

"No!" Jack laughed. "Greenhorn! You doona find gold in a lake. My claim is above the lakes and has the right look about it. Get yoor punch back, we'll go there. We're gonna get rich." Jack wasn't a good liar but he continued his good cause. "She's too hard to plow alone. Now if you were free for a time we could get started." Disappointed by Petr's lack of enthusiasm, he added, "You don't believe me. You want proof. I don't blame you. I'll show you proof."

Jack went up into his loft and retrieved a small leather pouch. Onto the table he poured a stream of gold flakes with a few smooth nuggets. Jack watched Petr's eyes.

Petr glanced at the gold. Then he stared out of the darkening window. Jack was a good man. Keep Petr busy and out of trouble. Jack spoke earnestly as a businessman.

"Split every *ting* right down the middle, you and me. I throw in my gear and know-how, which ain't a little. You throw in...well—how about that big red horse and yoor good sense? Call it fair and square."

He licked his thumb like a man turning a page. Jack had dark green eyes, the color of luck and hope. Petr sighed heavily.

"Jack."

"Eh?"

"Have you got your smoking pipe?"

Jack fumbled into his vest until his clay pipe and briar pouch emerged. He stared at Petr.

Petr said, "Smoke that and I'll tell you what we're going to do."

He couldn't show Jack Frazier The Luminah. But Jack had saved his life, wanted or not. That was no small thing. For that he owed him at least one big dream come true. Make *Jack's Place* a reality. Then pay Dain King a visit. That felt good.

Do good—then do bad.

What more to life was there?

"Tomorrow, Jack, I'll find you a gold mine—just don't ask me how I do it." Pointing at his right eye, "I just seem to know where to look."

7

Mack Karras had been drinking all night in his room behind the hotel bar and he was drunk and more tired than he had ever been in his life—because he had tried to do the right thing.

Mack Karras had done his best to take his evil partner down.

But Dain King had the luck of Lucifer. Maybe the hammer god really was stronger than the do-good Christian god. Maybe gods (by whatever name) liked seeing a big dog rip the fanny out of a smaller dog. Mack drank one more 'last' whiskey and felt another wave on the ocean of drunkenness. But there wasn't enough whiskey in the world to drown his guilt. His plan had backfired in a terrible way.

King had wiped out the entire Valory family. Killed his own brother, John (half-brother, how well he knew *that* distinction), killed his own son, Petr, and somehow made the crazy Valory woman, Magya, run away; and made the little girl *disappear*. Mack shook his head and the room rolled like a boat on the waves.

"Sorry about that letter, John. Sorry about that map. They killed you. I guess...I killed you."

But he would be sorrier yet.

CHAPTER ELEVEN

THE GOLD SEEKERS

1

"Tomorrow" became ten more days of recovery for Petr before they could set out looking for gold. Big Jack awoke early on July 15th smelling good coffee. Laddybucks making coffee! That was a good sign. Jack couldn't wait to get going. He balled his hair into his hat and shoved it onto his head.

He opened the door, his shoulders filling the doorway, and he laughed. The lake was sparkling with golden sunshine, another good omen, and the burro was waiting for him in the yard looking bright-eyed and mad.

Jack walked over to her and rubbed her head. "Eat hearty, my big darling. You gwointa earn your feed today." He heard Petr calling across the lake. It was the same every morning.

"ANNA - BELL...ROW - CHELE?"

High on a cliff, bathed in light, his arms outstretched, he looked like a holy man. It reminded Jack of something he had seen when he was a young man.

He had been on Fremont's Expedition in 1844 starving its way across the Nevada desert. The Pah Utes had saved their lives. They were strong, peaceful Indians who lived beside a great pale desert lake that Fremont named Pyramid Lake. They had probably lived there for thousands of years. Each morning their holy man, Sun Eagle, called out his prayer across the lake: "Come Spirit, come—Good Spirit, enter me! Strengthen me! Make me a giver to my People! Let me do good until I die!" That's what Jack wanted—to do good with lots of gold. And never worry where your next meal was coming from.

A hawk jumped from a tall pine across the lake and flew away.

Petr watched intently as if the hawk might show him the way to Annabel.

That was hopeless. He would never see that girl again. He had to let her go. Jack walked quietly back to the burro munching in a feed bag. He practiced his speech on her. "Oh laddy, you have to let her *go*. We did what we could. The Good Spirit has her now."

Jack walked back to the cabin. He fixed breakfast.

Petr returned ten minutes later and they ate pancakes and discussed the menu for *Jack's Place*. He sounded normal as long as they didn't venture into the past.

"Iced lemonade," Petr said. "They'll want lemonade in San Francisco."

Jack scrawled charcoal on a white slab hung over the fireplace: Lemon-aid–10c. Above this was, Pan-cakes–$2. Above this, Troot Pan-cakes–$1. Above this, Just Plain Troot–50c.

Petr said, "Charge more so people think it's good."

He had returned from death without a smile and wasn't smiling now. He abruptly changed the subject, which jarred Jack badly the first time it happened.

"Gragg's rifle exploded when he shot us. It chain-fired all six shots because he didn't pack the cylinders with grease—it blew his jaw off. Papa was still alive, I felt him breathing. Then King shot him point-blank. Then he killed Gragg with an axe. I saw but I couldn't move. He chopped him open. Then he came back and shoved arrows in Pa's chest. He did it like it was natural and necessary, like putting down a wounded horse. Can't you see King is a monster who needs killing?"

Jack began to sweat as he drank boiling hot coffee. Petr made these abrupt revelations each time adding chilling details of the Valory murder, always delivered in a flat voice.

"God commanded us not to kill. But then God allows good men to be killed. That's evil and I won't follow such a foolish code anymore. Once I get Annabel back, I'm going after King. Count on it, Jack. Right after I get you a goldmine."

Jack chugged scalding coffee, stood abruptly, and made his

prepared speech. "You have'ta let her go, Petr...you have'ta let all that go! Can we do that, *now?*"

Petr stared at him, and then slowly nodded. "Sure, Jack. Let's go find your goldmine." He stuffed two pancakes into his mouth and winked. "Finding gold is the easy part, for me."

They loaded a hundred pound bag onto Tamsen's back and headed for the crest.

The rising valley was a silver poem carved from larger poetry called the Sierra Nevada. Gray granite appeared as if seamlessly poured around the boles of pine trees that formed choirs of green angels whispering in the wind. Small pines looked as if they would dance gracefully away once intruders passed from sight. One thing was sure. Mountains made man forget his troubles.

Petr whispered, "Time-drowsed prisoners of stone, reaching for glorious heaven."

Jack didn't hear him. He yelled, "You canna traipse here and not take notice of her beauty. Look here, boy. She's pretty as Scotland's bens and glens."

Petr smiled sadly. "Judging from you," he said, "Scotland must be a grand big place. Where is it?"

"Where is Scotland? Man—where is Scotland? Why, she's the edge of Heaven! And in a Scot-man's heart. But she's all rooned now. Big lairds throw folks off the land, to raise sheep."

They stopped to stare at a pretty sight.

Three deer drank from a small waterfall, lifted their heads, poised, and then darted away. Petr nodded. "In America we push Indians off the land." Petr spoke with passion Jack had never heard before.

"We need religion of forests and rivers and mountains, clean and beautiful—maybe we once did have such a religion, Jack   long ago when a better race of men walked the earth."

Jack nodded. "The Indians love trees—and so do the real people of Scotland."

Petr said, "Well, let me die and be born a tree in Scotland."

Jack laughed. "Let's not die just yet."

Tamsen sulked past, dragging her rope. Jack knew the signs of temper. She was mad that Petr walked in her place, and slept in her bed.

Jack made his booming cry, "*Haughh*! We've gone two hours now. Seen any gold yet?" Not that it mattered. The important thing was to keep Petr busy, keep him moving upward.

They climbed the Sierra crest until dark.

2

Petr broke sticks. Then he struck a sulfur match into a tuft of orange pine needles blazing up like a Roman candle. Next he smoothed all the pebbles from their camp while Jack cooked cornbread and heated a tin of ham. Good smells filled the air. Jack heaped bowls with food and handed one over.

"Corned ham—$100 a plate. How's that sound, partner?" He held out his palm. "Sir, leave yoor goldbag at the door when you leave, sir." Jack laughed loud. His burro brayed.

Petr didn't laugh. He said stonily, "You don't believe I can find gold, do you."

Jack ate and talked at the same time. "Gold's where you find her, like a beautiful-good woman. You think you know the country exactly—but you don't." He poked cornbread into his mouth. "And the good one—and the gold—will take you on a chase you don't expect. Then she takes you by surprise. No man knows what he's doing with woman—or gold." Shoveling chunks of ham into his mouth, "My theory is that if you can find gold, you can also find the rarest thing of all: a *good* beautiful woman." Jack chewed thoughtfully. "We have na' found her yet. That's why we're out here alone. That's why I brought the whusky jug." Jack wiggled his eyebrows and laughed again.

Petr didn't laugh. "I don't know about women, I haven't tried. But I'll find you gold. You saved my life and I owe you a life and I don't know when I'll have a chance to save you back. But I'll get you a goldmine. That's the deal."

He had barely touched his food when Jack pushed his empty bowl away grinning.

"Aye, that's the deal."

It was perfect. Finding gold in high country would take months. By then Petr would be back to normal. Jack lit his pipe. The boy's bowl was still full because for once he was talkative.

"I went someplace I shouldn't," Petr said, "where things were different than they ought to be, so powerful, ordinary men should never go there. It was an Indian place for visions, a special place for dreaming. Anyway, I think it changed me." He stopped for a full minute both men looking at the stars blazing like a silvermine. Then Petr said something crazy.

"I *sense* gold. I can feel it. I really can. I know right where we're going to find gold."

Jack blew smoke into the fire, trying not to laugh. "All greenhorns think that. Just walk around till you get an inspiration, stick your trowel in the ground—and there's your gold."

Jack hunted gold for two years and it was the hardest work on earth.

"You doubt me," Petr said. "I don't blame you. But when your pockets bulge with gold, you'll believe me. Now let's ask you something." He plunged into a strange topic.

"Papa received a letter. It was rain-smeared. He couldn't tell who wrote it, but it was music to his ears. It spoke of big trees, free for the taking. A man named King buys all you can cut. Did he mention it?" Jack shook his head. Petr continued. "Dain King was mad when we showed up. So he didn't send the letter. John and King were half-brothers. King didn't want John telling his dirty past. Now my question is, Jack: Who sent that letter? Who knew Dain King and John Valory couldn't live in the same valley without tearing each other apart?"

Jack yawned loudly. "Some things we canna know, Laddy. Things like that keep you awake. We need sleep. Let philosophers wonder about the mysteries of the world. Nothing is worth more than sleep." Jack turned over and in a minute he was snoring.

Petr fell into something, too, but it wasn't sleep, it was a vision-like dream.

A falcon screamed in the dark, from a distant world, a different time. Petr knew the falcon was returning from Death, from the Invisible, once again visiting the living world.

For some reason he felt happy. But then the dream changed into something unforgettable.

3

Above him sat a shining boy cross-legged in the air, veiled in a bright red cape. Petr held out his hand. The shining figure held out its hand as if in a mirror. Petr spread his arms. The figure spread its arms. Then magically they changed places.

Petr was sitting on air viewing his body snuggled below in a sleeping brown lump, with Jack beside him, sound asleep, all seeming very real. Yet there were telltale signs of a dream.

The sky was a solid gold sheet—speckled with *black* stars. He began rising towards it as if to a magnetic mirror. His shape changed into a golden scimitar—falcon wings flying into night, flying high above vesper valleys black with sleep. Below him mountain domes became a string of moonlit pearls strung across the world. The truth of the world was very clear.

Earth was house of the body and sky was house of the Soul. Below, all things were visible as stone. Above, all things were invisible as air. Long ago his imperishable Soul had descended from its imperial home. Fallen from heaven into earth! And magical words whispered to him and for just one moment he understood their full meaning—

You shall ascend from earth to heaven, And descend again to earth, And thereby acquire the power of both worlds.

Below was a spectacular view of Earth.

Rivered deep with gold: veins, eddies, skeins, streamers of gold radiating out from within the mountains. Gold dripped from volcanoes like shining milk of pagan breasts. He realized—

"Earth is my mother. Sky is my father. Here is my religion of my Soul."

Why did no one know what the mystic poet tried to describe: *I sent my Soul through the Invisible...Some letter of that Afterlife to Spell...And by and by my Soul returned to me and said, I Myself am Heav'n and Hell.*

Before his eyes the world became wind and rain-tilled gardens of light.

Valleys exploded with light glimmering from golden battles waged ages ago. Gazing far north of the Valoryvale he saw a gleaming volcano, deep whorls of gold spiraling down into its heart. Gold flowed from shattered valleys, hidden floes of shining wealth.

Gold was scattered *everywhere* as if blasted out from a giant shotgun.

Mountains rose and fell in slow-motion waves of rock. The Sierras welled up immense warps and weaves of time—with dotted lines of gold trailing deep into earth, stopping and starting at unknown depths. Antlike men scraped crumbs from their Mother's breast.

Mountain valleys undulated in fields of flickering gold fireflies deep within whirling starbursts of gold. Mountains formed spokes of a giant Ferris wheel tipped sideways shattering, turning very slowly to the vision of time-altered mind. He commanded himself.

Blaze every detail in golden memory! Remember every golden line. You are no long the gold hunter. You are the Goldfinder.

Wild canyons roared with waterfalls of gold piling into sinkholes, then buried by sand. Millions of years passed in minutes. Gold palaces blazed riotous ruin beneath molten mountains as fractured quartz columns crashed sideways in perpetual slow-motion falling of golden debris. He penned everything with golden ink of memory.

There was Gold Nation.

Beneath this pitiful alignment of tents, saloons and cabins was a *roaring* tiger of gold. King couldn't help grow rich, ripping out its golden teeth. King would own the mountains. Who could stop him? Cold realization hit hard. *Petr Valory must stop him.*

Four thousand years ago he was a greedy, totally selfish Egyptian boy—no different than Dain King was now. Why doesn't God kill him? Push him off a cliff? Drown him in a river? Why should King control these mountains? Why should his big hands dip its bottomless wealth?

Much of what he saw tonight was buried so deep men would never find it. But King had only to scratch the surface and he would be madly wealthy, and cause lots of trouble.

Petr discovered he could speed up time or slow it down simply by wishing it. That made him enormously curious. Where did it all begin?

Go back to the beginning.

Earth broke from the Sun like a small egg yolk of gold. Its surface boiling with volcanoes, molten mouths showered a sky red as blood—all sparkling with gold. It would be paradise someday, but earth began as hell. Petr speeded up time and found rain rushing into melting volcanoes, sinking and rising like corks. Again he speeded up time.

Sky gushed a millions of years of rain—beating mountains into gravel—rushing down the rivers. Gold tumbled beaten down, smoothed, polished. Cold creeks held heavy secrets and washed the gravel away. Deposits fell sorted into layers of lighter, heavier, heaviest—gold was heaviest. Water always moving, sweeping away debris, always hoarding gold into holes, bends in creeks, sluggish channels, into riffled bars, and then dropping gravel, then sand on top, hiding the secret. Why do you do it, God?

Why push mountains up and then pull them down? Why raise men and crush them into the ground? What he observed was—

The Luminah repeated itself, but why? What for?

Why the aching endless eternity: year upon year, deposit after deposit; century after century the big Bank of God—heavy with gold, heavy with life and death, deposits sinking to immobile bedrock. Exposed gold was the result not of a lifetime, but of hundreds of lifetimes. The mystery of deep Earth welled up and spilt forth where men might find it. Why, God?

Who taught men to love gold? Why so universally treasured? Beyond the Stone Age—men loved the color of the sun—gold.

It was revelation: *This is my religion, my art, my life—to see the super-abundant God of Earth.* But if he saw magnificence, who on earth could he tell? Who would believe him?

Not all was gold. Many creeks held stretches meteoric with gold (Gold Nation was one such meteor) but many others lay still and lusterless. Vast stretches sparkled with glitter, but not enough for miners to exploit. The stream that poured through the Valoryvale was devoid of gold, as was Jack's big lake. Jack would never find any gold.

Next he studied the ridge above Gold Lake, a nameless bulge dividing the green valleys of Valoryvale and Long Lake—dividing them from Gold Nation.

He studied the Valoryvale with its burned cabin. He could see it easily, and in his exalted state he felt no sadness. The little creek ran from Long Lake to the Feather River, a very short race indeed. Its entire wealth was beauty and delicious water.

Gold Lake was another matter. That crater cup of water beneath a nameless ridge was a sunrise of gold. Gold spouted like a beam of light from the depths of earth. The Gold Volcano had spilled yellow ichors fifty miles all around. No other mountain was so spectacular. Most were merely crushed, sunken pumps. Extinct volcanoes.

This was true in every direction as far as he could see. Eastward, beyond the gap in the mountains that led to the deserts, where brown mountains repeated in ridges across yellow basins and dead plateaus, very little goldfire glowed beneath them. The deserts hid blue earth that would someday be recognized as silver ore. Did the super-abundance never end? His vision made him realize—

Gold Lake was the greatest of them all, the mother of gold: The Motherlode.

And the Indians kept it hidden.

And I must keep it hidden? How do I do that? But the answer was clear.

Stay away from it—The Luminah—and stay away from Dain King.

Staying away from a volcano was certainly reasonable. But stay away from Dain King? Walk away from murder? What chance did reason ever have against passion? He could not stay away, no doubt about it! *I'm going to kill Dain King—he killed my pa!*

But first do something for Jack Gorgius Frazier, the man who saved your life.

His falcon view fell away from Jack's cabin, drifting west and south, to hills not so rich in gold. He spotted a ledge containing just enough ore to make a man happy. Wild onions grew in a gentle valley below the ledge. He saw why the ledge contained gold. He couldn't wait to show Jack.

He descended to earth, to normal sleep, descending to normal life. He fell back into his body.

4

July 16, the second day of goldseeking, they awoke to silver jets of rain. They crawled beneath a towering tree, its massive, tent-like branches providing clean sleeping space, a miner's dry hotel. Because it smelled like pencils, Petr guessed it was a cedar tree.

They ate biscuits; they listened to songs of rain; they dozed.

When sunlight punched golden shafts into the great tree they headed out under a sky of powder blue. Two hours of uphill marching later they faced a knee-popping decline.

Jack hotfooted down like a bear, short sturdy legs pumping rapidly, eyes bulging madly. Petr followed close behind until they both began slipping on wet gravel and jittering helplessly down a sharp angle. They became happy, yelling boys.

Jack skied to a greasy halt with hands on knees at the edge of a foaming creek emptying into a deep green pool. Petr slid into view covered with mud, and grinning.

Jack bellowed, "Hey boy, ain't it fun!"

Petr was going way too fast. He leaned to the right and headed for Jack, yelling, "Help me! Can't stop!"

Jack spread his arms and then stepped aside. Petr sailed into the pool, making a good splash, and began dogpaddling in icy water. Jack made a whooping laugh.

"You have to admit, you needed that refreshment. Let's make camp."

Petr treaded water and seemed preoccupied with studying the field beyond. "No!"

Jack flung mud from his hands with great dignity, "No, what, Laddybucks?"

"Just ahead: the Jackpot Goldmine."

Jack clapped his hands. "Scuse me while I take a bath." He jumped waving his arms, screaming, "Aihh God!"

No matter how many times you experienced it, Sierra ice water was always shocking.

Jack tore off his boots and flung them ashore and began slapping his arms and hugging himself. "Lordee—God, its cold!" Both of them staggered on hidden boulders as they splashed ashore. Suddenly they heard the burro coming, rocketing down the slope with terror in her eyes.

"Eeee-awww!"

Like a brown locomotive hitting the pool, she threw up a sheet of whitewater—and romped through and out onto the other side—and then shot across the valley bucking and braying.

When Jack got out he noticed a strong smell of onions. Pale green shoots everywhere springing from the wide valley. Nodding his head, "I know her. There's no gold here, or in that creek. I spent a month in icy water up to my crotch to prove that, and be childless on account. But like me father, Gorgius Frazier said, If she makes you laugh, she's good for you. It's a lovely valley for all that."

They plodded across Onion Valley.

Jack laughed. "We need onions—to give our menu extra punch and extra price."

Petr didn't answer. He was crossing the meadow to a rocky slope rising from the valley floor, a ledge shelved against the valley. When he got there, he began climbing without pausing. Jack sighed and followed. Petr pointed at an orange streak above the shelf. "There it is, Jack—there's your goldmine."

They climbed fifty feet above the valley to a waist high apron of exposed bedrock like rusted iron. Above this level was a clear band of blue boulders embedded in crumbling gravel.

"Dig here and you'll be rich."

"Dig among blue skulls, huh! Sure *thinng*, sunny. Yoor more likely to find hoola girls than gold."

He tapped his lips. He looked at the blue boulders. They looked like powdery blue eyes. A chill raced up his spine; noisy flies buzzed around his head; bluejays screeched in the pines; sun poured down like hot yellow paint. Jack said patiently, "Listen, Petr. The crik doon there, that's where you find gold—running doon a crik. Not up in the air."

Petr brushed his fingers over the round boulders. "Think these got *round* all by themselves? Water smoothed them long ago. The river died and was buried and then earthquakes pushed up the mountains. Here's where the river ran before the earth pushed. It's very ancient riverbed."

Jack laughed nervously. "You've got wonderful imagination, lad," shaking his head. How much damage had the fever done to his brain? Jack smiled, thinking, humor him. He said, "Let's just go see."

They clambered down to the valley floor again, unfreighted tools from Tamsen and left her grazing in the onion field—and hotfooted back to the boulder ledge and began digging for gold even though Jack knew it was a waste of time—he would put on a good show of digging for gold in a dead river.

5

Jack dug with a pickaxe while Petr shoveled away debris. Three hours of hot sun and no talking, at least not to each other. They gouged out a trench that became a tunnel, man-high and five-feet wide. Jack studied various rocks, clinking them together, and mumbling. "Man-o-man... old Jack inna old river." Five hours later, covered with sweat and dirt, he grumbled, "I'm a river miner...not a hard rock miner." After six hours he muttered, "I'm the unluckiest man on earth...and this proves it. I hope my burro can't see me now."

Petr shoveled the dirt into a broad fan outside what looked like a big red rabbit hole. They dug down to a floor of bedrock; it wouldn't chip with an axe. Then they dug into the hill into a cake-layer of unbreakable boulders; then a nice soft layer of sandstone—all running uphill at twenty degrees. This made Jack's digging work brutal and Petr's shoveling-out work easy. Petr figured they'd reach a bend in the ancient creekbed pretty soon. He began whistling softly, shoveling and thinking.

This is a black room where only one corner contains treasure or nothing at all.

But gold was here. He had seen it in the dream. He could feel it warm as a stove.

Jack plunged his pickaxe to the haft and levered out blue and white quartz along with red debris. Grumbling, "Gold runs doon—anybody knows that! Nobody finds gold high on a hill. Stupid...stupid!"

He struck an upraised wall of bedrock ten feet inside the hill. He collapsed and began puffing. "I'm dying...dying." He faced the wall, groaning. After a moment of puffing and staring at the wall he stopped breathing. He said, "It canna be!" At the floor of the bedrock was something sticking out at him. "Aihh God, Petr! Look at that!"

6

They worked until dark making a comfortable uphill shelter out of the cave. Petr started a fire at its mouth, and moments later good smells filled the air. Tamsen, fed and hobbled, brooded below in the onion valley. Somewhere in the forest an owl asked, *Who-oo?* Later a coyote made its lonely cry across the dark valley. Jack lay wrapped in rabbit robes, while his clothes dried on a rock, and he was groaning, "Ochh. Me back, I'm dying, and me stomach, too."

Around the campfire lay amazing chunks of rock—giant quartz teeth with crude gold fillings. Jack's mine was an ancient bed where the old river had dropped its gold long ago. How much gold? They would dig until they found out. Jack could barely speak.

"Don't bother cooking. Just pop a wiggling troot straight in me mouth."

Petr sketched a menu in the air. "Raw trout. Dollar extra. It'll sound extra special if you call it...Mandarin Trout. Get the idea, Jack? I'd go with you if I didn't have a job to do."

His vision did a sudden flip, and his stomach trembled, the warning signs he was getting ready to have a fit. A strong voice whispered from the Invisible: *Stay away from Dain King.*

Jack said. "You go with me to the City—you can be my cook."

Petr shook off the spell by dishing out beans and deer jerky. They ate in silence staring at the valley fading under a vast windless night. Becalmed stars were tiny silver ships wrecked in deep blue space, beautiful and lonely. Petr shook his head. "No...I can't go away, not now."

Jack scraped the bottom of his bowl. "Don't say can't. No thing is final." He held a scholarly pose, a finger poised in the air, then expelling an earthy, gassy tune.

Petr lost his self-control, gasping in rising tones, "You eat too fast... you fart...."

Jack patted his back, saying, "Yoor struggling a bit yourself, old lad. Pack meat does that to you. Let's settle doon with another bowlful."

Jack finished four bowls to Petr's two, in fifteen minutes. Then he began polishing hunks of gold. "Pretty soon we'll have our own cantina, Petr." Glancing at him, seeing him hunkered over his bowl, frowning. Jack added, "Sarved by pretty dancing girls. What say you?"

Petr became serious. "You've got enough for a strong start." Then as if a goodbye: "Remember, Jack. Sell good meals, but make it sound like it's made for an emperor. Do that and your dreams will come true: Big Jack's Restaurant. Big Jack's Hotel. Big Jack's—"

"Enough of the restaurant blather!" Jack sounded hurt. "Let's drink to lucky partners." Lifting a small oak cask he pulled the cork and poured two cups. Raising his cup in the air, he roared, "Let'r buck!" Snapping the whiskey to his lips, tears leaked from his eyes as he made noisy *rot-rotting* swallows. He gasped, "God, how it burns!"

Petr sipped his cup thoughtfully. Enjoy your dreams, Jack. Not everyone gets good ones. Jack shook and his eyes sparkled and Petr wondered if whiskey could lift him, too.

Jack shook himself like a dog. "Aihh! That scrapes the moss off the shingles!" He saluted his cup, drained it, and refilled it. "Aihh, nothing beats neat scotch and home." Speaking now in hushed tones, "One thing I got plenty of was this killbrew. Only thing Scotland got plenty of—and so I left her. Aihh, God help me!"

Petr sipped whiskey trying to understand its appeal. It tasted like juice squeezed from a gnarled oak. Sweat from a sow's teat. Piss from a trodden seahorse. He gulped bigger swallows, searching its flavor for meaning. Men drank this strong misery-brew on a regular basis. Why? Petr filled his cheeks and took great walloping swallows. It swirled down his throat with fiery ease, and his vision blurred into long, slow spirals as if on a carousel. Finally one clear thought emerged: Jack's doing his best right now to father me—and introduce me to—he groped for the word until it came. *Consolation.* Petr raised his cup.

"Hail to whiskey, the prize for second place!" Feeling giddy, he shouted, "To the sweat o' Scotland." He drank and became bitter like a man, bitter like the sorrow in his heart. When he looked around the world swam lazily before him. He was a popeyed fish squeezed hard by the cruel hand of life.

He muttered, "Men drink...because they're broken-hearted!" Tears swelled in his eyes.

Jack took his cup away, saying, "Older a man gets, the more reason he drinks. Look at me. I'm too hard on a place where-som-iver I go." He gazed off. "For me, gold's the way to freedom—the only way I'll live ta forty—but five years hence for Jack G. Frazier. Where but to the grave leads this, unless—" He hoisted two gold chunks. "God, I believe you now! God, I thank you, Petr Valory! You tiptop gold hunter! Now I christen you—the Goldfinder."

Petr nodded holding his head because it seemed only loosely attached to his shoulders. The world was strangely hollow and full of too-loud noises. The distant *whirring* crickets were grindstones in his ears. Petr gulped cold water and threw up. Jack seemed not to notice.

"Since it's late and we can say anything we want," Jack smiled shyly, "I wonder if—" He stopped a full minute to load his pipe. "I never did see such a lad with such a gold speck in his eye. Is that...a f-f...I can't say it!—a *family* trait?"

In firelight the lad's eyes were hard gold planets.

Petr closed his eyes and looked away. "Does it look very bad?"

"Notta-tall! Makes you look like some fine roguish gentleman.

Scottish hearts would say you have the *taisch*." Petr looked back at him confused.

"Magic eye." Jack tapped his brow. "Second sight: they looka-roond in the future. Behind that curtain they see which string pulls what puppet next." Jack looked sheepish. "C-can y-you...I can't say it! Can you *do that*? See the future?"

Petr thought about it. Wondering: How much do you *really* want to know, Jack?

He bowed his head wishing for sleep, but his head was spinning like a rubber ball on a string. He mumbled, "Can I see, Jack? That's so funny I should laugh."

Except it wasn't funny. Closing his eyes he began thinking of all he could never tell Jack.

There you sit Jack with your halo glowing blue. Did you know, Jack? We are fallen angels in clay? Over there I see dozens of volcanoes spouting orange geysers. They happened long ago—but I see it *now*. Shall I tell you about volcanoes, Jack? My head's a storm of pictures right before my eyes. Oh, and I travel time, too, Jack. Did you want to know that? Far away west of here is a beautiful blue bay with a white city rising from the clay. Across the harbor is a bridge arched like twin golden harps. Ships pass beneath it. Crazy stuff, huh, Jack. Can I see, Jack? There's no such thing as a golden bridge!

Petr sat hugging himself, so Jack spoke calmly. "It's okay if you don't have the *taisch*. Probably a good thing." He tapped out his pipe. "Let's sleep now and have some happy dreams. We'll find that big restaurant and wagons of food coming to our door every day and pretty girls wiggling at the table. You wait and see, partner."

Petr mumbled, "Don't worry. I won't let you down, Jack."

In a moment Jack was snoring, but Petr didn't sleep. He was picturing Annabel Rochele, how the honey-colored child might look in a few years. A vivid vision: royal, sweet, slender; a real Danish dazzler with a dash of Russian spice. Not robin-breasted like her mother but a queen's beauty all the same. Barely awake, he whispered, "I'll see you... in heaven."

Beneath the liquid stars of midnight, he fell into a death-like asleep.

7

Annabel dabbed the back of her head for the hundredth time and couldn't believe her hand. At least her fingers no longer came away gooey red.

The bad Indian had cut her ponytail off leaving a bloody circle, all the time smiling his rotten smile. There was a name for what he'd done; she just didn't care to use it right now. She guessed the bare spot on the back of her head would heal and not grow hair anytime soon. Supposing there were other parts of girlhood that weren't going to *grow back* ever. She shook her head: Things to worry about later.

For now, she had plenty of water, plenty of meat and nuts. But for some reason she was losing strength day by day, probably from old food and not enough sunlight. Probably be a gray old hag when I get out.

She sat in darkness rubbing her sore knee, another parting gift from the bad Indian. He had wedged her leg into a crevice trapping it with a flat rock. The more she wiggled it, the more it hurt. Her ankle was swollen and scraped raw. Her toes seemed floating a hundred miles away. She had tried to move the stone but it wouldn't budge. She supposed the Indian was tired of replacing all the stones she smashed at the entrance. She had awakened this way after he'd bashed her head, after he had—*Skaal*....No. Don't say it. Never admit that.

She had plenty of time to think about all the events and catastrophes of the last few days—or was it weeks or months? Kinda spooky you don't remember. All the events blurred together: the swim under the lake; the blazing gold chamber; and then the crawling time in the tunnel. Petr said you couldn't do it. It was boy's adventure. Ha! She clutched her doll and tears welled and she rubbed them away.

"Don't worry, Miss Daisy. Petr will find us." Actually this doll was a replica of the doll made from the head of Daisy with rags ripped from her clothes and tied on using a tress of her hair which she had found laying beside her. Yes, this bloody doll, sad to say, was: Miss Daisy the *Third*.

She regretted now all the events of her boy's adventure, all of the time in the tunnels. She was inside and couldn't get outside. Pigeons were cooing somewhere *outside*. She could hear them, and they sounded very far away. And this Indian hideout was so good Petr would never find her. And if the really bad Indian decided just to forget about her, just leave her?

That wasn't even the worst question that plagued her. *Petr, are you really....*

Dead?—Are you *really dead?* She'd seen the stones piled in front of the Valory cabin.

She pulled out the Lover's Watch and opened it and looked at the time. Twelve midnight, same as always: Eternal Midnight. She snapped it shut and kissed the Lovers goodnight, same as always. And then she began to cry.

8

Petr was moaning, clutching at the darkness. He had been dreaming of Annabel again. In a moment he remembered where he was: The Jackpot Mine—ten feet dug out of a mountainside above an ordinary valley filled with onions. Jack sprawled at the cavemouth blowing like a beached whale.

Petr gripped his head. Headache—felt like he had been kicked by a mule. Let me be unconscious, drunk, dreaming. Let me go back to my beautiful dream.

She was so real. Deer-wide eyes, cheeks flushed with excitement, upturned pixie nose sniffing at the wind, so real he could scent her tangy little-girl smell, a mingle of crushed flowers, and sweat. So sure he'd smelled that particular scent *now*.

"Annabel...are you there?"

On the verge of waking, he'd heard her quick, hiccupping giggle. Sure sign *she* knew *he* knew she was here, and she could not contain herself any longer. His dream-self asked her: Are you waiting under the lake? Her tiny voice trailed away from the dream like a vapor—*No*.

He was awake now. The lingering thrill of Annabel skittered up his spine, because the impression was real as the lingering odor of bread, faint, nearly gone now. He called to the dark night, hoping spoken words created magic power, saying what he could never say in real life.

"Annabel, I love you! I always loved you—only you!"

Gray silence spread over him, the dank fog of stark reality slowly returning.

Awful reality: dark loneliness; Annabel *gone*. Just like the awful dream of the Lost Lover. *Gone, gone, gone!* Reality was Dain King *happy* with the murder of John Valory—and Petr Valory doing *nothing* about it.

He gazed from the dark hole of the mine. The dark hole flipped and Petr ignored the warning. Reality was Big Jack sleeping with no worries, no confusions. Jack could doze between the words "good" and "night". That kind of man might get some good out of gold. He gazed at the sleeping giant.

"Well. Goodbye Jack...I guess I gave what I could...now I go...do what I must do."

He put on his boots and went into the forest of night.

Go in darkness. End in darkness.

In a few minutes he was running for Gold Nation knowing what he must do.

Kill Dain King.

9

Running when the sun rose, still running as the sun blazed noon, he felt as if he'd been running forever and must go on running to death.

He stopped at streams and drank handfuls of water, and nothing mattered. Because—

It was July 17th and Annabel hadn't been seen anywhere on earth for a whole month. "Annabel is—"

He couldn't say it. He threw himself onto a flat slab of granite and began sobbing, "No...No...NO!"

Crying until his face hurt, until his body felt like a dissolving block of salt, in wracking sobs of despair, this was the moment—the final acceptance of gut-punching truth.

"Annabel...you're...*gone!* I have to...let you...*go!*"

He lay face down for a long time. Then a miracle occurred. He became unconscious.

❊❊

Late morning, Petr gazed around with a sense of fresh wonder. Birds sang, the sky was blue, the mountains and valleys blushed silver green. He stood feeling rinsed clean and hollow. Sorrow had distilled into something hot and dark as whiskey.

He walked calmly the rest of the way down to Big Jack's cabin.

The red horse greeted him eagerly prancing back and forth in the small corral.

"Rubaiyat, for this one thing—I will use you." She trembled as he saddled her.

They couldn't go straight up the ridge as Jack had done with his sturdy burro. They must go around the mountain. She took him rapidly down from Long Lake and he marveled at the big horse's speed and stamina as she carried him down to the Valoryvale. Again, the beloved home ground—and he saw that it was being worked.

Tall pines lay felled everywhere, ripsaws tossed aside gleaming in the setting sun. Papa never would have left saws lying about. Anger surged through him. So—life goes on for Dain King.

The horse sensing his need, charged at full gallop to the river and north to Gold Nation.

10

When the sun rose, Jack knew the lad was gone, and where, and what he was going to do. He boomed at the burro. "Tamsen, get over here! We must hurry to Gold Nation!"

Tamsen looked very curious, her nose green and slimy, and Jack smelled trouble.

"Aihh, honey! What have you done, gone and made a pig of yoorself?"

The burro had the bloat and she might die within the hour. And Petr might die within the hour if Jack didn't hurry to Gold Nation. Dain King would finish what he started at the Valory cabin. Jack took out his smoking pipe and sharpened the stem into a point.

"Oh honey, this is gwointa hurt."

This completes *The Gold Hunter*, the first of four books called *The Goldfinder*.

In the second novel, *The Gold Shaper*, Dain King sends Petr Valory down the river tied in an old Indian canoe to scare him into revealing the location of his gold. The canoe goes over a waterfall where Petr is rescued by Paiutes trying to locate a missing band of warriors. He falls in love with the Indian medicine woman, Minoah. A bad Indian named Sabbah kidnaps Annabel and uses her to make Petr lure Dain King and his men into a trap. The Indians are killed including Minoah's father. Now love turns to hatred.

Petr Valory ventures to San Francisco to make a beautiful gold gift for Minoah. There he will remember the secrets of gold shaping from the whispering Redhaired Man. There he meets the impetuous Valencia who will try to make him forget Minoah. There he will discover the terrible price of finding gold.

The Gold Shaper, available August 2017

CPSIA information can be obtained
at www.ICGtesting.com
Printed in the USA
FSOW01n1712220217
31130FS